Let it Happen
The Story of Jess and Tate

Jaimsss P.

Copyright 2024 by Jaimsss P.

All rights reserved.

No portion of this book may be reproduced in any form without written permission from the publisher or author, except as permitted by U.S. copyright law.

Disclaimer:

♥

If you're new to Jaimsss P.'s romance world, please know I pride myself on writing love stories that are sweet, realistic, and built to last. The romance I craft requires the characters' relationship to have an unshakable foundation that takes time to develop. With that said, this novel is a bit of a slow burn, so if those aren't your preference, you may want to skip this one. However, if you're down for the ride, I promise Jess and Tate's journey through life and love is *so* worth it.

Trigger Warnings

♥

This book briefly discusses the following sensitive topics:

-fibroids

-infertility

-suicide

Dedication:

♥

This one is dedicated to Chrissy, Alyssia, and Harlem Lottie. Chrissy and Alyssia, I've been trying to write this one for years, and y'all are the reasons I finally got it done! Your journeys inspired the heroine of this story. I aimed to honor you both by making Jess as strong, resilient, and amazing as y'all are, and I pray that comes across as you read this story. Harlem, you are a living reminder that God always has the last say. I'm so grateful for your life and light, baby girl. I love y'all *down*.

xoxo,

Jaimsss P.

The (First) Cut Off

♥

Jessica "Jess" Brielle Westin

Four Years Ago

I walked down the hall to my hotel room with my heels in hand—I was beyond tired. The wedding weekend had been fun, but now that the happy couple tied the knot, it was ending, and I would be going home the next day.

I tried not to sulk as I approached my room door, but it was hard, considering. I was on this beautiful island for my best friend's wedding, but Julian Tate had completely ruined my mood. He had basically ignored me the entire weekend. For the longest time, we had been playing a cat-and-mouse game that he had already admitted to being sick of. He swore he wanted to date me seriously, but I was perfectly content with hooking up when we were in the same city and going our separate ways after.

I sighed. I kept telling myself I was cool with how we left things, but if I was honest, it was all a front. I knew I could love him, but ultimately, it wouldn't work out. Before it was all said and done, Julian would hurt me. I knew it would happen.

He was a player before I met him, and to be honest, so was I.

Men as fine as Tate couldn't be happy with just one woman. Joseph was the exception to that rule, and I was happy for my best friend, but I didn't see marriage in my future.

Sighing again, I pulled my room key out of my clutch. Julian's signature scent filled my nostrils as I was about to unlock the door, then a palm slammed against the door above my head. I took a deep breath and swallowed the smile that was threatening to surface before I turned to face him.

Rolling my eyes hard, I looked at him with feigned disgust. "Could you move, please?"

He smirked. "You know damn well you don't want that."

"I actually do. You've ignored me all weekend. Why should I want to talk to you now?"

"Why have I been ignoring you, Jessica?" he asked with squinted eyes.

I shrugged. "Because you're rude."

He shook his head. "Nah, because you're in denial."

I let out a short breath. "What am I in denial about?"

"Wanting me."

I laughed arrogantly. "Everybody doesn't want you, Julian."

He stepped closer so our bodies were touching. I could have fainted right then and there. He leaned down so that his lips were brushing against mine.

"You do."

"So?" I asked in a breathy tone.

He chuckled and bit my bottom lip before devouring it in a passionate kiss. After a few minutes of kissing as if we weren't in the hallway of a very populated hotel, he broke away from me.

Biting my own lip, I looked up at him with seductive eyes. "You wanna come inside?" I asked.

He stared at me without words. Seconds passed before he asked, "You wanna give me a real chance to make you happy?"

I rolled my eyes. "We're good like we are, Julian."

He removed his hand from the door and backed away from me. "Then good night," he said before turning to walk away.

I groaned. "You're really going to act childish because I don't want to be in a relationship with you?"

He stopped in his tracks and backtracked to me. He stood close so our bodies were touching once again.

I loved the way this man smelled.

"If you gon' keep lyin' to yourself, go 'head, but stop lyin' to me. You want me, and I want you. You're the only childish one in this equation, and I'm done playin' with you. When you're ready to build with me, I'll be here. Until then, I'm off-limits to you." He smirked and kissed me again before walking away.

"I don't care, Julian! Nobody wanted you to come in anyway!" I yelled behind him. He kept walking and threw up deuces at me.

It took me a minute to pick my face up off the floor before I could finally enter my room. I headed straight to the bathroom and started the shower. I undressed and replayed the encounter I had just endured; I couldn't believe he had shut me down so quickly. So easily.

He called my bluff about wanting him, but that didn't mean I was ready to act on those feelings. I was sure he thought the little show he had just put on would break me down, but it did just the opposite… it reminded me of who I was.

Jessica Westin could have anyone she wanted, so begging a man for his time was laughable. I let him knock me off my square once, but never again. As I stepped into the shower, I decided to get back to me—traveling, dating, and having fun. I was officially done with Julian Tate.

I took a deep breath and lathered up my loofah. For the duration of my shower, I decided to repeat that last statement in my head until I actually believed it. I was determined to move past him, but in my heart, I knew Julian and I were far from done.

Transparency

Jess

Two Months Ago

"Happy birthday, boss!"

I smiled and extended my arms toward my assistant's voice. With my hands outstretched, I wiggled my fingers, but nothing graced my palm. Turning my lip up, I kissed my teeth. I was tempted to open my eyes but wasn't in the mood to hear Margo's mouth.

She was one of the best makeup artists and hairstylists in the industry, but she had been working on just my eyeshadow for the last thirty minutes, and I was beyond over it. She hadn't started on my hair, so I knew I would be in that chair for the rest of the afternoon.

"Okay," Margo said as she swiped the brush against my eyelid again, "you can open."

Finally.

I opened my eyes and immediately glared at my assistant. She was grinning with both hands behind her back, and I groaned. Shania played entirely too much.

I rolled my eyes. "Whatever you're holding behind your back better be for me," I said with a pout. All my people knew how much I loved opening presents. It had become kind of a birthday tradition for my inner circle to present me with my gifts on sight, because waiting for the party was just *too much* waiting for me.

I honestly didn't care what it was as long the person bought it with me in mind. I was a spoiled princess at heart, and my birthday was the one day of the year I got to own it shamelessly.

Shania, or Shay as I called her, rolled her eyes and revealed one of her hands. She was holding a beautiful bouquet of red roses, and just the sight of them had me giddy.

With raised brows, I glanced at Margo, who was just about to put setting powder under my eye, and she rolled hers.

"Girl, get them flowers and get back in this seat." She sounded annoyed but couldn't hide the grin that broke through.

"Aww, Shay, you shouldn't have," I said, cheesing.

Shay chuckled and handed the flowers to me. "I didn't."

I frowned and grabbed the bouquet. Looking for the card, I asked, "Who did, then? And where is my gift?"

"I stopped by the office first, and these were sitting at the front door. You already know who they're from," Shay said with a grimace, making my frown deepen as I pulled out the card and opened it. Her words made sense as soon as I started reading.

> *Happy birthday, Jessica Brielle Westin. You know I never miss one. Enjoy today, and know that my dreams are filled with you and me in a different space and time when we can celebrate days like this together. I love you, beautiful.*
>
> *Forever and only yours... always.*
>
> *MAC.*

I sighed and placed the note on the makeup table beside me before sitting back in the seat.

"It's been a year. I almost forgot about him," I said.

Picking up the card, Margo asked, "Forgot about who?"

I shrugged. "Whoever sends me these notes and flowers every birthday."

I had been modeling professionally for the last seven years, and this mystery admirer had been in my life for over five. When my career began, I gained popularity in the industry fairly quickly. I started on *Shutter* as a social media influencer, and at that point, my goal was to let the world know how dope of a designer my best friend Davi was.

I was only rocking Davi's designs, and people fell in love with her pieces and how *I* looked in them. Emails and phone calls about brand deals and modeling opportunities started flooding in, and it wasn't long before I decided to go all in with it. With the help of my parents, I eventually hired a personal assistant and purchased an office for her and me to work out of.

My birthday came around a couple of months after we moved into the office, and the first card was waiting on the doorstep. They hadn't stopped coming since.

Margo placed the note on her working tray before picking up the setting powder again. I shifted my gaze upward as she applied it.

"He does this every year and drops them off to your office? Uh-uh, Jess. That's weird," Margo said.

I shrugged. "I guess it *is* weird, but I never really thought too much about it. I feel like everybody with even a lil bit of publicity has superfans. This person is just my one," I said with a chuckle.

I had made so many friends in the industry who were bigger than me, and they got letters similar to mine on a daily basis. In my opinion, it just wasn't that serious.

"Whatever you say, girl. You can chill for a minute while the powder sets," Margo said, making me smile. I loved how my face looked when she did it, but I hated how long it always took.

"Okay, now that we have *that* outta the way, here's my gift," Shay said, taking her oversized purse off her shoulder. She reached inside and pulled out a large bottle of my favorite tequila brand, then a rectangular box with a bow.

"Wait! Let me get on live before I open it!" I said. Lately, I had been livestreaming a lot more on *Shutter*. I loved interacting with my supporters. This was the easiest and safest way to do that.

Pulling out both my phones, I opened the *Shutter* app on one of them and went live. With only my face in the frame, I waited with a smile as supporters started to trickle in. After about thirty seconds, two hundred people had joined, so I spoke up.

"Heyyy! What y'all doin'?" I asked.

My assistant took the phone from me and put it on a tripod that was also in that big behind bag of hers. She always thought of everything. I read the comments as some people typed what they were doing. There were an overwhelming amount of birthday wishes, and my audience grew by another three hundred viewers before I could even say thank you.

"Aww, I appreciate y'all so much! I got on here 'cause Shay just walked in with a gift for me, and I wanted us to open it together. Lemme get that, Shay Shay," I said, cheesing at her.

With a small smile, she rolled her eyes and handed me the box. I opened it slowly, careful not to rip the paper, and as soon as the leather cover was exposed, I knew what it was.

"Nah! You showed out, didn't you, Shay?" I asked as I continued to slide the paper off. Once the gift was completely unwrapped, I showed it to my viewers.

"If you're a real day one Jess supporter, you know this is my favorite sunglasses brand!"

I knew I would love whatever pair she purchased, but when I slid them out of their case, I was unprepared for just how *fire* they really were. The frames had an ombre emerald tint, and all the other details were gold, my two favorite colors. I was in love.

"Shay! Thank you so much, sis. I love 'em! I'm wearing these to my party tonight 'cause they match my outfit perfectly!"

I wanted to slide them on my face but knew I needed to wait until Margo was done.

Shay laughed. "I knew you had to have 'em when I saw them in the store, girl. Let me get a few glasses so we can pop open your other gift." She headed to my kitchen and returned a few minutes later with three shot glasses. Once she poured them, I held mine toward my phone screen and said, "It's Jess Day, y'all, so make sure you celebrate. Cheers!"

We all downed our shots, and I couldn't help the ugly face I made as the alcohol entered my system.

"Alright, now sit back and let me finish this face so we can get started on your hair," Margo said, fussing.

Rolling my eyes, I did as I was told and continued chatting with everyone who joined my livestream. After two more shots with Shay, I was tipsy. Just as I was about to end my stream, a viewer joined that caught my attention immediately: @*jtate*.

Mr. Ali, himself.

I hadn't seen him in months, but just that quickly, I wanted him in front of me. Julian Ali was the finest man I had ever met and had the personality to match it. He was the only man I'd encountered who matched my energy, and I loved that about him. I probably *loved* him, but that wasn't a fact I was in the headspace to consider. *Not today.*

I peered at the screen and waited a moment to see if he'd comment to tell me happy birthday, but I saw nothing. Still, he hadn't left the stream, so I wasn't ending it. He must have joined because he wanted to see me, so I was going to let him get that.

Shay poured the two of us another shot, and I clinked it against my phone screen before taking it.

"Y'all, why is Shay trying to get me drunk hours before the festivities begin? That's the last one until my party," I said, grinning. As the liquid went down, my chest heated, and my thoughts of Julian multiplied. When I couldn't take it anymore, I grabbed my other phone from my lap. After opening the *Shutter* app, I typed his username into my search bar and began scrolling through his feed. He didn't post much, but when he did, the visuals never disappointed. *He was so sexy.*

I had the urge to tell him so, right there on my livestream, but I knew it was the alcohol talking, so I resisted and did the smart thing.

"Alright, family. Thanks for helping me celebrate for a minute. I love y'all so much, and I'll make sure I call y'all back tomorrow to let you know how the party went!" I smiled and blew a kiss before ending the live.

Margo stepped in front of me and peered at me. After a minute, she grinned and said, "I did that. You look bomb, birthday girl." She handed me a mirror, and as I admired my reflection, I had to agree—she did her thing.

I couldn't wait to see how my hair turned out, but Margo never missed, so I knew I would be a whole problem in a matter of hours. I glanced at my phone's screen again and studied Julian's latest picture. I wondered if he was going to make it to my party later.

Julian worked for the FBI with my best friend's husband, Joseph. The three of them moved back to Atlanta a few months ago for some kind of task force they were joining, leaving me up North alone. I knew Davi and Joseph had flown up for the party, but they hadn't mentioned Ali.

I tried to keep him off my mind, mainly because whenever he entered my thoughts, there was no shaking him—this time was no different. If I were ever going to settle down, he would be the man I'd want to spend forever with. That kind of life wasn't in the cards for me, though. Unfortunately, I had nothing to offer Julian but a temporary fix, and he had made it clear a long time ago that he was no longer interested in that.

He wanted something real, but I knew it wouldn't work long-term. He would eventually want things I couldn't give him. Not because I didn't want to, but because I literally *couldn't*. Since I couldn't commit, he cut me off, and I had no choice but to let it happen.

Sighing, I opened my text messaging app and sent Davi a message.

> **Transparency Moment - Vi, Ali is on my livestream, and now I'm stalking his *Shutter* page. I wanna kiss him... like real bad. Is he coming to my party tonight? He never responded to the invitation I sent...**

With that, I dropped my phone again and closed my eyes as Margo started on my hair. I hoped I would see him that evening, but only time would tell.

Playing Games

♥

Julian Ali Tate

"Hey, baby! I expected you an hour ago. Was traffic bad? I told you you could have stayed here last night."

I frowned as I stared at Shondra. She kept trying it with that *baby* word, and I was about to cuss her out for it. I met her a few months back when I was in New York for Davi's fashion show.

She was at my favorite New York lounge, and we ended up in her bed later. Shondra was cool, but I wasn't interested in building on our one-night stand. I made that clear to her five months ago *and* when I ran into her at that same spot the night before. She said she was cool with that, but I wasn't convinced.

"Nah, traffic was straight. I told you I got a room, and that's where I like to lay my head," I said as she stepped aside, giving me room to enter her home. I had a feeling I needed to turn her brunch offer down, but I loved to eat, and homemade pancakes sounded about right.

I walked in and glanced at her just as she rolled her eyes. She got it together quickly and smiled. "I know, Tate. I was just saying. Come on in the living room and get comfortable. Brunch is almost ready."

I chuckled. "Almost? I thought you were expectin' me an hour ago, Shondra?" I asked, following behind her. Instead of responding, she turned to me and waved her hands in the direction of her sofa as if she were presenting it to me.

She left the room, and I took a seat. When I focused on the television, I realized she had the sports channel on. I knew that was for my benefit, and I honestly found her attempts to present herself as wifey material funny. Shondra had her hand in my pants twenty minutes after I met her, and I'd never cuff a woman that eager.

I stared at the television, trying to decide if I was about to dip. I was hungry as hell and wasn't trying to wait for her to whip nothin' up. I came later than she asked because I wanted to make sure the food was done, but she was playing games.

I chuckled.

I couldn't believe I was back at this woman's house for breakfast, and no food was in sight. I didn't even smell anything cooking. I shook my head just as my phone chimed. When I pulled it from my pocket, I realized it was a *Shutter* alert, letting me know Jessica was livestreaming.

I wasn't one to spend too much time on social media, but I for sure had my alerts on for Jessica Brielle. I had been meaning to turn those off, but that was shut down every time one of her posts graced my timeline. I loved seeing her pretty face, and since she lived to play games with me, pictures and videos were the only things I allowed myself to indulge in where she was concerned.

We met about five years ago, when her best friend and mine found their way back into each other's lives. Our first interaction was a damn argument, but it was all good because I respected the love she had for her girl, Davi. I rode for Joseph the same way, which caused us to bump heads initially, but the attraction was there from the jump.

After Davi and Joseph got it together and made it official, I wanted to be on the same thing with Jessica. Our vibe and bond were unmatched, but she was committed to running from it. Anytime we would start connecting on an emotional level, she would make up an excuse and dip.

I got tired of that and let her know I wanted something real with her. She shut me down twice, and after that, I stopped trying. She wanted to maintain our physical relationship, but I cut that off too. I slipped up plenty of times after that, but I hadn't been with Jess in about a year. I didn't have time to play with her.

I tapped the notification, and her beauty blessed my phone's screen seconds later. She was talking about something when I joined the live but stopped mid-sentence and leaned closer to the screen. I had to readjust myself when her teeth sank into her bottom lip just before she sat back in her chair again.

She looked good.

I remained focused on her as she and her assistant took shots and talked about her party later that night. She couldn't stop grinning, and I already knew what that meant. Jessica always tried to play it cool when she was drunk, but I spent too much of my time studying people. Studying *her* used to be one of my favorite things to do, and that grin was her tell—she was tipsy.

"I know you aren't grinning at some other woman while you're sitting on my couch, Tate."

I kissed my teeth at the sound of Shondra's voice and stood right after. The fact that she brought her loud ass into the room and made me miss whatever Jessica had just said pissed me off, and I was done acting like I had a real reason to be there.

"What you yellin' for? Aye, I'm out. Come lock up behind me," I said, moving toward the front door of her apartment.

I heard her footsteps behind me.

"Wait!" she said as she approached me from behind. I continued to her door but stopped cold when I felt her foot on the back of my custom off-white *Glides*. I didn't play about my got damn sneakers.

"Back up."

I glanced behind me, and she was slowly doing as I requested with a nervous look on her face. Once she was out of my personal space, I continued to the door.

"You haven't eaten yet," Shondra said in a desperate voice that would have turned me off if I wasn't already over it.

"Shid, I know. That's why I'm leavin', girl," I said, turning her doorknob. I burst out laughing as soon as I opened the door.

"Aye! I know you ain't do all that talkin' 'bout how good you can cook just to order breakfast from *Calvin's*?" I could barely get the question out because I was laughing so hard, and the delivery guy outside her door was low-key chuckling too.

I stepped out of the house and got my wallet from my pocket. I pulled out a couple of bills and handed them to the guy before dapping him up.

"Thanks, man," he said and smirked.

"No problem, dawg. Aye, take care, Shondra," I said and headed out of her building with her calling me all kinds of names behind my back.

Once I made it to my rental car, I started it up and was about to tune back into the livestream, but Joseph was calling, so I answered.

"Wassup, dawg?" I said.

"Shid, chillin'. I'm tryna make sure you got on that flight. You know Davi is gon' be ready to cuss you out if you ain't at Jess's party tonight."

I chuckled, knowing he was stating facts. Davi didn't play about holidays and birthdays. She made sure everybody showed up for everybody, every time.

"You know I'm here, J. I'ma prolly be a lil late, though."

"For what? You ain't got nothin' to do up here."

I laughed because he was right, but I would find something to get into. I'd never deny I wanted Jessica, but she made it clear that it would never happen with us. I had to limit my time around her.

"You know I got motion in New York. Don't try to play me, dawg," I said, pulling out of my parking space.

"Whatever, bruh. Just make sure you're there. You know my wife likes to take family photos."

I laughed. "I'ma be there."

J hung up without saying anything else, but that was expected from his rude ass. Almost as soon as I was out of the parking lot, I was at a standstill in traffic. This was the reason I would never officially move to New York. Atlanta was busy, but this place was on a whole other level. My phone chimed, and I received a text message.

I'd never tell a soul breathing how my insides started dancing when I realized it was from Jessica.

> **Jessica Brielle: Transparency Moment- Vi, Ali is on my livestream, and now I'm stalking his *Shutter* page. I wanna kiss him... like real bad. Is he coming to my party tonight? He never responded to the invitation I sent...**

My smile got wider with every word I read. She had to be tipsy because the Jessica I knew would never give me the satisfaction of knowing I was on her mind. For her own dumb reasons, she would rather pretend she wasn't feeling me at all.

I chuckled. This text was meant for Davi, but I was glad she slipped up. Jessica always tried to act like I didn't affect her, but I knew what was up, and this message was proof of that.

Instead of responding to it, I tossed my phone in the passenger's seat and headed to the mall. I'd deal with the birthday girl later.

Issa Celebration

♥

Jess

"Oh. My. *Goodness.* I *did* that!" Davi said as soon as I opened my front door for her, Crissy, and Demi.

Rolling my eyes, I laughed and spun around to give them a three-sixty view of my birthday look. Davi designed my dress, and it was stunning, as usual. I had been looking at myself in the mirror since Shay helped me into it.

It was a golden masterpiece. The floor-length, backless gown was completely sheer and covered in rhinestones. The plunging neckline stopped just under my navel, and the deep slit trailed from my hip to the floor. Because the dress had a hood, Margo straightened my wig to perfection and gave me a sleek middle part. Yeah, I looked *good*.

"You're gorgeous, sis," Demi said, and Crissy nodded.

"Yes, I'm lovin' this look."

I grinned. "Thank y'all. You *did* do your thing, Vi," I said, turning toward Davi.

She smiled. "Thank you very much. Did you get pictures already? I'm gonna need those."

I kissed my teeth and placed my hands on my hips. "First of all, yes, I got pictures. Valerie just left, and she took plenty. Second of all, don't be coming in here demanding photos when your behind hasn't even said happy birthday yet."

Davi rolled her eyes and opened her arms wide before pulling me into a hug.

"I could have sworn I was the first person to tell you happy birthday at *exactly* midnight... then again when I brought your gifts first thing this morning. Happy birthday, big baby."

Crissy and Demi joined in on the hug and wished me another happy birthday. It was true; I had already talked to all of them that day, but Davi knew I was a spoiled brat on my birthday.

"I know you like getting your presents off the top, so here you go," Crissy said with a smirk, handing me the small green gift bag in her hand. Vi and I met Crissy and Demi over a year ago in Atlanta. They were cousins and married to Joseph's friends, Aason and Aaron Legend. Although Davi and I didn't really bring new people into our mix often, we clicked with them immediately and had been something like a happy family ever since.

Crissy had gotten me a luxury brand robe I knew I'd be wearing every chance I got. It was white, plush, and had my name embroidered in gold letters. Demi's gift was next: a fire pair of leather sneakers with emerald-colored accents.

"Ooo! Both of these gifts are so *me*. Thank y'all!" I said, giving each of them a hug.

"Who the hell is this from?" Vi asked, bringing my attention to her. She was standing a few feet away, holding the card Shay brought earlier that day.

"You already know who it's from. Shay went to the office, and it was on the doorstep with those flowers over there."

Davi rolled her eyes. "Jess, this one is even more disturbing than the others. He's talking about meeting you."

"Who is *he*?" Crissy asked with a frown.

"Her stalker."

"My secret admirer."

Vi and I answered at the same time, and I rolled my eyes at her response.

Kissing her teeth, Vi said, "He's a *stalker* who has been sending her weird letters on her birthday for the last few years. This is the weirdest one yet, and I'm giving it to Joseph."

I rolled my eyes again. "Vi, *no*. It's really not that serious, and I don't need your FBI profiling husband blowing things out of proportion."

She kissed her teeth and dropped the letter back on the table. "I bet you my FBI husband will get these letters to stop. Anyway, let's go. I know Steph is wondering what's taking us so long."

I grabbed the bottle Shay got me and my bag for the evening, and we headed outside to meet Davi's driver. Once we were all in the SUV, I frowned at her.

"Um, why didn't your rude behind text me back?" It had just occurred to me that she never acknowledged my text about Julian.

Vi picked up her phone and said, "I have zero messages from you today, so fix your face."

Crissy, who was seated behind us, laughed and said, "Y'all argue worse than me and Demi, I swear."

"That's 'cause Vi is always tellin' stories," I replied and opened my message app. "As you can see, I texted you at…" My voice trailed off as I realized what I had done.

"Oh my God," I said, barely above a whisper.

"What's wrong?"

I could barely make out Davi's question over the loud thumping of my heart. Unable to respond, I just handed her the phone. Because she was messy, she read the message out loud.

"Transparency Moment - Vi, Ali is on my livestream, and now I'm stalking his *Shutter* page. I wanna kiss him..." she stopped reading and gasped just before she started giggling.

I elbowed her in the arm and rolled my eyes. "That ain't funny, Vi! I can't believe I did that." I buried my face in my hands.

"Did what?" Demi asked, confused.

Still laughing, Vi said, "She accidentally sent Tate a text telling him she wants to kiss him."

"Oh my God," Crissy said, sounding like I did a minute ago.

"He ain't gonna let me live this down. I hope he isn't coming to my party," I said, dropping my face in my hands.

"Oh, he's coming. I made Joseph call him earlier to make sure."

I groaned.

Vi stopped laughing but still had a stupid grin when she said, "I don't know why you're so worried about it. You didn't text Tate anything he didn't already know."

I cut my eyes at her. "So? That don't mean I need to be out here admitting it."

Vi sighed. "You *do* realize you could kiss that man whenever you wanted if you'd just stop playing?"

Here we go.

I rolled my eyes. "I'm not playing. I told you, he wants something I can't give. We're better as friends, Vi."

She gave me a knowing look, and I looked away and focused on the window because I wasn't going there tonight.

I told everybody I wasn't interested in settling down, so Crissy and Demi most likely figured that was what I was referring to. That was a lie I told myself and others because the truth hurt too much to talk about.

The *truth* was I couldn't give him a baby. A bunch of fibroids and a complicated surgery years ago ruined that possibility, and I knew Julian wanted them. He loved to have a good time, and in the beginning, I thought he wasn't the type to settle down. Over the years, though, I realized he was going to make a great husband and father for someone.

I saw him with Davi and Joseph's kids. Whenever he was ready to settle down, he would eventually want that. He would never have it with me, so it was best we remain friends to avoid a heart-shattering breakup in the long run.

Davi sighed again. She placed a hand on my leg and said, "I think all he wants you to give him is *you*. Stop overthinking it, and go be happy, girl."

I was *never* going to stop overthinking this situation, and I knew it. I still didn't want to get too deep in my feelings thinking about it, so I smiled and said, "I hear you, but this conversation is getting too deep, and I'm ready to turn up."

Getting my phone from Davi, I went to my music app and pulled up my birthday playlist before handing the phone to Steph. Seconds later, one of my favorite songs was blasting through the car, and I opened the bottle and took a shot before passing it to Demi. Crissy was four months pregnant, and Vi was a lightweight, so I was officially giving Demi the role of my drinking partner.

I closed my eyes and vibed to the music, allowing the tequila to do its thing in my system. I needed it and the music to help me forget the message I sent Julian, but I knew that was easier said than done.

***

Jess

"If you wit' me ain't no worryin' 'bout nothin'."

I swayed my hips to the beat as I rapped the lyrics to *With Me*, one of my favorite songs by Unique. The DJ played it at just the right time because I was feeling *nice*.

We had been at my party for about two hours, and I couldn't have been happier about how everything turned out, from the emerald carpet rolled out in front of the building to the amazing decorations and food. It was all perfect, and I had been having a ball since I walked through the door.

The song faded out, and the next voice I heard was my best friend's. She was standing beside the cake table, holding the microphone and wearing a grin. I wanted to laugh because I knew she was drunk, but I couldn't really talk—I was right there with her.

"Gather around, everyone!" she yelled into the microphone. Joseph, standing a few inches behind her, shook his head and laughed. Everyone in the room headed over and crowded around the table while Davi beckoned me to her. Once I was front and center, she spoke up again.

"Thank y'all so much for coming and helping to make my bestie's birthday just as special as she is. Let's go ahead and sing *Happy Birthday* so she can cut her cake."

Vi started the song off, and everyone in the room started singing. Grinning, I closed my eyes and sang to myself right along with them. Presents were my favorite part of my birthday, but the song and cake ran a close second.

I opened my eyes, and my smile grew as I surveyed everyone around me. I had really built some close friendships since being in New York, and although I was excited about moving home, I'd miss everyone in the room dearly. I turned my head toward the cake table. When I did, I caught a whiff of something that made me freeze and inhale a little deeper. The buzz I felt from the liquor intensified as I consumed one of my favorite scents on Earth, and it was followed up by a sound that made me feel lightheaded.

"Happy birthday, dear Jessica."

That line of the song was sung extremely close to my ear by a voice I hadn't heard in quite some time. His deep and silky tone sent chills through me, but I trembled when his chest pressed against my back. On its own accord, my body melted into him.

Julian.

I turned to face him as the song ended. Everyone began to clap and cheer, but I couldn't bring myself to care about anything other than the sexy man in front of me. *He was here.*

Usually, when he and I went a while without seeing each other, we would pretend not to be happy to see each other, or I'd start up an argument about nothing. The love-hate vibe had kind of become our thing, but I couldn't think of one smart thing to say. He had been on my mind all day, and I felt giddy to finally be in his presence.

"You're here," I said. I wanted to grab his hand and drag him out of the club, but I knew my best friend wasn't having that.

As if she were reading my mind, Vi cleared her throat in the mic and said, "Girl, get your fast behind over here and cut this cake."

I kissed my teeth, but my eyes never left Ali's. He smirked and said, "I am. I ain't goin' nowhere, either, so go cut your cake, Jet."

My cheeks warmed on cue. *I loved the way he said my name.*

Both Julian and I were from Georgia. I knew I was country, but *his* Southern accent was on a whole other level. He swore he called me *Jess* like everyone else, but because he cut almost every word in existence short, it came out as *Jet*.

"Come help me," I said softly. I couldn't even try to play hard with this man today. I hadn't seen him in months and was excited to have him standing in front of me. He completely entranced me, and I wasn't ready to be out of his space yet.

With a chuckle, Julian grabbed my hand and led me behind the cake table.

When I made it beside Vi, she smirked. Moving the mic away from her lips, she looked from Julian to me and said, "Mhmm."

I rolled my eyes and lifted the cake knife. "Y'all better have taken a picture of it first, Vi," I said. It was beautiful, and I hoped the photographers got nice pictures.

"Girl, don't try me. Cut the darn cake."

The music started again, and I just laughed while doing as I was told. Once I had a couple of pieces on some of the plates she had laid out, I handed her the knife and picked up one of the plates.

"Okay, I'm done, Vi. You can take care of the rest.

Now, it was her turn to roll her eyes.

"Y'all need to quit doin' that. When ya eyes get stuck up there, you gon' be pissed, and I am too, 'cause I ain't gon' wanna be around neither one of y'all funny lookin' asses no more," Julian said from behind me.

Davi cut her eyes at him.

"Don't make me slap you in front of all these people, Tate," she said, making him laugh.

He reached around me and picked up a piece of cake, then grabbed my free hand with his.

"My bad, sis," he said to Davi before whisking me away. We didn't stop moving until we reached an empty loveseat in the back corner of the room. He sat first and brought me down on his lap.

I held my breath for a second before inhaling through my nose deeply and letting it out. I hoped I was being subtle, but the smirk on his face told a different story. I rolled my eyes. This man missed nothing, and it aggravated me.

I didn't need him thinking I was pressed about being this close to him—even if it was true. Everything in me had been buzzing since he wrapped his arm around me, and now that I was on his lap, that had amplified. I was sure he felt me shivering, and I hated that I couldn't seem to calm myself down. He licked his lips.

"Happy birthday, pretty," he said, his eyes penetrating mine.

"Thank you," I said and rolled my eyes at the delivery. My words came out barely above a whisper, and there was no confidence in them.

I had to get it together.

Clearing my throat, I kissed my teeth and glared at him.

"Where is my gift, Ali?" I asked with an attitude I didn't possess. As far as I was concerned, his fine ass *was* the gift.

Still staring into my soul, he chuckled.

"I'm Ali tonight?" he asked with a smirk.

My cheeks warmed as I admired his sexy smile. I loved Julian's entire name, but I preferred to use Ali. I only called him that when we were playing nice, and that was *usually* only in the bedroom. I was happy to see him, so he was Ali tonight.

Instead of acknowledging his statement, I said, "You didn't get me a gift. You know better than that."

"Nah, *you* know better than that. I ain't get you *a* damn gift. I got three."

I bit my lip to hide my smile.

"Well?" I asked, holding a hand out. He reached into his pocket just as one of the floating bartenders approached us with her rolling cart in tow.

Smiling, she said, "Happy birthday, Miss Westin. Can I get you anything?"

I was about to answer her when my exact response fell from Julian's lips.

"A Lemon Drop with top-shelf tequila. Sugar on the rim."

"You're so aggravating." I cut my eyes in his direction, and he chuckled and pulled his wallet from his pocket.

"Gotta be quicker than that, pretty."

Shaking my head, I smiled at the bartender. "Thanks, Fascia," I said, reading her name tag.

"Got it. And for you, sir?"

Wearing a smirk, I answered for him. "An old-fashioned, stirred, with the best bourbon you got."

I stuck my tongue out at Julian, and he sat up a little. He positioned his lips less than an inch away from my ear before his deep, silky voice flowed into it, inspiring a different type of flow in my lower region.

"Don't think you're upsettin' me, girl. You know I like that."

Fascia began pulling things from her cart and making our drinks, and I focused on her, trying to ignore the heat of Ali's gaze. The man had me ready to explode, while he sat as cool as a cucumber. I hated how much I loved it.

She finished my drink first, so I lifted off Julian to take it from her cart, but his strong hand gripped my waist and brought me back down onto him. Holding me in place, he leaned forward and got it for me. I grabbed it and sipped silently, then a few minutes later, she handed him his glass.

After pulling out a crisp twenty-dollar bill, he handed it to Fascia.

"It's an open bar, so drinks are free tonight," she said.

"I still want you to have this, baby girl," he said, making me roll my eyes.

Fascia smiled and took the money before heading to another section.

He pulled out his phone and tapped the screen a few times before turning it so I could see. At first glance, I knew I was looking at tickets to something, but my tipsy state had me reading slower than usual. I frowned and squinted my eyes, really trying to focus on what he was showing me, and after a few minutes, I gasped and looked at Julian with wide eyes.

"Those are for me?" I asked, feeling my excitement build. They were VIP tickets to Unique's Atlanta concert. Unique was *the* best rapper alive, in my opinion, and to know me is to understand how much I loved him. I had never seen him in concert because he rarely toured. When the tickets went live, I tried to purchase them but was too late. They sold out quickly, and I had been stuck on the waiting list for weeks.

The tickets on Julian's phone had my name on them, so I knew the answer to my question already, but I was in disbelief. It was the best gift ever.

He kissed his teeth and smirked. "Hell nah. They're for *us*, 'cause you ain't goin' with nobody but me."

I laughed and shook my head. "I guess that's aight with me."

He smirked. "Girl, stop it. Securin' a date wit' me just made your whole night."

I rolled my eyes but didn't give him the satisfaction of a response. He was right, though. When Julian and I spent real time together, we always vibed. We liked a lot of the same things, and both loved having fun, so sharing company was easy for us. It just worked.

I watched as he sipped from his glass and casually surveyed the room. We sat that way for quite some time until, without warning, he glanced at me and asked, "So, you wanna kiss a nigga, huh?"

My eyes widened, and I immediately covered my steadily heating face with my free hand. I tried to stand when he started laughing, but he held me in place.

"Where you goin', pretty?" he asked, amusement evident.

I dropped my hand and kissed my teeth. "Forget I sent that text, Julian."

He shook his head and smiled. That one gesture made me want to grab his face and claim the kiss I texted him about. His smile always made my insides do somersaults because of what it did to his face. His smile was bright and childlike. It put all thirty-two of his perfectly white teeth on display and always reached his eyes. He was a ten without it, but when he wore that smile, he broke the scale.

"I'on want to," he said and grabbed my chin. Then, he placed his lips on mine lightly. I moaned into his mouth instantly. Our kiss tasted like bourbon and lemons, and it had me more faded than every drink I had consumed that day. Unable to help myself, I draped my arms around his neck and deepened our kiss by slipping my tongue between his lips.

Julian's hand moved from my waist to my backside, and when he squeezed it firmly, I was done for. I wanted him—*bad*. Just as I was about to break away from our kiss and tell him that, he beat me to it. His next words were nowhere near what I was going to say, though.

"My bad, Jet. We need to chill." He set his drink on the table in front of us before lifting me off his lap and placing me beside him.

"Chill for what? I'm just getting warmed up," I said, trying to make my way back into his lap.

He chuckled and shook his head. "Prolly 'cause we in a room full of nosy people."

I shrugged as I looked around. The fact that we were in a room full of people and making out like teenagers didn't concern me. Besides the fact that I was feening for Julian something serious, I was sure none of them cared about what was going on in this small corner of the large room anyway. Everyone in attendance was either someone I trusted or another celebrity who had nothing to gain from minding my business.

"Nobody in here is worried 'bout us, Ali."

He leaned over and kissed my cheek. "Maybe not us, but they're damn shole worried about *you*. You the reason they here, Jet."

I huffed and crossed my arms. "Whatever, goofy."

That caused him to laugh, making me roll my eyes harder. Everything he did was sexy to me, and the fact that he loved denying me of him was frustrating.

"And here I thought we were doin' good. You ain't called me that shit all night."

I wanted to laugh but resisted. The first time we met, I saw him as the enemy because he was the best friend of the man who had hurt my best friend. He was riding for Joseph the same way I was for Vi, so I called him out of his name a few times that day. Goofy was the one that stuck, and I pulled it out whenever we were beefing.

Rolling my neck, I said, "You haven't pissed me off all night either. Not until now. Give me my other two gifts, *goofy.*"

"I already gave you two. Here's the last one," he said, reaching into his pocket. A second later, he handed me a small black box with a gold engraving I knew all too well.

With my eyes glued to the velvet box, I said, "You gave me the tickets. What was the second..." My voice trailed off as I realized what the second "gift" was. I snapped my gaze up to him, and he was smirking, just as I knew he would be.

"Don't flatter yourself. That kiss wasn't a gift, and it wasn't even that serious."

He laughed arrogantly. "Tell yourself what you need to, pretty." He placed the box in my hand, and I opened it slowly.

My eyes bucked when I saw it. I was staring at a princess-cut emerald ring with a fourteen-karat gold band. Because of the box, I knew this ring was quite expensive.

I didn't own an authentic emerald, which was crazy since green was my favorite color. Gold was the other. I worked one or both of them into my ensemble almost every day, making this ring perfect for a girl like me.

Just like the man who gifted it to me.

I shook that thought, not in the mood to get down about the reasons we could never be together, and looked up.

"Ali, this is too—"

"Don't start wit' me. I saw it, thought of you, and wanted it to be yours. Now it is, so put it on, and don't say nothin' 'bout it bein' too much, Jessica Brielle."

He and my father were the only two people who referred to me as Jessica Brielle. Ironically, they both only did that when they were trying to put their foot down with me. Any other time, I was *Jet* or *pretty*. Not wanting to kill the vibe, I did as he asked and put it on my right ring finger.

"'Preciate ya, now let's go dance. I ain't about to be cooped up in this corner wit' you all night." He smirked and stood before reaching for my hand. I simply placed it in his and allowed him to lead the way.

***

Tate

"I'on like it when you deny me of your time, Julian." I glanced at Jess, and she was pouting next to me.

Pretty ass.

We had just sat down after at least an hour of dancing and rapping along to every song that played. She also had me taking shots, which I rarely did. Now I was lit and needed a minute to chill, which was why we were back in our corner on the loveseat.

I had been enjoying my time with her, but I always did when she wasn't running from me. Our ability to bond over anything, no matter where we were, was the reason I fell in love with her in the first place. I never thought I would desire one woman for the rest of my life, but Jess was who my heart wanted. I found it ironic that the one woman I wanted to lock in with was running from commitment at high speed. Jess refused to let us happen.

She knew that was the reason I stayed away, but if she wanted to go there tonight, I was *just* tipsy enough to tell her somethin' she needed to hear.

"I'on like it when you play wit' my time, Jessica," I said, mocking her voice.

She cut her eyes at me.

"Don't call me that."

"Did you not just *Julian* me? I'm just matchin' your energy, pretty."

I chuckled and sat back before closing my eyes. For a minute, she was silent, and I figured she would drop the subject, but just as I opened my eyes again, she spoke up.

"Me telling you I don't want to settle down isn't playing with your time, and it doesn't mean I don't want to be around you."

This really wasn't a conversation we needed to have while I was drunk, because I felt myself getting a lil too pissed at her words.

I laughed arrogantly. "Girl, I *know* you wanna be around me. I know you wanna settle down wit' me too. You're just scary, and you like to stay on that bullshit. I'm straight on that."

I glared at her, daring her to say I wasn't telling the truth, but she didn't. She sighed and leaned back also. She rested her body against my chest, and that had me bricked up immediately. Jess wasn't the most affectionate person, but she had been showing me plenty of that tonight. She almost always had something slick to say or dumb to argue about. I didn't know if it was because we hadn't seen each other in a minute or if it was the liquor, but she hadn't been on that.

Her touch always tested my control, but I wasn't about to give in. Our little cycle always left me wanting something she wasn't willing to give, and I promised myself I was done with that.

"I don't wanna argue with you," she said softly. She lifted her head and looked at me. As bad as I wanted to turn away, those eyes had me stuck. For a long time, we stayed like that—staring at each other with our faces inches apart.

Our closeness was breaking me down with every second that passed, and if she didn't back up, she was going to be in my bed sooner than later.

"Move," I said, making no attempt to remove her from my personal space.

Biting her lip, she shook her head before pressing her mouth against mine.

This fuckin' girl.

My intentions before coming to Jessica's party were to give her the gifts I purchased and the kiss she was feening for. I was supposed to wish her a happy birthday and dip. The problem with that plan was I forgot just how defenseless I was in her company. My inability to reject her was the reason I resolved to stay away from her in the first place.

I had cut Jess off plenty of times in the past, but I slipped up plenty of times, too. This last year was the longest I had gone without touching her, but it looked like that was changing tonight.

Now, we were in the back of this club, engaging in what I knew was foreplay because, with the way she had me feeling, there was no way I wasn't laying up with her before the night was out. That was exactly what she wanted too. It was *all* she ever wanted from me, and that was why I didn't wanna give it to her. She broke our kiss but remained close when she asked, "Can we leave?"

With my eyes on hers, I sighed, already knowing my answer. If I kept messing up with her the way I was about to, it wouldn't end well. The last thing I wanted was to consent to Jess playing with my feelings for the rest of my life. At some point, I was going to have to cut her off and mean it. Not tonight, though.

"Come on," I finally said. Her eyes widened in surprise, but only for a second before she hopped up and grabbed my hand. Without another word, we slipped out of the back of the building without saying goodbye to any of our people.

This is the last time.

***

Jess

I walked into the hotel suite and looked around.

"This is nice," I said, kicking off my shoes by the door. I turned slightly and glanced at Julian, just in time to catch him removing his jacket. He set it on the sidebar, next to the box my ring came in, which he had just placed there. As he took off his sneakers, he replied, "'Preciate that."

Turning again, I headed through the living area and down the short hall. I realized there was a bathroom in the hall that didn't have a shower. That meant a full bathroom was in the bedroom, and that annoyed me.

This expensive room for one night meant he intended to have some company. I supposed it was none of my business, but I knew he didn't expect the company to be *me* when he purchased the suite. The fact that he came to New York on my birthday weekend planning to entertain hos pissed me off, but I finished my tour of the suite without finding any signs of another woman.

When I exited the bathroom, I saw that he was removing his watch and placing it on the desk across the room. I sat on his bed, crossed my legs, and observed as he removed the rest of his jewelry then his shirt.

My tongue found my bottom lip while I watched him undress. If he noticed I had returned to the bedroom, he didn't make it known. With his back to me, he placed the shirt neatly on the back of the desk chair, then repeated the same process with his pants. Once, he was down to his boxers, he turned to face me. I had to work hard to hide my smile.

I missed him.

There wasn't a man on Earth who could measure up to Julian Ali Tate, and I was willing to bet my last on that. From his smooth, light-bright skin and those luscious pink lips to his solid, muscular frame and perfectly positioned tattoos, he was simply untouchable. I thought so, at least, and whatever woman he planned to bring to this room tonight undoubtedly thought so too.

"This is a nice room for one night, Julian. Who did you plan on sharin' it with?" I asked with a raised brow.

Instead of responding to me, his eyes danced over my entire body before he made his way to the bed. He stood in front of me for a minute, staring silently.

I kissed my teeth, trying to distract myself from ogling him right back.

"I know you heard me, goofy."

Still ignoring me, his arrogant ass came closer and pushed at my knee until my legs were no longer crossed. He then used one of his knees to pry his way between my legs, opening them wide and exposing the black lace panties I wore.

"So, you just gon'—"

My complaint was cut short when he caught me off guard and grabbed me up by my waist. He tossed me to the middle of the bed, then climbed on it himself, spreading my legs even wider.

Starting at my right ankle, Ali began kissing his way up my leg. His kisses were slow, sensual, and wet.

I missed everything about this man.

I hadn't had sex in about a year for several reasons, but the biggest was that no one had ever been able to compare to Julian and the things he used to do to me. *Never.* Ali knew my body better than I did because he took the time to learn her, the same way I learned his. He was an expert at pleasing me.

When he made his way to my calf, he opened his mouth slightly and began to tongue-kiss the area.

As tough as I wanted to act since he decided he didn't want to acknowledge my question, I couldn't help the moan that escaped my lips at that point.

"Mmm."

His breath tickled my skin as he chuckled, then he continued his trail up my body. I sucked in a sharp breath when he licked just above my knee. He slowly swept his tongue from that spot to the top of my thigh. I bit my lip in anticipation of him finally devouring my center. But... he didn't.

My eyes flew open, and I lifted my head so that I could properly look at him like he had lost his mind. His eyes were on me too.

"The hell, Julian?"

He kissed my inner thigh before responding.

"You been lettin' niggas taste you, Jet?"

I kissed my teeth. With my lip turned upward, I said, "Don't try me like—"

Again, I was cut off. This time, it was his fingers grazing my area that made me speechless.

"Calm ya ass down, pretty," he said, stroking gently. His eyes were on his own movements when he spoke again. "Just answer the question."

"You didn't answer miiiine." The last part of my reply turned into a moan when he dipped his fingers inside me quickly. Because he lived to piss me off, he only did it once.

"I'm ignoring your question 'cause you only wanna know the answer if it's the one you wanna hear. *I* want the got damn truth. So tell me."

I rolled my eyes but relented because he was right. Hearing about him with other women hadn't ever been something I handled well.

"You told me not to let anybody else put their mouth there, and I haven't. Oh my goodness, Julian. Stop playin' with me," I said, beginning to feel desperate. He was killing me, and he knew it. The silky sounds being produced as he stirred his fingers in my throbbing center were auditory evidence of my desire.

I was dripping with lust, but the man I craved had yet to give in and let me have him. Instead, he pushed me further toward the edge by allowing his saliva to fall from his mouth to my flesh as if I weren't wet enough already. Then, he blew against me gently.

"I haven't touched you in a year, Jet. Since when your hardheaded ass start listenin' to me?"

I let out a sigh that was mixed with frustration and longing. Little did he know, *nobody* had touched me since the last time he did. He was already on one, though. I wasn't about to feed his ego anymore.

"I've always listened to you when it came to *that*. Nobody else has put their lips on me. Now, can you *please*—"

Since shutting me up seemed to be the theme of the evening, I should have seen it coming, but he blindsided me once again. Before I could complete my sentence, he entered me fully... with his tongue. With it buried inside me, he moved it in a circular motion that I was sure he'd never done on me before.

It was the sweetest kind of torture, and he kept at it for what felt like a lifetime. Just when that familiar heat began to bubble in my gut, he slid his tongue out of me and relaxed it before using it to caress my wet folds.

Allowing his index and middle fingers to penetrate me, he focused his tongue on my clit, applying just the right amount of pressure.

"Please... please, don't stop," I said with a tight voice. I could feel his conceited smirk on my skin, and I bit down on my lip, determined not to give him the satisfaction of moaning one more time.

That plan was short-lived, however, because he *didn't* stop. He actually went harder. Simultaneously, he began spreading the fingers he had inside me apart and sucking the same spot he had been licking.

My whimpers sounded foreign to me. Julian and his mouth had made me a stranger to myself because nothing about what was happening within me felt familiar. The heat in my core turned into a full-blown fire, and I began convulsing.

"Ooo, yes. I fuckin' love you, Ali!" I cried out as my essence flowed from me.

"Shid, I know," he said against my ear.

My body continued to shudder long after he had removed his mouth from my body *and* slid his fully erect penis into my opening.

His entering me so suddenly sent me into a complete frenzy, and I felt myself releasing again.

"What are you tryna do to me?"

"Just let it happen, pretty," he whispered against my ear.

Tears were welling in my eyes as he drove himself in and out of me steadily.

"Damn, girl. You're wrong as hell for keeping this from me," he said with a deep groan.

Through labored breaths, I replied, "I'm not. You just wo—"

He slammed into me forcefully, and my words dissipated. I had a feeling he didn't want to hear the rest of my statement, and I couldn't say I didn't understand that.

He gripped both my ankles and bent my legs, spreading them even more, if that were at all possible. This man pushed himself even deeper, and I felt as though all the air left my lungs. Usually, I would try to keep up with him. I hated to let Julian show me up in the bedroom, but he wasn't playing fair. I was defenseless against his powerful thrusts, and my only recourse was to surrender completely.

"Fuck, man." Julian grunted and began moving faster, letting me know he was on the brink of a climax. I was glad because I felt my third one mounting quickly.

"Gone let me have that, Jet. You know I need it," he whispered, lifting his head. I knew exactly what he was asking for. He never came until I got everything I needed, but luckily, his request was coming right up.

Leaning down, he devoured my mouth with his, and that one gesture opened the floodgates once again. I began to tremble uncontrollably around him, and I felt his dick pulsating as he spilled into me.

Seconds later, he collapsed beside me and pulled me into his arms. We lay that way for the longest time. I didn't know what he was doing, but I was deep in my thoughts. I had just told him I *loved* him. In our entire history of being friends with benefits, those words never escaped my lips before. They were *true*, but I was the only one who knew it.

I knew he heard me, but I was hoping we could pretend it never happened. My loving him didn't change the fact that I couldn't give him children. That meant we could never actually be together, so my confession was pointless.

Not wanting to fall into a depressing rabbit hole of thoughts about my issues, I reminisced on the amazingly intense session we had just shared. He had no idea, but he had just reminded me why I had no wish to give myself to anyone else. If it wasn't Julian, I didn't want it.

"Happy birthday, Jet."

I looked at him and smirked. "Thanks, goofy."

He sat up and ran a hand over his hair.

"Come shower with me," he said and stood.

I hopped up a little too quickly—I was sore already—and placed my hand in his without hesitation. It was likely he would cut me off once again when we woke up in the morning, so I planned to make the most of the time he was giving me.

Happy birthday to me, indeed.

A Woman?

♥

Tate

Present Day

I sat staring at the evidence board with an elbow resting on the table in front of me.

I allowed my eyes to scan every photo, item, and word on the board for the millionth time as I listened to Joseph tell me his thoughts on the case we were working on. When he finished, I mulled over his words for a minute before letting him in on what I had been considering.

"I think the unsub is a woman."

He frowned.

"When you start thinkin' that?" he asked.

Sitting back in the desk chair, I drummed my fingers on the desk. "Since the last guy went missing. I was sittin' on it 'cause I thought it was a lil out there, but I'on know, man. I really think it might be a woman."

He studied me silently for a minute before nodding his head.

"Tell me why," he said. I sat up again and leaned forward.

"Aight, these two victims, the CEO, and the doctor are around the same age, they got the same build... they resemble each other all around. What if the unsub is a woman targeting men who resemble an abuser from her past?"

Joseph sat back and rubbed his chin for a minute.

"But these men we're talkin' 'bout ain't small," he said, pointing to their pictures on our evidence board. "How would she subdue 'em? And where they at? All we have is two missing persons' cases right now, and the fact that no bodies have turned up yet suggests they're still alive. If it's a woman, and they're still alive, how is she keeping two grown men in check?"

I sighed. "Yeah, you right. But also, I think the fact that bodies have yet to be discovered is another fact pointing to a woman. A man kidnapping other men would just kill 'em, right? There's something this unsub is getting out of this that I just don't see coming from a man, J."

After a minute, he said, "Yeah, I feel you, and you prolly on to somethin', but we gotta work all our angles, bruh."

I nodded, and he stood before walking out of our temporary office.

Joseph and I usually disagreed at certain points in all the cases we worked together, but our difference in perspective was what made our partnership work. Usually, when it was all said and done, we would realize that we were both right—*and wrong*—about different things regarding the case.

At this point, though, one thing we agreed on was that the abductions weren't random. They had to be connected. We just needed to figure out how. I was hoping we could do that sooner than later because the truth was, I didn't move back to Georgia for this.

J and I were profilers for the FBI, and while we had spent most of our careers on active cases, both of us got into this field because we were genuinely interested in the way the criminal mind worked. What caused a person to perform certain acts was the big question, and we had finally gotten to a place in our careers where we could explore it.

We were in Atlanta on a long-term case study, interviewing serial killers in Georgia prisons. No one else in our unit wanted to take the job, but we saw it as an opportunity to move closer to home and have a relaxed life for a change.

J was a husband and father of two. Whenever we weren't on a case, he would spend his time with his family, but we would work cases ten out of the twelve months a year. I didn't have kids, but I was hyped to be settled for a while.

The deal was that we interviewed criminals three days a week, and we had the rest of our time to ourselves. The only time we would have to work outside of those parameters was when the local police department requested FBI assistance or insight on a case. That was what happened two weeks ago and why we were still setting up shop in this precinct.

Two men had gone missing in the city, and the locals didn't know what to make of it. That was where we came in, but so far, we hadn't been able to find them. It was frustrating me to no end.

"Aye, it's four o'clock. Let's dip up outta here," J said, now standing at the door. I looked up at him and frowned.

"We ain't stayin' late today? It's Thursday," I said. Each of the victims had been abducted on a Thursday, and they were a week apart. It had been a week since the last one, and we both were pretty sure we'd get a missing person's call soon.

"Yeah, I know, but when the call comes, we'll be back. We gotta go help Jess move in, remember?"

My jaw tightened at the mention of Jessica.

"I ain't know nothin' 'bout that. Me and Jessica don't communicate."

He lifted his arms and gripped the top of the door frame. With a smirk, he said, "Y'all's asses coulda fooled me. I peeped y'all at her birthday party. You left with her, right?"

I was silent for a moment, considering whether I wanted to let my boy in on what happened that night. Blocking it out had been easy for the last two months because we went back to our normal lives. I was back in Atlanta, and she was in New York, so she was out of sight and mind. *Now,* she had moved back to the A, and I knew we would be seeing more of each other because of who our friends were.

Knowing he was going to force me to help him move her in, I figured it would be best to get my feelings about the situation off my chest first. I smirked.

"She left wit' me," I finally responded.

"Same difference. How did the rest of y'all's night go?"

"It was cool 'til it wasn't."

J stepped into the room and closed the door behind him. He didn't say anything until he was sitting across from me at the table.

"What happened?"

I glanced at him, and the serious expression he wore made me chuckle. *Ole concerned ass.*

"What you think happened? You know she be doin' too much, and it's only so much a man can take."

Now, he was smirking. "I thought you wasn't takin' it there with Jess again."

I cut my eyes at him. "I didn't mean to. She was tryin' me, and it just happened. She... she said she loved me after."

I laughed when J's eyebrows shot up.

"That's a new development, ain't it?" he asked.

I kissed my teeth. "Ain't nothin' new about it. Jessica *been* lovin' me; she just loves to play games."

"Aight, so what did you say to that?"

I smirked. "I told her I already knew that shit."

"Cocky ass. I ain't seein' the problem, though. It sounds like y'all had an okay night."

"We did. Then I woke up the next morning to her tryna leave without sayin' somethin' to me. That pissed me off, so I cussed her out and told her to hurry and get up outta my hotel room."

J chuckled and shook his head. "Y'all can't get right to save your lives."

"That's all her, dawg. I'm over it too," I admitted.

"What you mean?"

"I mean, I'm done wit' Jet, man. I put my cards on the table three times too many. I ain't 'bout to beg her to let us happen. Before her birthday, I had successfully cut her off for a minute. I ain't goin' there with her again. I mean that too."

Joseph chuckled. "Yeah, aight. You still comin' to help move her in, so come on."

Shaking my head, I stood and followed him out of the precinct. Moving her furniture didn't mean I had to talk to her.

***

My eyes found Jessica as soon as we pulled up to her new crib.

She and Davi were out front. Davi was taking pictures of her in front of a moving truck.

I studied Jess as she posed. She was rocking a deep green sweatsuit. The jacket hung off her shoulders and was only zipped halfway. The white tank top she wore matched her sneakers, and she had on the same sunglasses she was showing off on her livestream for her birthday.

I loved to see Jess on her chill-type vibe, and the fact that she was wearing my favorite color made me like her outfit even more. I chuckled as J stopped the car, and we got out. I never even had a favorite color until I met Jessica Brielle, but I now appreciated the color green because of how well she wore it.

I shut the door before heading toward them. Jessica's eyes were on me as soon as I was in her line of sight, and for a minute, she stopped posing. She looked surprised to see me. I didn't say anything because I was still trying to decide how I wanted to handle our encounter.

Davi, realizing they were no longer alone, turned to us and smiled. J made it to them first, and he kissed his wife.

"Wassup, Sunshine," he said, causing her to grin.

"Hey, handsome. Tate, where have you been?" Davi asked as J walked over and hugged Jess.

I pulled Davi in for a hug before responding.

"I been here. What you mean?" I asked.

Davi rolled her eyes. "You know what I mean. You haven't been to dinner at our house in forever."

I laughed. Davi cooked Sunday dinner every week. I went on a date with a woman I met the previous Sunday and ended up at her crib afterward, so I never made it to dinner. That was the only one I had missed since we all moved back to Georgia.

"Forever is an exaggeration, Sunshine, but my bad. It won't happen again."

I chuckled when J cut his eyes at me. He hated when I called Davi the nickname he used for her, but I did it just to get on his nerves.

She rolled her eyes and grinned. "Better not."

"Where my boys at?" I asked her, referring to their sons.

"Inside, doing who knows what." Davi held up the phone and started scrolling through the photos she had taken of Jessica.

I was low-key admiring them until Davi said, "Jess, come look at these. I need to start charging because I got skills."

Jess cleared her throat and walked over to us. She avoided eye contact with me and stood on the other side of Davi before taking the phone from her. I watched her as she observed the photos. Her chest rose and fell quickly, and her teeth had a vice grip on her bottom lip. She was nervous, and I had a feeling I was the reason why.

Initially, I planned to ignore her, but if I was honest, I couldn't do that if I tried. I decided to mess with her instead. I walked up behind her and left just a little space between our bodies. I heard her gasp, and I chuckled under my breath.

She kept her eyes on the phone, but I knew her focus was on me. I examined the pictures with her for a minute before finally speaking up.

"Don't post these."

She took a step forward, trying to remove herself from my personal space. With her back still to me, she asked, "Why not?"

"'Cause you're a celebrity, and these pictures show too much of the front of your house. You don't need people knowin' where you live. As a matter of fact..." My voice trailed off as I stepped forward and plucked the phone from her fingers.

That got her attention, and she finally turned toward me as I went to our message thread on her phone. I selected all the pictures and sent them to myself before I started deleting them from the thread on her end and her photos app. She tried to snatch the phone from me, but I held it out of her reach. She folded her arms.

"You ain't my daddy, goofy."

I ignored her. It wasn't until I went to her recently deleted folder and removed them permanently that I acknowledged her again.

"Go stand right there," I said, pointing to a part of the house that was more obscure. I opened the camera and held it up, waiting for her to move to that spot. She kissed her teeth instead.

"I don't want you to take my pictures, Julian. I want you to give me my phone back."

I chuckled and placed the phone in my pocket before heading over to the moving truck.

"Julian, that's my phone."

All that *Julian* shit was pissing me off, and I knew that was her intention. Because I was still committed to cutting her off, I didn't even react to it.

Instead, I glanced at her with a frown. "What the hell you say that for? You know I know that."

She was fuming at that point, and it was low-key hilarious. Not concerned about her attitude, I glanced at the moving truck before asking, "Where's the key to open the back?"

Jessica stood there for a minute, looking mad at the world, before she turned on her heels and stomped inside the house.

Davi laughed. "Y'all are a hot mess, Tate. Here's the key."

I took it from her and smirked. "Nah, she's the mess. I'ma let her have it, though," I said as I opened the back of the truck. My choosing not to fool with Jess on an intimate level didn't change the fact that I cared about her. I wasn't about to let her put herself in harm's way by letting the world know where she laid her head.

She could be mad all she wanted, but those pictures weren't getting posted.

***

"Where you want this, Jet?"

She didn't respond, so I glanced at her. She was standing in the center of her living room, not facing me. I set the small dresser down and walked over to her. J and I had carried everything in from the moving truck, and now she and Davi were supposed to be unpacking and organizing things.

She was surrounded by a bunch of boxes but hadn't moved to touch one of them. As I neared her, I realized she was staring blankly at the wall, which struck me as odd, but I had noticed her zone out a few times in the hours I'd been there. Something was up with her, and I wanted to know what it was. I couldn't be in her presence, knowing something was wrong and just *not* care. As frustrating as she was, my love for her wasn't built that way.

I tapped her shoulder, making her jump a little. When she turned to face me, her eyes softened, and for a second, she resembled the vulnerable woman who couldn't keep her hands off me and told me she loved me two months ago. After that second passed, though, her expression transitioned to one I could go the rest of my life without seeing again. She now looked like the woman who constantly pretended she didn't want a nigga.

"What?" she asked, making me chuckle.

"You good?" I asked.

She kissed her teeth. "Don't I *look* good?"

Her smart mouth got on my nerves and turned me on every time she opened it.

"Nah." She cut her eyes at me, and I shrugged. "Shid, you don't. You look like somethin' is botherin' you, and you actin' like you can't hear. I been callin' your name for the last thirty seconds."

Rolling her eyes, she said, "All that's bothering me right now is you, *Tate*."

I chuckled. She had been pushing it all day, but she *knew* I hated when she called me Tate. It didn't even sound right leaving her lips.

I chuckled again before lifting a hand and gripping her chin. Immediately, she gasped, then tucked her bottom lip between her teeth. Her confident gaze faltered, and she was now staring at my shirt.

Leaning down so that my face was barely not touching hers, I said, "You and I both know that's a damn lie, and I ain't gon' let you tell it to me," I leaned in closer and watched as she closed her eyes and parted her lips slightly.

I shook my head and released her. I stepped back, and her eyes shot open before she cleared her throat and tried to compose herself.

"You're bothered by somethin', but it damn shole ain't me. You ain't gotta tell me what it is, but you need to get it off ya chest, 'cause that stress you've been rockin' all day ain't a good look on you."

She was about to respond, likely with another lie she had just cooked up, but my work phone rang. I slid it out of my pocket and answered immediately.

"Tate," I said after placing the phone to my ear.

"Agent, there's been another abduction," Detective Hodges said. "Judge Raymond Rogers. I called your technical analyst and gave her a heads up. She said she'd be sending a file on him to you and your partner ASAP."

With a sigh, I said, "Aight, we'll be there in twenty," then I hung up.

"Aye, J! We have gotta head out," I called while opening the email Moreau sent seconds ago.

The hell?

I frowned as I scanned the information. The judge was white and almost seventy years old. His profile was the exact opposite of the other missing people, so if it was connected to our case, I didn't know what to make of it.

A second later, Davi and Joseph were coming down the stairs. There was no telling what their in-love asses were up there doing. He had his phone in hand and wore a frown, so I figured he already knew what was up. That was confirmed when he said, "What are we dealin' with, Tate?"

I sighed. "I'on know, but we gotta go."

Nodding, he turned and kissed Davi before heading outside. I glanced at Jess, and there was no longer hostility on her face. She looked worried and like she wanted to say something. At that point, I couldn't even worry about it.

"Hit me up if you need help movin' this furniture around. I should be available tomorrow."

With that, I turned and headed toward the door, telling Davi I'd see her later before closing it behind me.

An Instant Forever

♥

Jess

I watched silently as Joseph and Julian left my house.

How was he able to do that?

I managed to avoid him for the majority of the time he'd been here helping, but he still picked up on the fact that something was going on with me. I had a love-hate relationship with how sensitive he was to my emotions.

Ali was the most observant person I knew. He picked up on the little things, and because of that, I was sure he knew me better than anybody. Well, maybe everyone except my mother and Davi. *Speaking of my best friend...*

Her silence prompted me to glance at her, only to find she was already studying me intently. I rolled my eyes.

"What?" I had the same attitude in my tone that was there when I asked Tate that very question.

She frowned and folded her arms.

"I was just about to ask you that."

"Why?"

Now, she was the one rolling her eyes. "Jess, please. You've been quiet since Tate got here, and that's not like you at all. In four hours, you didn't find one thing to argue with him about, and every time I look at you, you're staring into space, looking like your dog died. Something is going on with you. Now that they're gone, I'm ready for you to be honest about it."

I almost laughed at the stern look she was flashing, but I couldn't even find a smile. My lip trembled as I tried to formulate a response, so I just closed my mouth. Something *was* going on with me, and seeing Tate pushed me even further in my feelings about it than I already had been.

I wanted to tell him exactly what was up, but I couldn't bring myself to open up just yet. What was weighing on me would change my relationship with him forever, and I wasn't ready to pull the trigger on that.

Realizing my best friend wasn't going to let me off the hook, I said, "Come here." I quietly walked over to the sofa where my purse was and sat. Davi plopped down beside me while I retrieved a small plastic bag from it. I placed it in her hands and said, "Here."

I watched as she studied the bag's contents. After a few silent moments, she finally spoke up.

"Who took these?" Davi asked with misty eyes. Her voice was barely above a whisper as she held up the bag of positive pregnancy tests. Her emotional state activated mine, and I felt my first tears fall.

"I did," I whispered, sounding like someone else. I didn't *feel* like myself, so it made sense. I watched as Davi's eyes widened and her lip quivered. Her expression displayed almost everything I'd felt since I took the tests a week ago. These tests contradicted everything I had accepted as truth about myself nearly seven years ago. They negated what the doctors said was possible.

My mom and Davi always told me God had the final say in my ability to reproduce, but I blocked that out and focused on accepting my childless fate. *But now...*

Davi interrupted my thoughts when she wrapped her arms around me. I returned the gesture, and we stayed that way for quite some time. Eventually, I pulled away and wiped my eyes.

"You're having a baby," she said, shock evident.

"I am."

More tears fell from her eyes when she said, "I'm so freaking happy for you, best friend. Congratulations."

For the first time in weeks, I smiled. "Thanks, Vi."

We both went silent again until she snapped her head in my direction and hit my arm.

"How are you? Like, how are you feeling about this?" The concern in her voice had me tearing up again.

How was I feeling about this? Two weeks ago, I knew something was different. At first, I thought it was food poisoning, but when it persisted, I was able to rule that out. I was fully aware that Ali and I hadn't used protection, but pregnancy was the last thing on my mind for obvious reasons.

I continued to feel sick and miserable for a couple more days until I decided to just buy pregnancy tests. Once I reassured myself there was no way I could possibly be pregnant, I was going to go to the doctor to figure out what the problem was. Turns out, pregnancy *was* the problem. Well, it wasn't a *problem*, but it was an overwhelming realization. The only way I had made it all this time without breaking down was by trying to block it out. I decided to pretend I hadn't taken the tests until I moved back to Georgia and told Julian about it, but now here we were.

"I don't know how I feel. I mean… if I'm really going to be a mommy, I'm happy. I've wanted that for so long, but I can't act like I'm not scared, too. I don't want to get hype about a baby only for something bad to happen because of my health history. I guess I feel all kinds of ways, Vi," I said and sighed heavily.

"I can understand that, but I'm not receiving it, sis. God knows how badly you want motherhood, and I refuse to believe he's presenting it to you just to tease you. It's not how He does things. So I get being scared, but I'm gonna pray that those fears be replaced with faith that He's got you. Because he does."

I nodded as I allowed her words to sink in. She was right, but letting go of these worries was a lot easier said than done. I was hoping I would feel better once I went to my old doctor. I visited a doctor in New York, and they confirmed the pregnancy and gave me some vitamins, but they didn't know my health history. Doctor Prestige knew my chart better than I did, so if she told me everything was good, a weight would be lifted off my shoulders.

"Wait… who is the baby's daddy, Miss *Celibate?*" she asked with squinted eyes. I laughed and wiped my tears.

"Julian," I said in a low tone, prompting her to hit me again.

"Girl, you just got to town yesterday. When did you find time to let him knock you up?" she asked before her eyes widened, and she gasped.

"Your fast tail had sex with him on your birthday! I knew you did, liar."

I rolled my eyes. "Sorry, but you know how you get when I tell you something about me and that man."

When she asked whether we had sex on my birthday, I did lie because I didn't feel like hearing her mouth about how we were meant to be together.

"All *I* do is tell the truth; you just can't take it. Now, tell me everything."

I told my best friend everything that happened on my birthday, from him singing in my ear to me singing his name in that hotel room.

"Everything was goin' fine until..." My voice trailed off before I told her the biggest thing.

She kissed her teeth. "Until what?"

"The sex was amazing. So amazing that I told him I loved him," I finally blurted out. Davi's annoying ass started laughing. I rolled my eyes.

"Something funny?"

"Yep, *you*. He knows you love him, so that wasn't a big reveal, Jess. While I do believe you about the quality of y'all's sex life, I know that's not the sole reason you said those words. That was drunk truth right there. You're in love with that man, and now there's no reason to pretend you don't," she said with a knowing look.

I sighed. Even though I had never expressed it to her—or even aloud to myself—I knew she was aware of the real reason I ran away from love with Ali. We always danced around the subject because she knew it was too painful for me to discuss.

I loved me some Ali, but unfortunately, he came into my life two years after I found out I couldn't have kids. My feelings for Julian were stirred up every time we were in the same space, so I knew they would grow with consistent time together. I dreaded falling too deeply in love with him, only to have him end it and find a woman who could give him everything.

No matter how much he said, he wanted a relationship with me, that one small detail would eventually matter. That was the reason I hid behind my jet-setting, party-girl lifestyle. I was grooming myself for a life alone.

"Maybe not, but... Vi, this is wild. I mean, I know Julian's a man who would eventually want kids, but this is so sudden, and who knows how it's gon' affect his life. What if he's seeing someone?"

My chest tightened at that thought.

"I don't think so, but if he is, he'd drop her the second you admit you want him."

I wanted that to be true, but I just wasn't convinced.

Davi continued. "Just wait. Once you tell him about the baby, he's gonna be ready to lock you down then. It's kinda funny that after one night of being grown and nasty, you secured an instant forever with the love of your life, who you've been runnin' from all this time."

I sighed. "Who said I secured forever with him?"

She rolled her eyes. "I said it. If you wanna be in denial still, then fine. It's an instant eighteen years, *minimum*."

"Maybe. Look, of course, I'm gon' tell him, but I need a little time to process first. I just took these tests a week ago and haven't had time to deal with them. So, I need you not to tell Julian *or* Joseph. *Okay?*" I looked her square in the eye, needing to hear her promise.

She looked conflicted, but she eventually nodded. "Fine, but Jess, you know how hard it is for me to keep secrets from Joseph. Don't wait too long. I'm serious."

"I got you, Vi."

"Does Mama Nelly know?"

I shook my head. "Nah, the second I tell my mother, she's gon' tell my father, so I'ma hold off on that. They were here earlier today, and it was killing me not to say anything."

My mother was like my best friend, and I kept nothing from her. For the most part, she kept my secrets, but I knew it would be hard for her to keep something this big from my daddy. As soon as he found out, he would want a sit down with the man responsible for my pregnancy, and I knew for a fact that I wasn't ready for all that.

"What about business?"

Davi was asking all the questions I had been avoiding, but I knew I needed to figure out the answers soon.

"I don't know, Vi. For now, I'm continuing with business as usual. I got a campaign to finish, and once that's done, I can focus on being somebody's mama."

"I'll let you finish the campaign, Jess, but I'm not going to let you *not* take care of yourself or my god baby."

I smirked. "Who said you were the god momma? I thought either Demi or Crissy might be a good choice."

She cut her eyes at me. "I will slap your pregnant behind, Jessica. Know that."

"I'm just playin', dang. I'm glad I'm finally back home, though. There's no way in the world I could get through this without you."

She hugged me again and said, "There's no way I'd let you. Now, let's go sort out your dishes. I know that's what you wanna work on first, anyway."

I rolled my eyes and stood with a genuine smile. I knew I still had a lot to figure out, but my best friend knowing made the burden feel a whole lot lighter.

***

"Hey, Val! Whatchu doin' here?" I asked, carefully taking one of my sculptures out of a box. I placed it on the desk before turning to Valerie, my photographer.

She smiled and walked further into my office. "I left one of my cameras here the other day, so I came to pick it up. It's coming together really well in here," she said, looking around.

I smiled as I gave the room a once-over. "Yeah, I'm determined to get it in order. You know I can't deal with chaos," I said with a chuckle.

Before I moved back to Atlanta, I not only had my dream home built from the ground up but also secured an office building. I was blessed enough to have a solid team of people willing to move with me to Atlanta, and I wanted all of us to have a legit workspace, just like we did in New York.

"Hey, Val! You come to help us out?" Shay asked, walking into my office. She and I had been there for the last few hours, sorting everything in the moving boxes.

Val shrugged. "I can, I guess—"

Shay's phone ringing halted Val's response. It was her business phone, so she placed it on speaker when she answered.

"This is Shania Paysinger, Jessica Westin's assistant. What can I do for you?"

"Hello, this is Tom Statin, the Creative Director at *Bodii Swimwear*." Shay's eyes widened, and Val smiled. I just stood in place, staring at Shay's phone with a lump in my throat.

A few months ago, I auditioned for a *Bodii* campaign, but they ended up going with another model. *Bodii* was the biggest couture swimwear brand in the country, so I was devastated when I didn't book the job.

Now, *they* were calling *me*, and my intuition told me an offer was attached. Two months ago, I would have been ecstatic, but now I felt a mild episode of depression coming on. I couldn't accept a swimwear gig unless they wanted to shoot like *tomorrow*. I was almost three months pregnant and knew I'd be showing soon.

I tuned back into the phone call just in time to hear him say, "The model we went with for the summer campaign has unfortunately had a terrible accident that will have her indisposed during our shooting schedule."

Oh God.

"We were hoping Ms. Westin was still interested in the spot."

Oh my God.

Shay glanced at me with raised brows, silently asking for my answer. Quickly, I grabbed the notepad and a pen from my desk and scribbled a note to give her. She nodded as her eyes scanned my message.

"When are you all planning to shoot the campaign?" she asked him. I saw Val frown at me, but I ignored it.

"In exactly six weeks."

Shay looked at me again, and I sighed. "I can't do it."

"One second, Mr. Statin."

I watched as Shay muted her phone. Now, she was frowning, likely because this was my dream job, and I wasn't jumping at the opportunity. "You want me to tell him no? You don't want to think about it?"

I didn't want to think about it because that wouldn't change my answer. My body was already changing. There was no way I'd be able to pose in bikinis in six weeks.

I sighed. "You can tell him we need to think about it, but I know I definitely can't do it."

Still frowning, she took the phone off mute and said,

"Uh, is it okay if I give you a callback? I am not with Ms. Westin at the moment, and I need to present the offer to her."

"Of course, I understand. Just give me a call within the next week."

"I sure will. Thanks again, Mr. Statin." As soon as Shay hung up, she turned to me.

"You've been wanting to work with *Bodii* since I met you. Why did we not just accept the offer?"

"I just..." My voice trailed off as I realized I didn't know how to respond. It had been three weeks since I found out I was pregnant, and only Davi and I knew about it. There was no way I was going to tell anyone else about my pregnancy before I told the father of my child. I was already feeling kind of bad about telling Davi before him.

"I just have a lot coming up in the next month or so personally... family stuff. I was going to tell you once we took a break from organizing that I have to pull back from booking gigs for a while."

Shay wasn't one to pry, but her mind was always on business, so I expected her next question.

"Okay, I understand. Does this mean we'll be sticking to social media content, or are you completely off the grid?"

I shook my head. "No, not off the grid. I just can't commit to brands outside of my own right now. I'll be able to tell you more in a few weeks, but things are a little in the air right now."

I didn't want her to think we had just moved to Atlanta just for me to stop grinding. I was still going to work. I just had to figure out how to center it around my life changes.

Val, who I almost forgot was in the room, spoke up then. "I get family stuff, but you don't think this can be the last gig you take before you step back? Like Shania said, you've been wanting a *Bodii* campaign for a long time."

I frowned a little because Val rarely gave her two cents on major bookings. She was my personal photographer and captured content for my social media pages and different sponsorships I got, but this type of job wouldn't involve her. My team consisted of Valerie, Shay, and Margo. I valued each of them and paid them an excellent salary. They knew they'd be getting paid whether I booked a job or not, so I was confused about what her problem was.

My expression softened as I realized it wasn't about money. It was about *me*. Our team became like a family over the years. It was the reason the three of them were so willing to move with me. Val wanted to see me win, and she knew how badly I wanted this job.

Sighing, I said, "This one is a dream of mine, but the things I have going on right now are what they are. All I can do is explain that to Tom honestly and pray he doesn't hold it against me. If it's meant to be, it'll come around again."

Shay nodded with a smile. "Agreed. We'll call him in a couple of days, but let's take a break from all this and get lunch." She turned to Val. "You wanna come?"

Val shook her head. "No, I forgot I have a few things to take care of before five. I'll catch up with you guys tomorrow."

"Cool." The three of us headed out of the office and to the parking lot. Once Shay and I decided where to eat, I got in my car and pulled out of the parking lot with my baby and their father on my mind.

***

I shut my car engine off, relaxed my head against the headrest, and closed my eyes. It had been a long day.

It had been four days since *Bodii* offered me a job, and I had officially declined this afternoon. After that, Shay and I mapped out a social media content calendar for the next month and finished organizing our office.

We hadn't told Valerie and Margo to come in today, but we planned to meet with them soon so we would all be on the same page about everything.

Lately, my fatigue had been at an all-time high. I had my first official doctor's appointment the next week, and I was hoping the doctor could give me something to increase my energy levels. I had too much to accomplish to be in bed for the next six months.

Davi wanted me to get an earlier appointment, but I wasn't about to have anyone by my side during this journey who wasn't Doctor Prestige, and she couldn't get me in until next week. She had been my doctor since I was a child and specialized in pediatric and women's health. She was the person who noticed my fibroids initially and was a big support to me during that time.

Eventually, I opened and exited the car and headed toward my front door. The garage was still being built on my home, so unfortunately, I had to park my car out front. Once I reached the door, I realized I had a delivery. I bent down and observed the bouquet. It was black roses, and a letter was attached.

Frowning, I unlocked my home and entered.

Who the hell bought me this?

Black roses weren't my vibe, and I didn't think anyone close to me would ever purchase something like this for me. I was a little alarmed but tried to rationalize the unexpected gift. I bought this land for my home because it was in a friendly community with only a few other houses nearby. Maybe one of the homeowners was trying to welcome me to the neighborhood.

I removed my shoes, left them neatly by the door, and headed for the living room. It wasn't until I reached my sofa and plopped down that I opened the note. As I read it, my heartbeat quickened. This definitely wasn't from a neighbor.

> *I can't believe you are this ungrateful. I did the unthinkable to get you that job, and you turned it down? I do so much for you... things no one else would ever do, but you just spit in my face. You're so unappreciative, and you don't deserve my devotion. But my heart wants what it wants, and that's you. I think it's about time for us to talk face-to-face so we can straighten this out.*
>
> *Forever and only yours... always.*
> *MAC.*

I couldn't even form words. To say the note spooked me would have been a significant understatement. By the signature, I knew the sender was my secret admirer who sent flowers to my office every birthday.

But...

These flowers were delivered to my home—my *new* home that was a thousand miles away from where this person delivered their other letters. My eyes watered as my heart began to pound.

What in the entire fuck?

I didn't have a secret admirer like I thought. I had a *stalker*, and that realization scared the shit out of me.

I reread the note.

I did the unthinkable to get you that modeling job...

What did *that* mean? With my brain working overtime, I picked up my phone, but my hands were trembling so much that it dropped from my hands. I had to pause and take several deep breaths before I was able to grab it and actually dial.

"Hey, sis," Shay said after the second ring.

"Hey," I said, my voice shaky. I cleared my throat and closed my eyes before continuing. "Do you remember the name of the model who got the *Bodii* campaign initially?"

"Yeah, it was Heather Thorne. You've done work with her before."

That's right. I remember her.

"Alright, thanks," I said before hanging up in her face.

I worked hard to steady my fingers as I typed Heather's name into my phone's internet browser. Sure enough, the result that popped up was about her accident.

Bile rose in my throat as I read. Tom Statin said she was indisposed, but he didn't mention that she was in a freaking coma. The article stated that she fell down a flight of stairs alone at home.

I looked at the letter again. If I didn't know any better, I would say MAC was taking credit for Heather's injury. Who was this, and what did they want with me?

I sat there frozen for the longest time. I didn't know what to do. I wanted to call my parents but had lied and told them I was out of town for a job.

I hated lying to them, but until I was ready to come clean about being pregnant, I had no choice but to avoid them. I needed to go to the police.

If I was on the right track, then this unidentified person who had been a part of my life for all this time was a criminal. That fact made me think of what Davi said on my birthday.

"I bet you my FBI husband will get these letters to stop."

Without letting another moment pass, I called Davi. She answered immediately.

"Hey, Jess. What's up?"

"Uh, can you and Joseph come over? I have a problem, and I'm..." I swallowed. "I'm scared," I admitted, my voice cracking.

Like I knew she would, Vi sprang into action. "We'll be there in fifteen minutes. Let's stay on the phone until we get there."

***

I released a shaky breath after explaining everything I knew about this situation to Joseph.

He was silently examining the letter as he had been since they arrived minutes earlier.

"Auntie, does the TV work in your room yet?" my godson Joseph, the second, or Two as we called him, asked. He was entering the living room from my kitchen with his little brother, David, behind him. They each had a bag of fruit snacks in their hands.

"Yeah, it works, baby."

He nodded and said, "Come on, D."

They headed upstairs, and Joseph finally spoke. "You don't have security cameras?"

I shook my head. "I haven't hired anybody to do that yet."

"Fuck," he said under his breath. He pulled his phone out and left the room.

"Jess... you have to call Tate and tell him right now," Davi said, looking at me sternly.

Tears began to fall as I tried to find words to negate her suggestion. *There* were none.

"Vi, I just—"

She held a hand up to stop me. "I don't wanna hear that. This is dangerous, and you need protection. It's *been* unsafe for you, and I had already told you that, but now it's bigger than *just* you. You need to be around someone who can protect you, and while you already know you can stay with Joseph and me, I don't think Tate would appreciate someone else stepping up for *his* family."

His family?

I hadn't thought about it that way, but she was right. No matter what, this baby had officially linked Julian and me forever.

"Come on, Jess. I already know Joseph's next call will be to him anyway, so you need to pick up the phone and tell him first."

I took a deep breath. This was the day the rubber met the road. I really had to tell Julian I was pregnant. Wiping tears from my eyes, I reached for my phone just as Joseph reentered the room. I was about to press Julian's name to call him, but Joseph's next words stopped me cold.

"I just talked to Tate. He's on the way over here so we can figure this out."

I was too late.

TF, Jet?

♥

Tate

Ring. Ring. Ring.

I grabbed my phone from my coffee table, low-key grateful for a distraction. This case was driving me crazy. This was the first Thursday since it began that we had no missing person's report, and I didn't know what to make of that. I was tired and irritated, to say the least.

"Wassup, J?" I answered, realizing Joseph was the caller.

"We got a situation. I need you to come to Jess's house."

I stood and immediately moved to my front door, where my shoes and keys were. Once they were on, I grabbed my keys from the hook and headed out.

When I had my car started, I finally asked, "What's goin' on wit' Jet?"

"She got a stalker. Some dude been sending her flowers at her office in New York on her birthday for the last few years."

"So the last time she got somethin' from dude was on her birthday?" I asked, annoyed that she didn't say something then. I knew how crazy superfans could get, and I'd be pissed off if something happened to her because she didn't know how to open her mouth.

"Nah, she heard from him tonight. They left flowers and a note on her doorstep."

"At her new office?"

"Nah, at her crib."

Tightening my grip on the steering wheel, I pressed the gas and sped through the streets of Atlanta to get to her house. None of us lived too far from each other, so I'd be there in the next ten minutes.

"I'm almost there," I said and hung up.

I needed a few minutes of silence to contemplate how I would approach this when I pulled up. Jessica was coming to my crib tonight; I just wasn't in the mood to fight with her about it. If this person knew where she lived, she couldn't be at her place until we found him.

Jessica lived to argue with me, so I knew she was about to try to stay with Davi and Joseph or her parents. Unfortunately, those options didn't work for me.

No disrespect to her pops or my boy, but nobody was going to be responsible for Jessica's safety but me. My heart was important to me, and if something happened to that woman, I was sure it would break. I couldn't put that type of pressure on anyone but myself.

As soon as my car came to a stop, I hopped out of it and jogged to Jessica's front door. I only had to knock twice, and J was opening it up for me. As soon as I stepped inside, he handed me a letter in a plastic bag.

As I read it, I tried to analyze it in every way possible. It looked as if it were typed on an actual typewriter, which was unfortunate because my first move was going to be to get a handwriting analyst to check it out.

I read the words repeatedly, combing through each character with my eye, trying to determine if there were any underlying messages within the note for me to decipher. I couldn't find any.

I pulled out my phone and dialed Moreau. It took her a minute, but she eventually answered. With a sleep-laced voice, she said, "You better be glad you're my favorite."

I couldn't even bring myself to smile or joke with her like I usually did. I needed answers.

"If an unsub typed a message on a typewriter, could we use the note to find where the ink ribbons were purchased?"

She cleared her throat, and I heard her shuffling around.

"Uh, depending on the quality of the note, it's possible. I need to look into it, but I'm sure I can find you an analyst down there who specializes in that sort of thing. I just need you to preserve the note as best you can until I tell you where to take it."

"Aight, cool. Can you look into something else for me too? A woman named Jessica Brielle Westin got a letter from a creep who signed it M-A-C. It's prolly a long shot, but can you see if anyone with those initials is in her past or present?"

"Anything for you, hun. Is everything okay?" she asked concerned.

"I'on know, but I appreciate you helpin' me figure it out. I gotta go, Moreau."

"I'll hit you back with something soon."

I hung up and turned to Joseph. "Where she at?"

***

Joseph led me into Jessica's kitchen, where she and Davi stood, whispering to each other.

Davi was leaning on the counter while Jess was wringing her hands together with her back to the pantry door. I zeroed in on her hands, and they were trembling nonstop. She seemed to be staring at the ground.

Anger began to bubble within me as I studied her. As annoyed as I was about not being her first call, her current state was all I needed to refocus on the real problem. Gone was the smart-mouthed, confident Jess, who walked around like she owned the world.

I realized that not only were her hands trembling uncontrollably, but her entire body seemed to be vibrating. It was clear she had been crying a long time because even with her chocolate skin, I could see redness on her cheeks. Her top lip looked swollen, and I assumed it was because she had been biting down on it just as hard as she was currently chewing her bottom one. She hadn't stopped rocking back and forth or shaking her head since I laid eyes on her.

The longer I observed her, the more red I saw. This stalker had stolen her and left behind a fragile, broken woman who was scared out of her mind. That didn't sit right with me at all.

Joseph and I fully entered the kitchen, and she looked up. Her eyes found me almost immediately, and what I saw in them stilled me. Aside from the fact that they looked bloodshot and were twice the size they usually were, there was something else there. She was terrified.

Whoever was behind that note was going to see me sooner than later for dimming the light in her eyes. That was a promise I knew I'd make good on in due time. I had to make this right for her.

After a few moments, I headed straight toward her. Standing inches away, I asked, "What's going on, Jet?"

She inhaled, but it got caught in her throat, and she broke into a coughing fit. I rushed to open her refrigerator and grab her a bottle of water, but by the time I closed the fridge door, she was leaning over the kitchen sink, throwing up.

Feeling a stinging behind my eyes, I made my way to her while untwisting the cap of the water bottle. I stood beside her quietly, giving her time to collect herself. Only... she couldn't. She continued to heave over the sink, and her body was jerking so aggressively that I placed a hand on her back, trying to steady her.

That connection seemed to calm her down a little because the heaving stopped, but she was still shaking like a scared kitten.

"Come on, pretty. Drink some of this."

I helped her stand again and handed her the bottle of water, but I quickly realized she might not be able to hold it on her own. Placing one hand under her chin, I held the bottle to her lips and tipped it just enough for her to drink. It took a minute, but she was able to take a few sips. Then I set the bottle on the counter and turned to her again.

"Jet," I said, trying again to talk to her.

She looked into my eyes briefly but immediately dropped her head again.

Lifting her chin with my index finger, I said, "Please, talk to me. As soon as you tell me wassup, it won't be your burden to bear no more, pretty, 'cause I swear I'ma take care of it."

She teared up at those words. Then her eyes shifted to something past me before they met mine again. With a quivering lip, she stuttered through her reply. "I-I, uh, I don't even know where to start."

"Start at the beginning, Jessica. I wanna know everything you know."

She shrugged, then sniffled. "I don't know much." Her voice shook as she spoke. "A little after my first modeling campaign, I got an office space in New York and hired a photographer and my assistant. My birthday rolled around a few months after I had the space, and I received my first letter from this person.

"It was attached to a bouquet of red roses, and the note just talked about how they were inspired by and proud of me. I thought it was sweet. I've been getting those notes for the last few years on my birthday."

More tears fell.

"And you're sure they're from the same person?" I asked.

She nodded. "I'm pretty sure. All the notes are signed, M-A-C, so I guess so."

My mind was working overtime as I listened to her.

She sighed again and licked her lips. "Today, I received this note, and it's different than the others. I think he's upset that I turned down a modeling job for *Bodii*. He said something about doing the unthinkable so that I could have that gig, and I researched the first girl who got it. She—"

"You turned down a *Bodii* campaign? Why?"

I didn't mean for my words to come out as aggressively as they did. The campaign wasn't even the most important thing at the moment, but it *was* a big deal. I never had a problem admitting my feelings for Jess, and those feelings didn't disappear because she made a hobby out of running from me.

Being aware of what was happening in her life was almost second nature to me, and I knew as much as I could know about her without turning into a stalker myself. I'd heard her talk about *Bodii* several times on her livestream and knew she wanted to work with them badly.

More tears started spilling from her eyes, and I frowned as I wiped them away.

"Fuck, I'm sorry, Jet. That don't even matter. Calm down, pretty. Please."

She shook her head. "Sorry, I just... I-I..."

Her voice trailed off, and she avoided my eyes. My frown deepened, and confusion consumed me.

I turned to look at Davi and Joseph. Joseph looked stressed, while Davi looked worried. Neither of them seemed confused. *The hell?*

The stalker didn't trigger these tears. The mention of the campaign did. I was now getting the sense that I was the weakest link. There were layers to what was going on with her, and it seemed like I had only scratched the surface. *What was I missing?*

"Jet, what's wrong? Please, tell me what I don't know."

She inhaled slowly and let it out shakily before she released two words that shook my entire world.

"I'm pregnant."

"What did you just say?" I knew my voice was filled with hostility, but forget that. I just knew Jessica Brielle Westin didn't let another man get her pregnant. That was supposed to be *our* future. If she really granted another man barrier-free access to her body, I didn't mean anything to her. I had really played myself to believe that this girl loved me and was scared of what that meant, but nah...

Hell nah.

If she was carrying another man's baby, I didn't know her like I thought I did, and she wasn't the woman I thought I loved.

She spoke up again, but it was barely above a whisper. "I said, I'm pregnant, and... and it's yours."

I barely registered Joseph clearing his throat and saying, "Sunshine, let's give them a minute. Come on."

I dropped my head as I listened to their footsteps retreat. Once I knew we were alone, I looked at her again. I opened my mouth to say something but closed it immediately after. My mind was telling me to be rational, but my heart was telling me to cuss her the fuck out.

I was standing here worried about this and formulating plans on how I was going to protect her—because I *loved* her—and she was keeping secrets as serious as this?

If *I* was the father of the child she carried—and I believed her as soon as she said I was—she was over two months pregnant. She had this information all this time and didn't say anything? Was that why she was acting weird the day I helped move her in?

Why wouldn't she tell me?

I chuckled as I answered my own dumb question.

Jessica had made it beyond clear to me that she was here for a good time, not a long time. I had heard her say plenty of times that she wasn't the "settling down type." I knew she wasn't one to spread herself thin when it came to men, but she loved to travel and party, and a baby would interfere with her lifestyle in a major way.

She didn't tell me because she didn't want the baby, and she didn't want my ass either. *Damn.*

"The fuck, Jessica?" My voice was strained, likely because I was trying to filter the anger out of it. As I listened to the words fall from my lips, the only emotion I could register in my tone was pain. That made sense because this shit hurt bad.

More tears fell from her eyes, and she dropped her head.

"I found out two weeks ago, but it is yours, Julian. You were the last person I had sex with even before my birthday, and I haven't—"

"I ain't doubtin' that the baby's mine, Jessica." As pissed as I was, I didn't want her feeling like she needed to prove anything to me.

She nodded and released a shaky breath. "I'm sorry I didn't tell you sooner, but I just—"

"You just don't want a baby, right? Your jet-settin' ass can't bear the thought of sittin' down long enough to get my seed into the world safely?"

She shook her head. "That ain't true, Ali."

"Then what the fuck is it?" My voice boomed through the kitchen, but I couldn't even worry about checking my tone. I couldn't worry about the feelings of a woman who clearly didn't give a damn about mine. I was pissed. "You want the baby, but you don't want me? Is that it? It's gotta be one or the other for you to keep it from me for two weeks."

"No, Ali, I—"

"Then, you get a whole threat at your door, and I *still* ain't enter your mind. Were you even gon' call me over here? Was this letter enough for you to finally decide to let me know wassup, or did Davi tell you it was time to stop lyin'?"

The look on her face told me everything I needed to know.

I chuckled and shook my head as I took a step back. I couldn't deal with this right now. I needed to detach myself from the situation long enough to come up with a game plan on how to keep her—keep *them*—safe.

"Do you still have the other letters from over the years?" I asked her. Finally, I was able to lower my voice to a reasonable level when I addressed her.

Still crying, she nodded.

"Yes, but they're in a box at my office."

I'd get them the next day. Turning away from her, I headed toward the kitchen door. Before exiting the room, I said, "Go pack a bag."

She frowned as she wiped a tear. "Why?"

I turned my head but kept my body facing the door. "Don't ask me shit, Jessica. Do what I said. I'll be in the foyer waitin' on you."

With that, I walked out. I passed the living room and saw Davi and Joseph sitting on the sofa.

Looking at Davi, I said, "D, can you help her pack a bag? She's still shaken up, but she's comin' wit' me."

"Of course," Davi said softly. I didn't miss the tears in her eyes. Nodding, I passed them and continued to the front of the house.

A few seconds later, Joseph was approaching me. I glanced at him and noticed his concern. I appreciated it, but I wasn't in the mood to hash anything out at the moment. I needed to keep my focus on this stalker and treat it like any other case.

I had to maintain tunnel vision until I got the will to deal with my feelings about everything else because if I gave in to my emotions, I wasn't going to be any good.

J was my boy, though—my brother—so I didn't have to tell him that. He just knew.

"What's the plan, bruh?" he asked.

I shrugged. "She's comin' home wit' me. Ain't nobody gettin' within feet of her without my okay until this is resolved, and that's as far as I've gotten in my thinking."

He nodded. "Understood. We'll figure this out, but Tate..."

His tone let me know he was about to say something I didn't wanna hear but probably needed to.

"What?"

He placed a hand on my shoulder. "I know you're pissed, and you got every right to be, but don't let your anger have you forgettin' the most important fact. She's pregnant, bruh. Pregnant women got enough to worry about, so you addin' to that by bein' cold to her ain't a good look. This is your kid we talkin' about, Tate. We need to get 'em in the world safely, so make sure you're doin' your part in makin' that happen. Aight?"

My jaws tensed, but I nodded. He was basically telling me not to be an asshole for the baby's sake, and I knew he was right. I couldn't lie, though. With the way I was feeling, that was going to be a challenge.

***

"You can sleep in here. We'll talk tomorrow," I said. We had made it to my house, and I immediately showed her to my guest room.

Our ride to my place was quiet, and I had no plans to talk to her any more than I had that evening. I needed time, and I'd have that as soon as she was settled.

"Okay," she said. Her voice cracked, and it was breaking me down. I hadn't ever witnessed Jess sad or emotional before this, but I learned quickly that I didn't like it one bit.

I already knew her smile could make me feel ten feet tall, but tonight, I learned that her tears made me feel powerless. I wanted to fix things for her but knew it wouldn't happen in the next few hours, and that had me feeling weak.

Every time I looked at Jessica, I began searching for ways to make her smile, even if only for a moment. I held back, though, because I was also slowly accepting that I wasn't the man she wanted to make things better for her.

I couldn't have been because when everything hit the fan, she called my best friend. That reality was enough to keep me from wrapping her in my arms and promising her I'd find who was bothering her. I had every intention of protecting her and fixing this problem, but I needed to remember that she didn't necessarily want or trust me to do that.

I left the room and headed straight for my bathroom. I turned on my shower, and almost instantly, steam began rising from the stream of water. Once I undressed, I stepped inside and let the hot droplets pierce my skin.

What am I gon' do?

A lot had been dropped on me that evening, and I was having a hard time focusing on just one aspect of it. I loved Jessica, and I knew I'd be perfectly content catering to her and my unborn child for the rest of my life. The fact that she wasn't interested in that kind of a future was messing with me in the worst way. It was humbling, to say the least, but the more I focused on that fact, the more clear my plan became.

Find the stalker and keep the mother of my child safe. Once my child was born, I'd be a dope father. Those were my priorities, and every feeling I had outside them was no longer my concern.

I Love Him

♥

Jess

"Wake up, Jessica."

His smooth, deep voice stirred me awake with a smile on my face, but as soon I opened my eyes, it faded. The memories of the previous night flooded my mind, and I teared up immediately.

He hates my dumb behind.

I slept on my side, so my back was facing the door, and I was grateful he couldn't see my face. I felt like an emotional wreck, and this was uncharted territory for me. It was rare that I wasn't able to reel in my emotions with one simple reminder: *I am Jessica Brielle Westin.*

That fact centered me daily and reminded me that *I* was the prize, and anyone who couldn't get with that could move around. It usually helped me let go of the day's problems and move forward with my chin up and my stride intact, but as I continued to repeat it in my head this morning, I realized it wasn't working its usual magic. Maybe it was because, in this situation, *Julian* was the prize, and I had fumbled it.

"Jessica." He repeated my name. His tone was soft, but the endearment that was usually there was missing in action. He could have been telling a stranger to wake up. That was how void of emotion he sounded.

That hurt because I knew I had done that to him. Julian was not a man who was afraid of his feelings. His usual bright personality was one of the things I loved most about him. He was always smiling and joking around, and he never had a problem letting me know exactly how he felt about me. As I listened to him try to coax me awake, I realized all that had been tossed out of the window in a matter of hours.

When I felt like I could face him without crying, I sat up and turned my body toward the door.

He leaned against its frame, wearing army green sweatpants and no shirt. I bit my lip as my eyes trailed his body. He looked good, and he knew it. When I made it back to his eyes, I realized he was studying me also, but it was different than any other time he looked at me. I could usually tell exactly how Julian felt about my appearance by his eyes, but this morning, he gave nothing away. He was a brick wall, and I hated every second of it.

"Good morning," I finally said, returning his attention to my gaze.

He stared silently for what felt like an eternity until finally, he said, "Mornin'. I need you to get up and get dressed. We got somewhere to be."

I frowned. Judging by how mad he was the night before, I assumed he would spend the day acting like I didn't exist. The fact that he wanted me to go somewhere with him surprised me.

"Where?" I asked.

Again, he stared at me blankly and took his time to deliver a reply.

"It's my momma's birthday, so we goin' to her party."

"In Concord?" I asked.

I knew Julian grew up on the outskirts of Atlanta, and his parents still lived there. The last thing I wanted was to be in the car with him for the next hour while he was treating me like chopped liver. With the way my emotions had been spiraling, I didn't think I'd be able to handle it.

"Yeah. We headin' out in an hour. Meet at the front of the house when you're ready." With that, he turned to leave, but I spoke up, making him pause.

"Ali, I don't think that's a good idea. Maybe I can go to Davi and Joseph's house while you're—"

He turned around quickly and closed the space between us. Now, his expression wasn't blank. He looked pissed.

"I bet you would like that shit, but it ain't happenin'. Quit bringin' other people up to me where your safety is concerned. Ain't nobody but me makin' sure my unborn child is straight, aight? You rollin' wit' me, Jessica, and I ain't willin' to debate that wit' you or anybody else. Get dressed."

He left the room, and I sat there momentarily, trying to hold back fresh tears. He wanted me with him because I was carrying his child, not because he loved me. I mean, I knew he loved me, but my silly behind had forced him to a place where he was no longer willing to show me that. I had really messed up my happy ending, and that was a hard pill to swallow.

Without another word, I stood and headed to the bathroom to prepare for the day.

\#

I sighed in relief when I realized the car had finally stopped. The hour-long car ride to his hometown was tense, and I was glad it was over.

Lifting my head, I looked out the window at a nice-sized apartment complex. I looked around the area and realized we weren't in the best part of town, but the building he parked in front of seemed almost new.

Julian got out of the car and rounded it before opening my door. His eyes pierced mine as he extended a hand toward me. My heart thumped against my chest as I accepted it and stepped out of the car. He opened his mouth to say something but was cut off by a woman approaching us.

She looked to be in her forties and wore a T-shirt and basketball shorts. She was holding a toddler who wore only a white onesie.

"Lee?"

Julian turned to her. When he did, the menacing glare he had just had on me faded and was replaced with that bright smile I loved to see.

"Wassup, Tash?" He hugged the woman before taking the little girl from her arms. "Wassup, Kayla? You can't smile for your favorite cousin?" he said to the little girl. He began tickling her, and she started giggling while wearing the most adorable little smile I had ever seen.

"I was wonderin' if the city would see you today. You know you only grace us witcha presence every blue moon," the woman said, her voice teasing.

Julian kissed his teeth. "Man, don't do that, cuz. It was hard gettin' down here when I was in Virginia. Now that I'm in the A, y'all gon' be seein' a lot more of me, aight?"

"Mhmm. What time you get here?"

"I just pulled up and wanted to check on things around here. Y'all good?"

She nodded. "Yeah, but you already knew that. We've been living better than good since you bought the building and fixed it up. It's shole been nice having a working air conditioning and a nice refrigerator, cuz, I ain't gon' lie."

Julian chuckled and dropped his head like he was embarrassed by her praise. I looked at the building again.

I knew he and Joseph had started a home renovation business on the side. They had flipped some homes in Virginia and made a lot of money from it. I understood that those homes were in upscale areas, which was why they were so profitable. I had no clue he had projects in Georgia. I shook my head at my thoughts.

I only knew the little information I did because of what Davi told me, so there was no reason I would know the ins and outs of his business.

"As long as y'all are straight, I'm happy. Aye, Tash, this is Jessica," Julian said, turning to me. "Jet, this is my cousin Tasha and her daughter Kayla."

I smiled at her and extended a hand, which she shook, wearing a bright smile.

"Nice to meet ya, Miss Jessica. You shole is a pretty lil thang, ain't ya?"

My smile grew at her kind words. "Thank you. So are you, and Kayla is adorable," I said, rubbing the little girl's back briefly. She smiled for a second before burying her face in Julian's chest.

"Aight, Tash, I'ma head in here and talk to Taylor for a minute," Julian said, kissing Kayla's cheek before handing her over.

Tasha kissed her teeth. "Taylor ain't in there. I just went to the leasing office to talk to him about the internet being out, and the office is closed."

I watched as Julian's face tensed. He lifted his wrist and glanced at his watch before kissing Tasha's cheek.

"Word? I'ma get that up and runnin' in a minute, and I'ma make sure that office stay open when it's supposed to. I'll see you at the party later."

Tasha grinned. "You already know I gotta come turn up for my favorite auntie. We'll be there."

"Aight, cuz. Later."

"See y'all," I said, waving to them.

Julian opened my car door before pulling his phone out, and by the time he got in on his side, he was going in on who I could only assume was Taylor.

"I'on understand why me and Joseph payin' a property manager who ain't managin' the property. It's ten o'clock on a Saturday mornin', Taylor. The office is supposed to be open 'til twelve."

He was silent as he listened to the guy's response.

"You clearly thought wrong. It's residents without the internet that they paid for, and they can't even tell anybody about it 'cause the office is closed. Get over there and get it fixed. If you can't, I will, but if I do, you don't need to come 'round here no more, man."

His tone relayed the warning that his words didn't, and I wasn't even sure if the man had a chance to respond because a second later, Julian was tossing his phone into his middle console.

I bit my tongue to refrain from asking him if everything was okay. I wanted to know, but he was still not my biggest fan. I didn't know if he ever would be again, but only time would tell.

Once he started the car, he zoomed out of the parking lot, and within a few minutes, we were at another property. This one was also in an underdeveloped area, and it wasn't in good condition at all. Once we reached the leasing office, I realized he was inquiring about purchasing the building.

We made a few trips like that, and after each one, he would call Joseph and debrief him on the meetings. My heart swelled as I realized Julian was on a mission to improve the place he was raised. I knew the city was predominately Black, similar to Atlanta, but Julian and I had two very different lives growing up.

Davi and I were raised with the best of everything. Our fathers met in college and started a business together that became a major franchise, and they grew extremely wealthy because of it.

Julian, like Joseph, didn't come from money, and both of them worked hard to live the comfortable lives they did today. I knew their humble beginnings were one of the reasons they bonded so quickly when they met, and I loved that they were helping to make children who were growing up in similar circumstances have better living conditions.

It was amazing and made me love Julian more. I wanted to tell him that but was afraid he'd look at me in disgust like he had been since the night before, so I just rode shotgun silently.

***

"Happy birthday, pretty."

I couldn't help but smile as Julian wrapped his arms around his mother's waist from behind. We had been all around his small city all day, and by the time we made it to his parents' house, the backyard party seemed to be in full swing. There was music playing loudly and people dancing everywhere.

She turned around and kissed her teeth.

"Don't 'pretty' me, child. I heard from too many people at this party that they saw you before I did, and I'on like that."

Wow. Julian's mother was the female version of him, and she was beautiful. Like... stunning. Her bright skin and the freckles on her cheeks matched her son's. Her hair was also jet black, but while Tate's hair was cut into a neat fade, her natural curls flowed well past her shoulders. She was much shorter than Julian, but I figured he got his height from his father.

Julian chuckled. "My bad, Ma. I had business to take care of at some of the properties we're tryin' to buy."

She rolled her eyes. "You need to take care of *business* on your own birthday, then."

Still smiling, he nodded. "I left your present in the car, but I'll get it in a minute." He then turned to me and extended his free hand in my direction. I took a few steps forward so that I was standing beside him.

"Ma, this is—"

She swatted at his arm. "Boy, I know who this is. She was just on my television screen earlier for a *Quench* commercial. I swear that ad is the reason I made ya daddy go buy all them sodas in that cooler."

I laughed and extended a hand toward her.

"I'm Jessica. Happy birthday!" Her eyes widened, and she swatted my hand away and brought me in for a hug.

"*You're* Jessica? Oh, honey, I been dyin' to meet you for years. I'm Celeste, Lee's momma."

She's been wanting to meet me for years? I glanced at Tate when she released me, but his focus wasn't on me. He was too busy glaring at his mother. He must not have wanted me to know that little piece of information.

"So, are you here because you and my son are finally a thing? Lord knows he wants y'all to be," she continued, completely ignoring her son.

"Nah, we ain't a thing, Ma, chill. She just wanted to come down for the party."

"Oh, chile, please. Lie to your therapist, not ya momma."

Ali shook his head and kissed her forehead.

"I'ma go get your gift out the car, pretty. Be right back."

"I done told yo' ass, when you find a wife of your own, you can call her pretty. *This* pretty woman here belongs to me."

I looked past Celeste and realized that a handsome older man was the owner of the deep voice we'd just heard. His skin tone was a couple of shades darker than Julian's, but they shared the same eyes, nose, and height. My suspicions about the man's identity were confirmed when he slipped an arm around Celeste's waist.

"Why you hatin', Pops?" Julian asked with a smirk.

"Don't make me knock you upside ya head in front of ya cousins, son. You wish I was a hater."

Julian laughed while Celeste playfully swatted the man's chest. "Be nice to your son, now."

The man kissed her cheek and said, "Only because you told me to, pretty."

Their exchange had me tearing up, not only because their sweet exchange was triggering my pregnancy hormones but also because, at that moment, I realized how badly I had fumbled their son. I found it hard to believe that he walked around calling every woman he met the same pet name his father used for his mother. But... he used it for *me*.

When you find your own wife, you can call her pretty.

Damn.

"Honey, this is *Jessica*," Celeste said, smiling wide.

Like Celeste, Julian's father's eyebrows shot in the air, and understanding filled his face a second later. He released his wife and brought me in for a brief hug.

"Nice to meet you, young lady. My name is Julian also, but most folks call me Senior."

"It's nice to meet you too."

Senior pulled his son in for a hug that lasted for a few seconds before he patted his back and stepped away.

"Have y'all eaten? There's plenty of food in the house," Senior said, gesturing toward the nice home behind him.

"We had a lil somethin' earlier, but you know I was savin' my appetite for one of your burgers, Pops. Come on, Jet," Julian said and grabbed my hand.

"Find me later, Jessica," Celeste called after us as Julian led me into the house.

"Yes, ma'am," I said, already nervous about what that conversation might consist of. When we reached the patio door, he slid it open and allowed me to enter first. When he closed the door, the music from outside was muffled, and I was able to hear the sports channel playing on the television in the house.

The home was beautiful inside. It had an open floor plan, so upon entrance, I had a view of the kitchen, family room, and dining room. The family room was decorated with burnt orange accents, giving the area a mature yet homey vibe. As a person who loved home decor, I appreciated Celeste's style. The parts of her home I could see were immaculate.

Tate didn't let go of my hand until we were in the kitchen, and I followed his lead with making my plate. There was a lot of counter space, all covered with several covered food tins. I went through the area, putting a little of everything on my plate because it all looked amazing. By the time we made our plates, we each had two.

The kitchen was empty, so Tate suggested we sit there to eat, and I nodded. We sat on barstools and ate in silence, much like we had all day. I contemplated saying something to him, but then the patio door slid open again, and a woman who looked a lot like Julian's father entered the kitchen.

When her eyes found Julian's, they widened. Because we were sitting so close, I noticed his chest rise and fall a bit quicker than it had been before. He dropped his head for a second and cleared his throat. I didn't know what was going on, but something about the woman's presence shook him. Without a second thought, I placed a hand on his thigh, and to my surprise, he covered it with his and squeezed.

"Lee. How are you doin', baby?" she asked with a smile. I couldn't help but notice that her eyes looked a little sad.

Julian cleared his throat again. "Hey, auntie. I'm aight; what about you?" he asked and stood. He walked over to where she was and leaned down before hugging her. The hug was brief and a little awkward, and once he pulled away, he returned to his seat beside me.

"Who's this?" she asked, looking at me with that same smile.

"This is Jessica," was all he said. The woman frowned a little, likely because my name didn't explain my relationship to her nephew.

"Nice to meet you," I added with a smile, trying to kill the awkward moment.

"Likewise. I'm Tracee, Lee's auntie." She stood there a moment longer before saying, "Well, I was getting ready to leave, but I'm happy I got to see you, nephew. We all miss havin' you around. Love ya, baby."

Julian dropped his head again, and there was a sadness in his eyes that I had never seen there before. Desperately, I wanted to know what was going on between the two of them. I wanted to make it better for him, but I knew we had our own issues to figure out before I could.

"Yes, ma'am. I-uh—I love you too," Julian finally said. With that, she passed us and left the kitchen to go to the front of the house. Seconds later, the front door opened then shut. Julian stood abruptly and said, "I'ma go to the bathroom real quick."

"Okay." An overwhelming sense of helplessness washed over me as I watched him retreat down a hallway. My eyes remained in that direction until someone else opened the patio door.

Three handsome men, who looked to be around our age, entered the home. One of the guys had deep chocolate skin and dreadlocks, while the other two were fair-skinned. Of the two, one had a fade and a rolled blunt tucked behind his ear, and the other had a curly fro and a toothpick between his teeth.

Each of them gave me a thorough once-over as they moved further into the kitchen. The one with the toothpick smirked. "You look good," he said. His southern accent was even more pronounced than Julian's, and that thought made me want to smile, but something in his eyes had me on guard.

"'Preciate that," I said before taking another bite of food.

"You came here wit' Lee, ainna?" he asked. I gathered hours ago that everyone in Julian's family called him Lee. The sound was in his first and middle name, so the nickname made sense. I nodded.

"Yep."

"I hate that for you, sweetheart. You better off fuckin' wit' another Tate 'cause the one you came wit' ain't it."

I rolled my eyes. I knew I didn't like him. "The Tate I came with is *everything*, so I'm good where I'm at."

The one with dark skin laughed arrogantly. "That nigga ain't nothin' but a sellout and a murderer."

I snapped my head in his direction and felt my attitude brewing. I didn't know what he was talking about, but I knew Julian well enough not to take this person's word about who or what Julian was. I also wasn't going to sit there and let anybody throw salt on his name while he wasn't around to defend himself.

I chuckled. "Aye, I don't wanna get disrespectful in his momma's house, but if you ain't got somethin' nice to say about your cousin in front of me, it'll be in ya best interest to shut up talkin' to me."

"Aye, bitch, who you—"

"Watch ya mouth when it comes to her, Floyd. Don't make me do it to you. *Again.*" I turned my head and saw Julian making his way back to the bar. Once he reached me, he glanced at me and asked, "You good?"

I softened my face, which had been twisted up from the moment the first guy said something to me, and smiled.

"I'm great," I said, cutting my eyes at the group again.

"You ain't beatin' nobody, Lee, and you know it," the one who must have been Floyd said. However, I didn't miss how he took several steps back before he continued. "I was just tryna put your girl up on game 'bout who she's dealin' wit'. I saw Auntie Tracee come up in here. I bet you couldn't even look her in the eye, could you?" Floyd asked.

The guy with the blunt piped up then. "Nah, he didn't, 'cause his punk ass knows he the reason her daughter is gone. That's why he ain't ever in the city. It's all good, though, because *we* got her for life. Know that," he said, eyeing Julian with disgust. My heartbeat quickened at his words.

I *knew* it was something going on between Julian and his aunt. I hated that I didn't have all the pieces to this ever-evolving puzzle. I needed them so that I could defend him properly.

Julian chuckled. "Move around—all you niggas." The three of them stood there for a few seconds longer before leaving out of the patio door they entered in.

Julian's face was even more tense than it had been, and his fists were clenched.

He sat down and placed his head in his hands for a moment.

"Ali... are you okay?" I asked, tearing up. My tears weren't because I was pregnant or because I cared about anything those guys were talking about. I felt myself about to break down because I could clearly see that Julian was hurting behind some unresolved drama—or *trauma*—with his family.

He stared at me like he had been doing all day before giving me a stiff nod.

"I'm straight. Let's finish eating so I can chill wit' my momma for a minute. She prolly lookin' for us already." He was definitely not okay, but he wasn't going to open up to me. I guess I couldn't blame him, either. With a sigh, I continued eating my food.

***

"You enjoyin' yaself?"

I looked up from the *Match Four* board and smiled at Celeste.

"Yes, ma'am. This has been nice," I replied before dropping another blue chip in. Julian's little cousin, Lucas, almost immediately dropped a red chip.

"Yeah! I won again, Jet!" he yelled, making me laugh. Lucas was eight years old and reminded me so much of my godson, Two. Since

Julian was ignoring me, I decided to find something to do to occupy my time. I had been playing games with the kids for the last half hour.

"Dang. You gotta let me win at least once, Luke," I said, pouting.

He grinned and shook his head, "Sorry, Jet. I like winning too much."

Celeste laughed and turned to Lucas. "Luke, go and get your momma to wrap y'all up some food before you go. The party's windin' down, baby."

"Yes, ma'am." I watched the handsome little boy run off, leaving me alone with Julian's mother. My heart was beating quickly from the moment she walked over, but now, I felt like I was about to faint.

She made it clear that this conversation was coming before the day was over, and now here we were. I looked around and realized people were hugging each other and reentering the home, likely to get to their cars in the front yard. Who I didn't see was Julian. I kind of wanted him to come save me, but I quickly reminded myself that he wasn't even messing with me at the moment. He probably couldn't wait for his momma to go off on me.

She sat beside me on the comfortable bench and turned her knees toward me.

"So, my son tells me you're pregnant."

My eyes widened. *Straight to it, huh?*

"Uh-yes, ma'am, I am."

"And he's the father?"

I cleared my throat.

I wasn't the type to explain myself to anyone, but I decided to give her that. She was a Black momma from the south. I had one, too, so I knew firsthand how hard they went for their children. The truth was, I loved her son something serious, and even though I had a hard time admitting it to him, I had no problem letting her know that.

"Yes, ma'am. Julian and I have known each other for a while and kind of rekindled things about two months ago. Before that, I had been celibate for quite some time."

She smiled. "I believe you, honey. My son doesn't seem to have any doubts about being the father, so I'm not gon' press you about that."

I released a breath I didn't even know I was holding but almost choked on it when she continued.

"I *am* gon' press you about the fact that my son been walkin' 'round here lookin' mad at the world, and you've been lookin' at him like a sick puppy. It ain't too much that he don't tell me, but he won't say what's goin' on with y'all. He's tryna protect you from me, and that means he loves you. I'm sure you already knew that."

I dropped my gaze for a minute before meeting her eyes again.

"Yeah, he may have mentioned his feelings before."

"Mhmm. I've been hearin' about you here and there for years. Whenever we talk, he'll just randomly mention what *Jet* is doin' or where she's travelin' to. My son ain't ever been interested in committing to anybody, but I've been knowin' it was somethin' about you that had him invested."

"Really?"

"Really. I need to know if you are too. My baby is tough as nails when it comes to a lot of things, but his heart is big, and he wears it on his sleeve. You're not gon' break it," she said with finality.

Rubbing my lips together, I nodded. "I'm not out to break it. If I'm honest, I…" I took a deep breath, unsure if I wanted to let her in on the ins and outs of my life. *Fuck it, man.*

"Your son is amazing, and I love him too. Honestly, I have for a long time, but I always told him and everyone else I wasn't the settling down type. I have a job that requires me to travel often and be a part of the social scene, and I just leaned into that heavily because… I had a complicated fibroid surgery a while ago, and my doctor told me I couldn't have kids. I watch Julian with our godchildren, and I know he wants them, so I decided not to get too attached to him because I knew I'd never be able to give him children.

"I figured we'd end up breaking up when he found out, so to avoid my own heartbreak, I just kept him at arm's length. The truth is, I'd be perfectly content with being your son's housewife, cooking, cleaning, and taking care of our baby for the rest of our lives. That sounds like a dream I never thought I'd have, but—"

"But now, things are different," she said, finishing for me. "I'm a woman first, so let me first tell you how sorry I am that you went through that. I'm sorry you went so many years feeling that way, and while I do believe Lee would want to be with you no matter what, I understand why you made the choices you did."

"Thanks," I said, rolling my eyes at the fact that my voice was cracking. I had to find a way off this emotional rollercoaster.

"My son is stubborn, so I can't say how easy it'll be for you two to get back on track, but if you care for him the way you say you do, I'm sure you guys will make it. I've been watching you all day, and I love your confidence. You came in and made yourself at home, and it's clear that you have strong family values because of how you made it a point to bond with mine today. I respect that you did it without Lee's help too. You were clearly raised by some great people."

"I was."

I smiled, but it faded as I thought about my parents. I had yet to tell them about my pregnancy, and the fact that my baby daddy wasn't even my boyfriend had me nervous about breaking the news.

Celeste lifted her hand and rubbed my back briefly. "It'll all work out, sweetheart."

As I was about to reply, Julian and his father approached us.

He looked at me briefly, and my heart fluttered. His expression showed no hostility or disgust, and I was relieved. I was used to princess treatment whenever I was in his presence, so the cold version of himself he'd been presenting had me deep in my feelings. Maybe he was about to let up a little bit.

"We 'bout to head out, Ma. I gotta work tomorrow."

Celeste rolled her eyes and stood. "I guess. I'm so glad to see you, son. Now that you're back in Georgia, I wanna see you more. Do better."

Julian dropped his head. "Yes, ma'am."

Giving him a stern look, she said, "I'm serious, son. Everybody here loves you. Stop letting the enemy tell you differently."

"I hear you, Ma."

Senior cleared his throat. "Well, it was lovely to meet you, young lady. From what I hear, we gon' be seein' a lot more of you in the future."

I smiled and glanced at Julian. He shifted his focus to the right, and I sighed but responded to his father. "Yes, sir, y'all will. It was great meetin' you too."

We all hugged goodbye, then Julian led me to his car. Without words, he helped me into the passenger seat, got inside, and drove off.

"Your family is cool people," I said once he turned onto the interstate.

"Yeah, they're aight."

"You told your parents I'm pregnant?" It was a dumb question because I already knew the answer, but I was tired of silence and didn't know what else to say.

He cut his eyes at me. "I'on keep secrets from the people I love, Jessica."

I sighed. "I didn't say you did, Ali. I just... never mind."

As we traveled back to Atlanta in silence, my hopes that he was ready to stop being mean dissipated. If we couldn't communicate, I couldn't be around him. This silent treatment hurt too much.

"When we get back, you can take me home," I said.

He glanced at me and chuckled. Eventually, he responded. "Nah."

I exhaled deeply. "You're mad at me, and I get it, but why make me suffer under your roof when you're clearly not ready to talk to me? If it's that serious, I can stay at my parents' house."

I was about to say I could stay with Davi and Joseph, but mentioning them in this situation didn't seem to sit right with him.

"It is that serious, and I'm not gon keep havin' the same tired conversation wit' you, Jet. You're wit' me, and that's what it is until somethin' changes. Leave me alone, nie."

I rolled my eyes hard and turned to the window.

His mother said he was stubborn, and for the first time since I met him, I was learning just how true that was.

Somebody's Gotta Try

♥

Jess

"Mmm." I moaned as I slid into the warm bubbles.

I was past due for a bubble bath, and while I believed the tub in my new home was better than the one in Julian's guest room, his was nice. I rested my head on the bath pillow behind me and sighed.

It had been a long and depressing week. I hadn't gotten any work done because I wasn't ready to tell my team the big news, and I hated how lazy I felt.

I closed my eyes so that I could fully immerse myself in my self-care. Baths were one of my favorite ways to cater to myself. I wanted to come up with a plan to be able to work and remain safe, but Julian had made himself my head of security and wasn't even willing to talk to me about it.

He was still giving me the silent treatment, and I was beyond over it. He didn't want me to go anywhere unless he was available to take me, but I didn't want him to take me anywhere until he started acting his age.

The whole situation had me deep in my feelings, and the baby growing inside me only put my emotions even more out of whack. I hadn't been able to get an appointment with my doctor until the next day, so I had been taking the vitamins from the New York clinic, and they didn't seem to be doing anything for me.

I was hoping my doctor could give me something that would help me get back to OG Jess because if I cried again, I was going to slap myself.

I had yet to tell Julian about my doctor's appointment, but I knew I had to. The only time he spoke to me was when he asked me about going to the doctor. I honestly had no reason to keep it from him other than the fact that he was hurting my damn feelings every day.

I felt myself tear up as his face appeared behind my eyelids. I hadn't seen him smile since his mother's party, and I missed it. *Girl, get it together.*

I lifted a hand out of the water and dried it using the towel on the bench beside me before I grabbed my phone and unlocked it. Not wanting to be alone, I video-dialed Crissy. Davi was my best friend in the entire world—my sister—but every time we talked about this situation, she was always so positive that things would work out.

I wanted that to be true, but it wasn't my reality at the moment, so I just wasn't in the mood to hear her tell me to keep the faith. I was tight with both Demi and Crissy, but Crissy was like my soul sister. She reminded me so much of myself, and our personalities just clicked, similar to how Demi and Davi bonded.

Crissy joined the call immediately, and I was grateful for that. She was married, but her baby was still in her belly, so I hoped I wasn't disturbing her and Air's evening.

"Wassup, boo?" Crissy said when her face appeared on the screen. A second later, her husband, Aaron, pressed the side of his face against hers and grinned into the phone. "Wassup, boo?" he asked, mimicking his wife.

Crissy rolled her eyes while I laughed and shook my head. "Hey, y'all."

"Move, Aaron, and let me have my own phone call."

I cracked up as he kissed his teeth but backed away. "Girl, I ain't worried about your stankin' phone call. I got shit to do anyway."

"Yeah, that's why you're over there poutin', right? 'Cause you got *so* much shit to do?"

"Leave me alone, man. Bye, Jess!" he called.

She started walking, and I knew their home well, so I noticed when she made it to their bedroom. Plopping down on the bed, she smiled into the phone but frowned almost immediately after.

"What's wrong?"

I frowned, too.

"I haven't even said anything yet. How you know something's wrong?"

"Um, maybe because your eyes are puffy and red," she said matter-of-factly.

"Oh."

She gave me a look that said, *Girl, start talking*.

I sighed. "I'm pregnant."

She moved suddenly, then groaned. I laughed because it was clearly a struggle for her to get to a sitting position.

"You're *what?*" She propped her phone up on her nightstand and sat back on the bed with a hand resting casually on her belly.

Still laughing, I repeated myself. I was grateful for a reason to smile, and her little pregnant self was that for me at the moment.

"First, let me say I'm excited as hell. Ooo, I hope it's a girl, 'cause our babies are gon' be best friends, I can see it now!"

That made me grin even wider. I hadn't thought about that, but it was an exciting thought. Both Davi and Demi's children were years older than our babies would be, so the fact that ours would have each other to grow up with was kind of lit.

"Yeah, I'm hype about that."

"*Second,* when did you get pregnant, and who knocked you up?"

I laughed again because I realized everyone would probably ask me who I was pregnant by when they found out. It was no secret that I was single and not looking to settle down.

"Julian."

She gasped. After a minute, she finally spoke up.

"Now, when you say *Julian*, you mean—"

I rolled my eyes at her. "I mean, Julian Ali Tate is my baby daddy, girl, dang."

She screamed. "Oh, bitch, you've been holdin' out. I'm so glad it's him, though, 'cause the love of his life havin' somebody else's baby was not gon' fly with him, I already know."

Fresh tears formed when she said that. Crissy, Demi, and their husbands had been in our lives for the last two years, so she had the chance to witness Julian and me interact a few times.

The fact that even *she* knew how he felt about me made me feel like a big dummy. I could have *been* had my man.

"Wait, sis, I didn't mean to make you cry. Tell me what's goin' on." Her tone was soft and filled with concern.

I took a deep breath and told her everything, from the fibroids up until Julian found out about the stalker and baby a week ago.

"So now, I'm in his house because he refuses to let me be alone while there's a stalker on the loose, but I can't take his cold shoulder anymore, so I honestly don't wanna be here. This has me miserable."

She nodded silently for a minute.

"You remember the night we met? When Joseph had that party for Davi at *Ace on Air?*"

I nodded.

"At that point, Air and I were still new. We were fresh off a bad argument about a dumb thing I did, and he refused to talk to me for like a week. He was being so mean, but he wouldn't let me go back to my own house either. Julian and Air remind me a lot of each other."

I chuckled and nodded because I thought the same thing the first time I met Air. They were both silly and funny as hell, and neither had a problem showing affection to the ones they loved.

She continued. "Aaron's biggest issue with me at that point was that I had lied to him. He felt like it was so easy for me to keep something from him, and it didn't sit right with him. Even though that wasn't the case, it was how he felt, and I had to respect it because I created the situation the second I answered a call from my ex. I had to eat that shit.

"Jess, I'm sorry you went through such a traumatic experience, and I'm so glad God had a different plan for you. I truly understand where you're coming from with all of it, and I even get why you were scared to tell him about the baby, but, sis, you gotta eat this.

"The fact is that Tate shoulda been your first call, just like Air should have been mine when my stupid ex was hitting my line. He loves you, Jess. A blind man can see that. He just doesn't feel good about the fact that you were able to keep it from him or that *his* best friend was your first call when you were afraid. He's *been* wanting to be your protector, and now he has a valid reason to do so, but he feels like you were trying to strip him of that opportunity."

I exhaled. "But I wasn't, I just—"

She raised her hands in mock surrender. "I get it, but this is how he probably feels, and you gotta accept that. Then you gotta figure out what you want to do about it. Let me ask you this. What does a perfect life look like for you in seven or eight months? What version of reality would make you most happy?"

I chuckled because the answer was easy. "My mini me in my arms with Julian standing beside me. A perfect future is me being Missus Jessica Tate."

Crissy grinned.

"I knew it. That *can* be your future, sis. You just gotta push yourself to do something you've never had to before. You're used to Tate putting his feelings out there while you play him to the left. You're used to him treating you like the sun rises and sets on your ass. It's time for you to do that for him.

"By the time I admitted my feelings for my husband to myself, he had gone and found a girlfriend and wasn't worried about me at all. I had to go get my man, and you gon' have to do the same. Make your feelings clear and let him know you aren't willing to do life without him. Somebody's gotta try first, and I ain't gon' lie, Jessica... it needs to be you."

Damn.

She was right... about all of it. I wasn't used to Julian treating me the way he had been lately, and I definitely never put myself out there like he had with me. I guess it was time for me to do something different.

"I hear you."

She smirked. "I know you do, so let's make a game plan for you to get your baby daddy, honey."

***

My stomach growled at the smell of the bacon I had just laid on a paper towel to drain.

I had been craving bacon and eggs, so I was making that along with pancakes. I was making enough for both Julian and me in an attempt to break the ice. My conversation with Crissy had been on my mind all night, and I woke up ready to get us on the right track.

Breakfast was now complete, but I wanted to wash my dishes before I tried to wake him up. I washed most of them as I went along, but I needed to dump the bacon grease before cleaning the pan and tongs I used.

Just as I was about to grab the pan, Julian's scent invaded my nostrils, and his arms were around me. I shivered under his touch, but it was short-lived. He grabbed the cast iron skillet in front of me, then backed away.

I turned around and realized he was taking it outside to dump the grease out.

"I was going to do that," I said.

He glanced at me. "And now you don't have to." With that, he headed out of his back door. Shaking my head, I took a deep breath. I planned to greet him with breakfast, but he caught me off guard. When he reentered the kitchen, I needed to try and turn our encounter around.

Moments later, he was back in the kitchen. He moved to the sink, and I watched as he cleaned a few remaining dishes. He didn't stop working until they were all dried and put away.

"I made you breakfast," I said after he closed the last cabinet.

Drying his hands with a paper towel, he turned and leaned against the counter behind him. He gave me a thorough once-over, but his expression remained neutral. Finally, he met my eyes again.

"'Preciate that."

"Can we eat together?"

He licked his lips. "Yeah, we can do that."

I released a relief-filled sigh, then made both our plates. I wanted to sit across from him so that I could see his face as we talked, so I placed our breakfast at his dining room table.

He joined me, and we began eating in silence.

"This is good, Jet. I ain't know you could burn."

I smiled. "I love to cook."

"Good to know."

Silence filled the room again until I cleared my throat.

"Ali, I have a doctor's appointment this morning. I apologize for not saying something earlier. I was just in my feelings about you not talkin' to me." I let it all out in one breath but watched his expression change. When I started, he looked annoyed, but his face softened once I got through the apology.

"Aight," he said. He then pulled his phone out and tapped it a few times before placing it on his ear.

"Aye, J. I'ma be a lil late. Jet's got a doctor's appointment. Aight, cool."

He then hung up.

"What time?" he asked.

"Eleven."

"Cool."

While he continued eating, I racked my brain for another conversation starter. I didn't think I needed to go right into my feelings for him. I needed to work on rebuilding our line of communication first. Right now, we were acting like strangers who had become roommates. I had to get us past that point first.

He placed his fork down and glanced at me. "You done?"

I nodded.

"Aight. I'll wash these. Go 'head and get dressed."

I sighed. "I can wash them."

"So can I."

He stood and took my plate before disappearing into the kitchen. I didn't know if that interaction did much to break the ice, but it was the most we had spoken in days. If nothing else, it was a start.

***

"What's up, Shay?"

Shay smiled. Because Julian and I were on the way to my appointment, I thought about ignoring the video call, but I wasn't about to do my assistant like that. I had been MIA and knew she was worried about me.

"It's good to see your face, boss. Are you okay?"

"Yeah, I'm good. I know I've been missing this week, but I've had a lot going on. I'm sorry."

"It's okay. You got a minute to talk?"

"Yeah, what's up?"

"I'm at the office right now with Val, and we were talking about when we would get started with the content calendar we created last week. Maybe Val and Margo could come to your house today, and we can take some photos in a few cute outfits to post on social media. You know, to keep your face out there."

I nodded. "That's not a bad idea, but—"

"That ain't happenin', Jet."

"Who's that?" I heard Valerie ask in a low tone.

I glanced at him with a frown. "Hold on, y'all." I placed them on mute.

"Why not? It's a good idea since I will be out of commission soon. I still have a career to maintain."

"I'on trust nobody until I do. I don't know them, Jessica. For all I know, one of them bitches tryna come over is who gave this stalker your address."

I shook my head. "No one on my team would ever do that."

He chuckled. "As true as that may be, I need to look into them before I feel comfortable havin' them where you lay your head. You ain't goin' back to your place 'til it's safe, so a home photo shoot would have to happen at my place. I'on let people in my crib that I'on know, so we can figure somethin' out, but that right there ain't what we doin'. Not today, anyway."

I just sat back and closed my eyes for the rest of the drive to the doctor's office. I understood that a person in the world was moving crazy when it came to me, but Shay, Margo, and Valerie were my people. They weren't out to hurt me, and the fact that Julian couldn't trust me on that was frustrating.

I Like Her, Dawg

♥

Tate

"You good?" I asked Jessica when I opened her door.

After I shut down her manager's little photo shoot plan, she tuned me out for the rest of the drive. I didn't care, to be honest. I was in a line of work that made me weary of everybody, especially when situations like this were happening.

I wasn't trying to run her life, but I was going to make sure she was safe. She would be my Velcro until I figured out how to do that while balancing my job and hers.

"I'm fine," she said and accepted the hand I extended to her. I helped her out of the car and walked slightly behind her as she headed toward the office. I held the door open and allowed her entry before I followed.

Once we reached the front desk, the woman behind it smiled.

"Jessica, we haven't seen you in quite some time. How are you?"

Jess smiled back. "Hey, Ange. You know I moved to New York for a while. I'm back home now; this is the only office I'll ever visit in this city. You know I love Doctor Prestige."

Ange laughed. "Don't we all." She typed a few things on her computer, and I turned to observe my surroundings. There were mostly women sitting around the office, and several of them had their eyes on Jess and me.

Most of them were gazing at me, but one in particular was grilling the hell out of Jessica. I wasn't feeling that. As the desk attendant checked her in, I moved closer to Jessica and wrapped an arm around her from behind. Homegirl was lookin' like she knew Jess. If they had bad blood from the past, I was gon' make sure the only thing she could leave this office sayin' about my baby momma was that she still looked amazing and had a fine ass man on her arm. Jess looked up at me with a surprised expression, but I ignored it and focused on Ange.

"Alright, I got you all checked in. Just have a seat, and I'll call you back when she's ready for you. Good to see you again, Jessica."

"You too." Jessica turned and headed for a seat, and ironically, it was closest to the woman who had eyes on her since we entered the building.

"Aye, can we help you?" I asked because she refused to look elsewhere. The girl finally peeled her big-ole eyes off of Jessica and looked at me. My question caused Jessica to lift her head from her phone to see who I was talking to. When she noticed the woman, she rolled her eyes. They knew each other.

"Nope," the woman said with all kinds of attitude in her throat.

Jess chuckled and refocused on her phone.

"Something funny, *Jessica*? You can't speak?"

"Sabrina, shut up talkin' to me."

The girl laughed arrogantly. "Still the same ghetto mess you were in college, I see. You never could string words together without using profanity."

"And you never could follow directions. My ghetto ass is 'bout to beat yours if you don't shut up talkin' to me."

I leaned over so that my lips were grazing Jessica's ear. "That ain't happenin'. Calm down, pretty."

"Sabrina Hamilton," a doctor called from behind the desk. The woman beside us stood. She turned to us again.

"Tell Davi I said hello," she said with a smirk.

Jess laughed. "Yeah, I'll tell her husband *Joseph* you said the same shit."

Sabrina's eyes widened. "They-they got married?"

Jess rolled her eyes and let out an exaggerated sigh. "Sabrina, I don't like you, and you know that, so I don't understand why you even started this conversation with me, girl. Gone to the back and get that STD checked on."

I couldn't help but laugh because Jessica was a damn fool. Still looking stunned, the girl turned slowly and headed to the back.

"Who dat?" I asked when we were alone again.

She rolled her eyes again. "A ho Joseph was messin' with before he met my best friend. She honestly is owed a beat down from back in the day, but I'ma let her make it."

She looked too serious, and I wanted to laugh again. I always respected how hard Jess went for her people because I was the same way about mine. I couldn't wait to mess with J about meeting his old cut buddy, though.

"You somethin' else, man."

"Jessica Westin," the same nurse called. We both stood, and I grabbed her hand before we went back. Once we reached the door, the nurse smiled and led us to a scale where she took Jessica's height and weight.

I stepped back a little to give her privacy while the woman recorded her data and asked her a few questions. A few minutes later, Jess gestured for me to come over.

"I'm about to get my blood taken and give a urine sample, but Nurse Martin is going to take you to my exam room," Jess said.

"Cool." I followed the nurse and made myself comfortable in a chair in the corner. The room had hella pamphlets, so I stood and started perusing them. I found one with the title "FAQs for Fathers About Pregnancy."

I picked it up and got to reading. As I read, I internalized everything in the pamphlet and ended up with more questions than answers. I was beyond ready for the doctor to come on.

A few minutes later, Jessica walked in with the nurse behind her.

"Jessica, Doctor Prestige will be in shortly. Go ahead and change into your gown," Nurse Martin said. She eyed me briefly before walking out and closing the door behind her.

Jess walked over to the exam bed and lifted the gown. She looked over at me.

"Close your eyes."

Rearing my head back slightly, I kissed my teeth.

"Why? I've seen what you got plenty times, Jet. Tasted it too," I said and smirked.

Jess rolled her eyes and shrugged. "Whateva." She turned her back to me and removed the sundress she wore. I kept my eyes glued to her because I'd never pass up an opportunity to admire her.

She put the medical gown on, and I was low-key disappointed. Jess looked good, and I wanted to touch her. I didn't miss how my body—my heart—reacted to having her in my arms again in the waiting area. That woman did something to me that was unexplainable, but the feeling had me praying we'd get right someday. I loved Jessica more than a little bit.

Just as Jess was sitting on the bed, there was a knock on the door.

"Come on in," I said, prompting Jess to cut her eyes at me. I frowned. "What?"

The door opened, and an older woman stepped inside, wearing a bright smile.

Jessica smiled wide also, and the woman approached her with open arms before pulling her in for a long hug.

"Hey, my girl," the doctor said.

"Hey, Doctor P. How have you been?"

"I've been great, and so have *you*." The woman glanced at me before looking at the clipboard in her hands.

"Congratulations are definitely in order because you are pregnant, my girl."

I kept my eyes on Jessica when the doctor delivered the news. She looked like I felt—happy. That caught me off guard because I was sure she wasn't feeling this pregnancy.

"Really?" Jess asked with tears in her eyes and hope in her voice.

Maybe she did want this.

Doctor Prestige nodded. "Really. You said on the phone that you're sure you're over two months pregnant, so it's time for an ultrasound. Before we get to that, though, we need to talk about your health."

Jessica's eyes turned fearful, and that had my chest tight.

"Calm down, Jessica. The only thing I'm noticing right now is that your blood pressure is higher than I'd like it to be."

"Okay," Jess said tentatively.

I frowned. "How do we fix that?"

The doctor glanced at me and smiled briefly.

"We ensure Jessica has plenty of fluids, eats balanced meals, and remains stress-free. I know how well Jess takes care of her body, so I suspect the culprit might be the latter."

She turned to Jess again. "Sweetheart, you and I have been on this journey for a while now, and this is one of those things we prayed for. Let's protect it at all costs, okay? Whatever is in your life that has you feeling overwhelmed or stressed, cut it out now. Whatever it is isn't worth your or your baby's health."

Jess glanced at me before lowering her eyes, confirming what I was just thinking. The stalker situation was probably weighing on her, but the reality was that I was what had been stressing her out. My feelings were hurt, and I hadn't even attempted to take Joseph's advice about not giving her the cold shoulder. I had been meaning to do better.

I was just mad about how everything played out. I was upset that I felt like she didn't want the baby and pissed that she kept it from me. Just from listening to her doctor speak, I realized I may have misjudged the situation a bit, but either way, she was right.

There wasn't anything more important than our baby and Jessica's health, so I had to do my part to eliminate the stress from her life, starting with my messed-up attitude.

Jess was quiet, so I cleared my throat and spoke up.

"She has had a lot on her plate, and I'on think I've been helpin' with that much at all. I'ma do better," I said, looking into Jessica's eyes, wanting her to know I meant that.

"She ain't gon' be stressed no more, Doc."

The doctor lifted her brows and grinned. "Well, alright then, I will hold you to that, mister."

The door opened again, and a nurse entered the room and started messing with the equipment beside the bed.

"While she gets the ultrasound equipment situated, let's do introductions, shall we?" Doctor Prestige said and turned to me.

"I'm Doctor Prestige. I've been Jessica's doctor since she was a small girl, and I love her to pieces. *You* must be Julian Tate?"

I chuckled and glanced at Jess. When did they have time to talk about me?

I extended my arm and shook her hand. "I am. Nice to meet you, Doc."

"Likewise." She glanced at the brochure I was holding and grinned. "I'd happily answer your questions while Nurse Holly gets Jessica hooked on the equipment."

"I got plenty," I replied with a smirk.

"I figured you would. Shoot."

"This lil paper says she shoulda come to the doctor at the eight-week mark. It's been 'bout eleven since we got it in, so is the baby aight? Like, is he missin' somethin' he should have gotten three weeks ago?" I asked before crossing my arms.

The doctor started laughing, and I frowned. *What was so funny?*

"I'm sorry about him, Doctor P. I told you he was a lot."

I cut my eyes at Jessica. *What was that supposed to mean?*

"Oh, he's perfectly fine, dear. The eight-week mark is ideal for the first prenatal visit, but we aren't far off from that. We are about to take a look at your baby to get a clearer picture of what's happening, but they haven't missed anything. I assure you."

"We're ready, Doctor," the nurse said. The doctor walked over to the bed. She squirted something on Jessica's belly and rubbed it around a little before she put something that looked like a joystick on her stomach.

The fuck is that?

The doctor looked at me and laughed, so I assumed my face looked as confused as I felt.

"This is called a transducer. I'm going to move it around, and if you focus on the screen, you'll be able to get a look at your baby."

I fixed my eyes on the television in front of us, and it was just a black screen for a while. She continued moving the transducer, and a few curved white lines appeared.

"Ah, here we go. You're spot on with how far along you are. You'll see baby's hand if you guys look at the top of the screen."

I squinted, unable to make out anything. "Nah, I'on see that, Doc," I told her.

She chuckled and moved the transducer again.

"What about now?" she asked.

I continued to study the monitor, and before long, my eyes adjusted to what I was looking at, and the picture became clear.

"Ah, shit. I see the lil fingers. That's the head right there, ain't it?" I asked, pointing to a big round figure on the screen.

"Yes, it is. Good job, dad," Doctor Prestige said, and I felt a smile tugging at the corners of my mouth.

"Dang, pretty, our baby's got one hell of a noggin, just like your bigheaded ass," I said, glancing at her. She rolled her eyes but grinned and said nothing.

"There's baby's heart," she said after moving lower. "We'll zoom in on it and do a heart tracing to get the beats per minute."

The screen zoomed in on a moving object, and it was thumping at a steady pace. After a while, Doc said, "The beats per minute is one forty-nine. That's perfectly normal."

Suddenly, the image shifted, and I whipped my head toward the doctor. "What happened?"

She smiled. "The baby's just moving around, that's all. Looks like they want us to work for these ultrasound photos."

I grinned and returned my focus to the monitor. "Can't sit still, just like their momma, that's all that is."

"Shut up, goofy," Jess said. The softness in her voice made me look at her again, and her expression made something start dancing in my core. I loved witnessing her more vulnerable side because it was rare.

Her expression was the perfect display of how I was feeling. Seeing my unborn child on that screen was surreal. I felt all my prayers had been answered, down to the woman carrying my seed. We had a lot to work through, and we both knew it, but there was no one I would have wanted to be sharing a moment like this with other than Jessica Brielle. That was a fact.

Without thinking about it heavily, I moved closer to the bed. I reached for Jessica's hand, and she gave it to me without hesitation. We remained that way for the rest of the doctor's visit, and I couldn't lie; it just felt *right*.

***

A couple of hours later, Jess and I walked into my home.

I was hella late to work, but I knew J would hold it down without me. I watched as Jessica headed to my refrigerator. She opened it, grabbed a water bottle, then leaned on the counter. I joined her since it looked like she would be chilling there for a minute.

We stood there, staring into each other's eyes, and I wondered what was on her mind. Mine was all over the place, and I couldn't focus on just one thing to save my life. The baby, the stalker, and the tension between Jess and me were at the forefront of my mind, but the case I was working on tarried there, also.

Knowing there was no telling how long I'd be out, I felt the need to try calling some type of truce with Jess. She was a hothead, and I didn't need her leaving the house before I got back.

"Look, pretty, I've been an asshole for the last week, and regardless of what we got goin' on, it ain't an excuse for me actin' like a simp. I apologize, aight?"

Her eyes became misty, and I frowned. *What did I say?*

She sighed and placed the water bottle on the counter.

"I'm the one who needs to apologize. Ali, you should have been my first call when I realized I was pregnant. I was afraid you'd be pissed since this wasn't planned, so I kept putting it off. That wasn't right."

My frown deepened. It bewildered me that she thought a baby with her could ever upset me. She really must have had no clue just how deep these feelings went when it came to her.

"Aye, I'm happy as hell that you're carrying my baby, Jet. I'm excited 'bout the journey, and more than anything, I wanna make sure you're straight. That means not stressin' you out. I'm done bein' an asshole."

She bit her bottom lip, and I had to take a step back to refrain from kissing it.

"And I'm done keeping things from you," she said.

"Cool. Look though, I need you to stay here while I'm at work. I'ma call Davi and get her to bring whatever you wanna eat over here, but a part of making you're straight is making sure nothing happens to you.

"I swear, when I get back, we can come up with a plan that doesn't make you feel like a prisoner, but for now, I need you safe. I haven't fully mapped out what that looks like when you're away from me, but I'm workin' on it. So, stay home today. Please?"

She remained silent and shifted her eyes as if considering my request. It honestly wasn't up for discussion, but if she were really about to give me a hard time, I would just have to miss work so that I could be her chauffeur and bodyguard for the day.

"Tell Vi I want oxtails and greens from *Miss Bessie's*," she finally said, smirking.

I chuckled. "Bet. I'll see you a lil later, Jet."

With that, I was headed back out the door, and my phone was ringing at the same time. I answered without looking because I knew it was J.

"I'm on my way, nigga."

***

"I'on know what makes you think I'm the one to ask about this," Joseph said, kissing his teeth.

I cut my eyes at him. "Prolly 'cause you went through a whole pregnancy wit' your wife, and David got here just fine. I already know what she likes. I just need you to help wit' the pregnancy-related stuff."

"Then call Sunshine. Davi was too much of a control freak to let me do somethin' like this for her. She used to order everything she needed online and make me pick it up."

"If I call Davi, she gon' tell Jet what I'm doin', dawg. You know she can't keep secrets."

J kissed his teeth again as we turned on the body care aisle of *The Exchange*. "Apparently, she can. She ain't tell me 'bout y'all's baby. Sneaky ass."

I laughed loudly. "I know you ain't mad 'cause Davi finally learned how to hold water. She tells you everything, but she knows you woulda told me, so she held it for her girl. You can't be mad at that."

J smirked. "Watch me. Here, get this. Sunshine was puttin' this on her belly every two seconds when she was pregnant." He tossed a brown tube in the buggy, and I reached over to pick it up.

Coconut Body Gel Oil.

"Jet be walkin' 'round smelling like coconuts already, so she'll love this here." I grabbed a few more of those before we left the aisle and continued through the store.

"How was Ma Duke's birthday?" J asked.

We had been busy with the tip hotline today, so we hadn't talked about anything else after I made it to work. We were both tired, but I made him follow me to the store so I could try and put together a care package for Jess.

My momma used to make them for me and mail them when I lived in Virginia, and I loved them. I figured I could hook up a pregnancy edition of that for my baby momma.

I chuckled as I thought about that day. My mind wasn't on my momma, though. I was thinking about how Jess was ready to go toe to toe with my cousins 'bout me.

"It was cool."

"You told them 'bout the baby?"

"Hell yeah. You know they're excited. I had a run in wit' Floyd them too."

J knew all about my family issues, just like I knew his story. Outside of family, he was just about the only person I trusted, and it was the same for him. We both had a lot of baggage where family was concerned, and I think it was one of the main things that bonded us in the beginning.

"What happened?"

I chuckled again. "Shid, I walked up on them talkin' shit about me to Jet. I ain't gon' lie. She handled business."

J laughed. "What else did you expect? As scared as Jess has always been about settlin' down with your ho ass, she ain't ever played about you. You know that."

That was true. Jess was a firecracker, and anytime I was around her and another woman looked at me too long or someone said something disrespectful, she was in their face, checking them. I'd be lying if I said I didn't love that.

"Her runnin' from me ain't got nothin' to do wit' me bein' a ho, so kill that. You right, though. She's always been crazy."

"Whateva. How was the doctor's appointment?" J asked.

"It was straight. Hol' on," I said, reaching in my pocket. I pulled out one of the ultrasound pictures. I intended to pass it to my boy but ended up staring at it myself.

"Nigga, let me see." He snatched it from me. "Damn, Tate. You 'bout to have a baby."

I smiled. "I know, right? It's crazy."

"It's *lit*. It's been time for you and Jess to lock in."

I chuckled and shook my head. *Didn't I know it.*

"Yeah, maybe, but I ain't even on that right now, dawg." We made it to the candy aisle, and I got a couple boxes of her favorite chocolate and tossed them in the basket.

J stopped a few feet behind me and folded his arms. "What you mean you ain't on that? She's havin' your kid, Tate. Y'all already love each other, so what's stoppin' you from gettin' wit' her now?"

I kissed my teeth. "Man, *I* love Jet. I ain't too sure it's mutual. Not like I want it to be anyway. Right now, I wanna concentrate on making sure she's healthy so the baby makes it here safely. The doctor said somethin' 'bout her blood pressure bein' high 'cause of stress, so—"

"The *doctor* said somethin'? *I* told you not to go over there stressin' her out, and that's exactly what you been doin', huh? That's why we in here makin' presents and shit, ain't it?"

"We shole ain't in here for you to be fussin' like you're my fuckin' parent. Lower your voice."

"Whatever. I know I'm right."

He was, but I wouldn't give him the satisfaction of confirming it.

"Anyway, her well-being is what I'm focused on. Everything else is on the back burner. Jet played me to the left three times too many, so I ain't even thinkin' about taking it there wit' her. I just need us to be cool so that she don't give me a hard time about protecting her the way I need to."

"What's the word wit' that? Was Moreu able to track down the ink?"

"Nah, not really. It's sold hella places in Georgia and New York, and the person coulda bought it online too. I haven't let her go to her office yet, but I'ma have to take her over there so I can get the other letters. Right now, I'm at a standstill, but I need to put somethin' in place so she can move around the city safely."

"What you thinkin'?" he asked.

"I been runnin' checks on potential bodyguards this week. I hired one I feel comfortable lettin' her go outside with. He starts next week, so I guess I'll tell her about them when I get home."

"Make sure you keep me posted. Both of y'all are family, so remember that you ain't goin' through it alone, aight?"

I smirked. "Let's hug, J," I said, opening my arms wide.

He cut his eyes at me. "You touch me, and I'ma punch you. Stop talkin' to me and focus on fillin' this basket up. Your gift lookin' real weak right now."

It's Happening

♥

Jess

It's happening. It's really happening.

That thought had been on repeat in my mind since my doctor's appointment hours earlier. The morning sickness, the fatigue, and the home pregnancy tests were all valid confirmations that I was pregnant. Today, however, I learned that there was nothing like actually *seeing* my little one moving inside me.

Hearing their heartbeat.

Holding the sonogram in my hands.

Now, I sat on the sofa in Julian's living room, staring at one of the pictures. Today hadn't been my first ultrasound. My first one was the day Doctor P confirmed my fibroids, and each one after that was related to my condition.

From the beginning of my fibroid journey, I knew it was likely I'd never procreate.

Doctor P mentioned the possibility, but it was the surgeon who told me there was no chance at all. My fibroids were large, plentiful, and caused me a lot of pain. Because they grew in my uterine cavity, reproduction was highly unlikely. It wasn't easy and took a very long time, but eventually, I began to accept that kids weren't happening for me.

But... it *was* happening. *It was really happening.*

Today meant so much to me. Every time I had to endure an ultrasound in the past, only to look inside myself and see my pain materialized broke something inside me.

The photos I held in my hands shattered those dreadful memories and replaced them with sweet expectation. I touched my belly and smiled. The life God had blessed Julian and me with was in there, restoring what I thought was broken.

I inhaled, but it was cut short because my nose was stuffed. Wiping my eyes, I laughed to myself. I had been crying for hours, and for the first time, I didn't even mind it. *I was having a baby.*

"Thank You, God," I whispered, tilting my head back and allowing the tears to flow. "Thank you so much."

The security system announcing a car approaching the house brought me out of my praise session. Quickly, I stood and walked over to Julian's security monitor. I watched as he backed his SUV into the garage before quickly tiptoeing back to the sofa.

I wiped my eyes but knew he'd realize I had been crying. Besides the fact that he seemed to notice everything about me, my eyes always doubled in size when I cried even a little bit. It was one of the main reasons I hated getting emotional.

"Front door open." Seconds after the system announced his entrance, he was heading toward me. He was eyeing me with a frown, and my smile grew as I stared at what he was holding.

"What's wrong, pretty?"

"Nothing. What's that?" I asked, pointing to the large basket.

Julian kissed his teeth before rounding the sofa. He placed the basket on the coffee table, making me frown.

"Nothing's wrong, but your eyes are bloodshot? I thought you were done keeping things from me, Jet."

I sighed and rolled my eyes. "Nothing's wrong, goofy. I'm pregnant, happy about it, and unnecessarily emotional, that's all."

He raised a brow. "So those are happy tears?"

I nodded and smiled. "Yep." He stared at me longer, likely trying to detect bullshit, but after a while, he nodded and smirked. "Cool."

"Now, what is that?" I pointed to the basket again. It was large and deep, but I saw my favorite chocolate peeking out of the top, so I was hoping it was for me.

"During my time in college and Virginia, my momma used to send me baskets like this—well, hers looked a lot better than this one—of all my favorite stuff. Them packages had a way of liftin' my mood, and I'm hoping' that's the outcome of this gesture, too. I guess I'on know *all* your favorites yet, but all the ones I am privy to are in this basket."

I scooted to the edge of the sofa to access the basket more easily. I was in awe as I pulled out every item. This man had purchased everything I loved, from the socks down to the potato chips. He had my favorite kinds of popcorn, hand lotion, and face masks. The basket was so thoughtful. Everything in it was tailored to Jessica Westin, and I didn't even know he knew this much about me.

I was about to spend time creeping on Julian because I wanted to learn him this well. I wanted to be able to do something like this for him.

When my hands were full, I set the items down and continued going through the basket. The next thing I pulled out was a notebook. It was faux leather and had a space for a photo on the cover. Right under the picture pocket was the title, "My Bump Journal."

"That's a pregnancy journal. I was looking online, and a lotta women use 'em to record their thoughts, feelings, and just updates about their pregnancy journey. I also read that journaling relieves stress," he said, and his words tickled my insides.

"You ain't gotta use it if that's not your thing, but I think it might be cool to try it—"

I leaned over and kissed his cheek, cutting his response short. Because I loved his scent and hadn't been that close to it in a while, I lingered in his personal space a little longer than I probably should have. I also didn't miss the subtle groan he released at our contact, but I ignored it, knowing we needed to work on several things before we thought about getting physical again.

"I love it. I love all of it. Thank you," I said, cutting him off. I had the best baby daddy on the planet, and I had to make him my man sooner than later. He was so everything.

"I'm glad. Listen, I hired someone to roll witcha when you need to go out, and I'm not here."

I sat back on the sofa and raised a brow. "You got me a bodyguard?"

"Yeah, I know you have a life to live and a business to run, and I ain't tryna hinder that, so this is my solution for now. His name is Kendrick, and you'll meet him Monday. Just know I checked him out, and I trust him with you."

I shrugged and sighed. "Okay."

"I hired him for when you *have* to go out, but I ain't feeling all that jet-setting you're used to, pretty. It just ain't safe out here, so I'on know what to tell you about that. I gotta figure this out before I let you just be out here wildin', so you just gotta hold off on all the extra stuff. Maybe you need a hobby or sum."

I grinned. Jet-setting was nowhere near my mind, but it had been a part of my life since he'd met me, so I understood where he was coming from.

"A hobby, huh? What do you suggest, goofy?"

"Aye, chill. Maybe you can work on startin' your sunglass line. You mentioned it before on your live as a joke, but that could be lit. You got style, and I knew the clothing thing is more Davi's lane, but if you get in your bag, I know you could design some fire shades. You know what you like, and that's the first step in creativity."

I wanted to take that moment to clown him about supposedly knowing the *first step* in creativity, but I couldn't. I was still stuck on the fact that he had somehow picked up on the fact that I wanted to start a glasses line.

It had been a thought for a few years now. I just never had enough time on my hands to flesh it out and make it happen. I shuddered as warmth bloomed in my chest. I wasn't sure when I mentioned it on my livestream, but he had caught it and tucked it away in his memory, along with everything else he had learned about me over the years.

Man, I loved this man.

"That's, uh, that's a really good idea. Look, Ali, I want us to be good again. We've been walkin' around this house like strangers, and we ain't ever moved that way before. We used to argue, joke around, and have a good time together. Can we get back to that?" I asked, holding my breath.

He grinned. "Hell yeah. Let's start now. Pick a movie, and I'ma go pop some of this nasty popcorn you got me buyin' out the store," he said, grabbing a box of caramel popcorn from my basket. He stood and headed to the kitchen while I grabbed the remote with a stupid grin.

I underestimated the power of Julian's smile because now that he was back to giving them out freely, I felt a high I never wanted to be without.

***

"I got the door, Miss Westin," Kendrick said once he parked the car in front of Julian's house.

It was his first day, and I was so ready to leave the house that I asked him to take me grocery shopping. I was a little hesitant about how we would vibe because my perception of bodyguards was that they were rude, stoic giants who acted like they couldn't speak.

Kendrick was cool, though. He *was* huge, but while we rode around in the car, we engaged in interesting conversation, and he was actually hilarious. He was about his business once we were out in public, though, and I couldn't lie. I felt safe in his presence. I was glad we got along because I felt we'd be stuck with each other for quite some time.

He opened the door, and I got out slowly. I wasn't showing yet, but my boobs had swelled and were sore. They'd throb if I moved suddenly or too fast, and I was tired of the sensation. Initially, the pain had me worried, and I went back to the doctor, but she assured me that it was a typical symptom of pregnancy and nothing to worry about. She said the tenderness would subside after a few weeks, and I honestly couldn't wait.

Kendrick opened the front door, then stood back so that I could enter first. I took my shoes off and placed them beside the door while Kendrick traveled past me with my grocery bags in his hand. By the time I made it to the kitchen, he had already taken everything out of their bags.

He looked at me and asked, "Do you need help putting everything up?"

I shook my head. "No, you've done more than enough, Kendrick. I appreciate your help."

"I'll be here at the same time tomorrow, Miss Westin." I frowned. I could have sworn Julian said Kendrick would pretty much be around until he got home from work. Kendrick must have sensed my confusion because he spoke up again.

"Mister Tate is home early, ma'am." My frown turned upside down quickly.

"Oh. Okay, thanks, Kendrick."

He nodded, walked back out of the door, and closed it.

Sighing, I eyed the groceries and contemplated my next move. The neat freak in me wanted to organize everything immediately, but the lover girl wanted to go find Julian. Now that we had called a truce and I was done locking myself in his guest room, we had been sharing space more often.

Being around Julian only increased my desire for him. He had been so attentive to my needs in the last week, and it felt like a glimpse into what a future with him could look like. I wanted that with him but was a little discouraged about the probability of us actually becoming something.

Even though he had been treating me like a queen, it differed from our previous interactions. He had officially placed me in the friend zone, and I wasn't sure he wanted that to change. I wasn't sure it *needed* to change.

Julian and I were having a baby together, and the last thing I wanted was for us to finally try a romantic relationship and fail at it, only to become enemies. I wanted us to always get along, for the baby's sake, so maybe taking it there wasn't the best move for us. That didn't change the fact that I wanted him badly, though. I sighed and headed down the hall.

My first stop was his bedroom, but the door was wide open, and the lights were off. I peeked in anyway.

Empty.

The other places he frequented in his home were his gym and office. Since the office was closest to his bedroom, I headed there. Sure enough, he was sitting behind his desk, focused on his computer screen. I should have figured he was working since he got home so early.

Not wanting to interrupt, I took a step back.

"Ow!"

Hopping on one foot, I turned to see that I had backed into his sideboard and stumped my toe in the process. I was about to hobble back down the hall and to my bedroom when Julian's voice sounded off from his study.

"Jet? What's wrong?"

Taking a deep breath, I turned again and slowly pushed his office door open. He was still sitting behind his desk, but now, his eyes were on me, and his eyebrows were furrowed as he gave me a once-over.

The throbbing pain in my foot subsided as I made my way closer to him. As soon as I was within reach, he pulled me closer. I inhaled sharply as his large hands glided from my waist to my thighs. They then slid under the hem of my shirt and up my stomach.

I stared down at Julian as he gazed intently at my flat stomach. He wore a small smile as he observed my midsection, and it made me smile. My baby bump was barely noticeable, but Julian observed it every chance he got. He was obsessed with our baby already, and it was clear that was where his mind was.

"Why did you yell out a minute ago?" he asked, still focused on my belly.

I took another deep breath, trying to focus on the question. The feel of his hands rubbing my stomach made me think about other places on my body where he could put them. We had just gotten to a point where he was acknowledging my presence, so I was sure sex was off the table. I needed to get it together.

"I was walking away from your door and hit my foot on something."

He looked up at me then. My teeth immediately sank into my bottom lip. Those dark, piercing eyes did something to me every time.

"What you walkin' away for? You ain't even come in."

"I saw you were busy. I didn't wanna bother you."

He stared at me silently for a moment before he kissed my stomach. Releasing his hold on me, he sat back in his seat and sighed.

"You bothering me is an impossibility, Jessica. If you need my time or attention, get it."

His words made my cheeks warm, and I looked away for a moment. He always said the right things.

"Okay," I said softly and rolled my eyes immediately after. I didn't know if it was my baby, Julian, or both, but I had been a little *too* soft-spoken and sensitive lately. That wasn't me... at all.

"So wassup?" he asked.

I shrugged as my eyes trailed from him to his desk. It was full of photos and documents, and the first to catch my eye were photos of houses that weren't in the best shape. There were addresses and other information located at the bottom of each.

"Are those houses you and Joseph are gonna buy?" I asked, gesturing toward the pictures.

"We're thinkin' 'bout it. We're tryna flip one of 'em into a nice rental spot for tourists, but it's gon' cost some bread to get either of them in good enough shape to rent out. We just wanna make sure it's worth it."

I glanced at the photos again.

Placing a hand on the one closest to me, I said, "If you want the most bang for your buck, I would go with this one. West End ain't the best part of town, but all the Black colleges are over there. People are always lookin' to rent a place close to campus for Homecoming and other functions."

I continued observing both pictures until I realized he hadn't responded to me. I looked over to find him already staring at me with an expression I couldn't quite read.

I frowned. "What?"

"Nothin', man," he said with a chuckle. "I forgot you're Atlanta-bred, for real. You might be on to something."

I smirked. "Might be? Tell yourself what you need to, goofy."

We both laughed and fell into a comfortable silence. I reveled in it because I had been wanting to just *be* around him since I moved into his home. The fact that we were back on speaking terms made me feel good, to say the least.

"You sure you good, though? You ain't need nothin'?"

I shook my head. "Not really. I mean... there is something I *want*, though."

He smirked. "I bet. What's that?"

"Can we do something?"

He raised an eyebrow. "Somethin' like what, Jet?"

I shrugged. "I'on know, anything. I'm bored, and you're home, so I want to do something."

Julian smirked. "Anything?"

I nodded. I just wanted to prolong my time with him.

He stood and grabbed my hand before heading toward the door. "Aight, bet."

All or Nothing

♥

Tate

"You for real?"

I glanced at Jess again and chuckled. "Yeah, I'm for real, girl. You said *anything*. And this shole ain't boring."

I patted the spot on the sofa next to me while extending one of my game controllers to her. I knew she wanted to go out somewhere, but I was still hesitant about that. I wasn't trying to hold her as a prisoner, but if we were gon' head out to do somethin' fun, I couldn't be in the moment with her *and* be on top of my game when it came to protecting her from whoever this stalker was.

Since I gave Kendrick the rest of the day off, I wanted to stay inside, but I'd plan something for her to enjoy herself soon enough. In the meantime, though, I wanted to see if she could hang.

She stood there with her arms folded for a moment longer before she smirked and grabbed the controller. She sat down slowly, and that had me frowning.

"Why you movin' like that? Somethin' hurts?"

She shook her head and sighed. "Not really. I'm just a little sore."

Sitting up, I said, "I need to take you to the doctor, then. Come on."

Jess shook her head again. "No. I already talked to Doctor P about it; she says it's normal. I'm good."

I took a minute to respond because I was trying to decide whether I believed her. She must have sensed that because she spoke up again.

"I'm good, Ali. Promise."

"And you would tell me if you weren't?" I asked, my eyes piercing hers.

She nodded immediately, and I relaxed a little. "I would."

"Aight. Come on, then. I promise I'll take it easy on you," I said as I fired the game up.

As I chose the game mode and my team, I heard her kiss her teeth. "Boy, my baby Two taught me how to play. I'on need you to take nothin' easy on me."

I glanced at her, and the serious expression she wore had me cracking up.

"Oh yeah? Well, I taught ya boy everything he knows, so don't take this whuppin' personal."

She rolled her eyes and focused on the screen. "Whateva."

I continued to talk my trash while she chose her team, and after I adjusted the settings, we were off.

The sound of sneaks squeaking and the basketball thumping against the floor quickly replaced the silence that filled the room when we got focused on the game. I sat back further on the sofa because I'd be lying if I said I didn't want the opportunity to steal glances at my beautiful baby momma.

The lights in the room were dim, so the television put a spotlight on her pretty face, and it definitely had me feeling away. As I refocused on the screen, I realized Jess was maneuvering on the court with ease. The fact that she was kind of nice with it had me sitting up a little because I'd be damned if I let her beat me in basketball. She was arrogant enough without the W, and I wouldn't ever hear the end of it.

"Aight, I see you, Jet, but I'm done playin' with you. You 'bout to see how a boss does this."

She kissed her teeth but didn't look away from the television when she said, "Whatever, goofy."

We were still early on in the first quarter, and I took the lead, sinking shots with ease.

I looked at Jess quickly, and she frowned as her fingers danced over the buttons. She was feisty on a normal day, so I wasn't surprised to see her competitive side come out, but I was loving it.

By the end of the first quarter, I was up by 15, and Jess was pouting. "Don't look like that. It's just a game, Jet," I said with a smirk.

"Leave me alone, goofy. Lemme focus."

I laughed. "Aight."

The second quarter commenced, and everything was smooth until it wasn't. About thirty seconds into it, something shifted, and Jess found her groove.

"How did I just let that happen?" I asked under my breath as she shot a three.

"You didn't *let* nothin' happen, goofy. I'm just good like that, and I ain't done either."

"Yeah, whateva."

This girl started weaving through my player like a pro, and she got another shot in on me. I still went into halftime in the lead, but as the quarters passed, the score tightened.

There had been a competitive tension between us throughout the game, but I couldn't lie. Something else was mixed in there too. We were both talking trash, but it was all love. The fact that she could always hang with me in the joke department did nothing to curb my attraction to her, either.

The thought of losing to Jessica Brielle annoyed me and turned me on at the same time. Every time she made a shot or blocked one of mine, I had to adjust myself.

Her determination to beat me was all over her face, and I welcomed the challenge. It was the first time we had spent this much time together in a minute, and it felt like a little more than a game for me.

It was further confirmation that we were supposed to be together. It couldn't have been a coincidence that we could easily bond over *any* damn thing.

Realizing I was spending too much time analyzing my feelings for Jess and not enough on playing the game, I cleared my throat and got back into it. Sinking another shot, she secured a tight lead, making me kiss my teeth.

"Aight, nie. Chill out before I have to stop takin' it easy on ya."

She rolled her eyes and laughed. "Oh, now that I'm winnin', you wanna try to claim it's 'cause you're takin' it easy? Boy, bye. Take this L like a real one."

Her smart mouth had my boxers tightening around my manhood, but I tried my best to block it out long enough to teach her a lesson. In the final minutes of the game, I was locked in. I was doing my thing, but Jess wasn't trying to let go of the lead.

She wasn't backing down, and as I continued to fight for the lead, all the other bullshit that usually plagued my mind dissipated. I wasn't worried about work or the mountain of issues Jess and I still needed to work through. All I cared about was this moment—this connection—with Jess.

Just as I was about to make the shot that would put me ahead of her, my work phone rang. For a millisecond, I thought about ignoring it, but I knew it wasn't a good look.

Instead, I paused and pulled the phone out of my pocket. It was the police department chief.

"Tate," I answered, trying to filter the annoyance out of my voice.

"Afternoon, it's Chief Donaldson. I know you were supposed to be working from home today, but there's been another incident that may or may not be related to the abduction case. How soon can you and your partner get here?"

I sighed.

"We'll be there in thirty minutes."

"See you then."

I hung up and tossed the phone then the controller on the sofa.

Jess set her controller down and turned toward me.

"Everything okay?" she asked. Her scrunched eyebrows and creased forehead made me want to crack a smile.

"You concerned about me, pretty?"

She bit her lip before rolling her eyes. "No. I was just trying to see if the phone call was important or if you were trying to get out of this L you were 'bout to take."

"You crazy if you think I was really gon' let you beat me. But nah, I do gotta head out. Somethin' popped off with the case we're workin' on."

"Oh," she said, disappointment clear in her tone.

I was disappointed too. We were having a good time together for the first time in a long time, and now the moment was gone.

"Yeah," I said, standing. "I'll call Kendrick and see if he can come back through in case you need to go somewhere."

She shook her head. "No, you don't have to do that. I'm just gonna chill here."

I observed her for a moment, wanting to know what she was thinking at that very moment.

"You sure?" I asked, not knowing what else to say.

She nodded. "Positive."

"Aight then," I said, grabbing my phone and slipping it back into my pocket. I headed out of the living room slowly. I almost wanted to laugh at myself. A part of me felt like going to work was canceling out all the progress we had made to be cool again. My lovesick ass didn't want to leave.

Just when I was crossing the threshold of the room, she called my name. I turned my head and asked, "Wassup?"

"Don't um… don't be tryna take too long because you're scared of a rematch."

I dropped my head for a second and tucked my bottom lip between my teeth, trying to keep my smile on lock.

"Bet."

As I exited the house and entered my car, I let myself grin as big as I wanted to seconds earlier. I had told myself plenty of times that I was never taking it there with Jess again. I didn't want to hand her another opportunity to disappoint me, but I couldn't help but feel like we had just started something. I needed to figure out whether I was willing to explore it yet again.

TiTi Jess

♥

Jess

"Ooo, these are fire," I said to myself as I bookmarked the sunglasses I liked.

I had spent the better part of my morning swiping through prototypes from the vendors I had come across the day before. Of the three I had received emails back from, two of the companies piqued my interest most. One had a broader range of color options, while the other allowed more creative freedom.

If I was really going to start a sunglass collection, I needed them to be different than anything else on the market, so I was pretty sure I would be going with the vendor who was more likely to go above and beyond design-wise.

I took a screenshot of the pair I liked and pulled the photo up in the design app on my tablet. The app allowed me to use my tablet pen to draw on images freely, and I needed to change a few things about the shades. I liked that particular oval shape, but if the top had a straight edge instead, it would give a sharper look.

I toyed with the design for a while until I felt like it was a *very* rough draft of what I would want. I had a vision, but my drawing skills were subpar at best. My best friend always sketched beautiful clothing designs, so maybe she could help me with the visual if I sent her what I had come up with.

My phone vibrating on my lap brought my attention to it, and when I realized it was my godson video calling me, I grinned.

"Hey, Two-Two!" I said, staring at his handsome little face.

"Wassup, Auntie? What you doin'?"

My smile grew a little, and I felt myself tear up simultaneously. I had known Two since the day he was born, and now he was a nine-year-old with a voice that got deeper each time I talked to him. He looked and acted more like his father every day.

That thought reminded me that my baby was a skilled artist himself, just like Joseph. Two loved to paint and draw. He also loved money, so I knew he'd be down to sketch out all the things in my head for a few dollars.

"Just workin' a lil bit. What's up?"

He frowned and squinted before leaning closer to the screen.

"Are you at Uncle Tate's house right now?"

I chuckled and dropped my gaze for a moment. His little observant self took after his father and his *Uncle Tate* in that department.

"Uh, yeah, I am. Is that okay wit' you?" I asked with a grin. I held my breath as I waited for his reply because he had no problem telling you how he felt about a thing. He was always very protective of me, and I believed it was because he thought I was a poor old woman who would be lonely for the rest of her life.

"I'on know," he said with a shrug. I chuckled. I had to respect my baby's honesty. "I haven't seen you in a long time. The last time I was at your house, you were cryin'. You okay?"

I bit my lip and willed the tears that were building to stand down. I swear I loved this little boy more than life. "Yeah, I'm okay, baby."

"I miss you. Can you come pick me up?" he asked, his face softening. My heart melted at his words. Two and I were like a dynamic duo before his brother was born. It was just him and me against the world, doing all the things he loved to do. We became a trio when David was added to the mix, but Joseph, the second, would always be my day one. I took my role as the fun, rich auntie very seriously.

"I miss you more, pumpkin. I would love to come get you, but—"

"Aye, we'll be there in an hour to get you, nephew. Ask ya momma to get David dressed, aight?"

Two's face lit up at Julian's words. "Aight! Wassup, Uncle Tate? Why is my auntie over there?"

Julian laughed as he approached. Standing behind the sofa, he leaned closer to me so his face was in the camera. His signature scent invaded my nostrils, and I closed my eyes to try to savor it.

"You remember how you were tellin' me 'bout that girl at school who told you to ask ya momma if she could come over?"

"Jaleesa? Yes, sir, she got a crush on me," my baby said with a smirk. I shook my head because there was no tellin' where Julian was about to take this.

"Well, ya auntie got a crush on me, my boy, so I let her come over. You cool wit' that?"

I opened my mouth but closed it instantly. I *did* have a crush on the man, so I couldn't really say anything.

"Yeah, it's cool. Just be nice to her, aight?" That made me laugh. My baby knew that his uncle and I argued about nonsense every time we got together, so I was sure he was confused about us actually *wanting* to spend time together.

Julian chuckled. "I got you, my boy. Gone 'head and tell your momma we on the way to get you."

"Yes, sir. See y'all in a minute!" Two said excitedly before hanging up.

I tossed my phone on the sofa and turned my head. Kissing my teeth, I glared at Julian.

"Why would you say I'm the one with the crush?"

Tate raised his brow. "You ain't?"

Again, I had no response.

He smirked and stood up completely. "Exactly. I be seein' you stare, man. I mean, I get it, so it's cool."

Chuckling, I dared to ask, "You get *what*, Ali?"

"That you can't get enough of a nigga. Your baby daddy is handsome as hell, Jet. You can feel good about that. You chose well, girl."

I burst out laughing at that. This man was crazy, but he told no lies. I set my tablet down and stood from the sofa.

"Tell yourself what you need to, goofy. I'm going to get dressed so we can pick up my babies," I said, starting down the hallway.

Before I made it too far, I heard Julian's voice again.

"What's this?"

I turned and made the few steps it took to get back to the living room. When I saw my tablet in his hands, I realized what he was asking me about.

"A very bad design for a pair of sunglasses."

He looked up at me with a grin. "So, you're really gon' do it?"

I licked my lips and nodded. "I think so. I think it could be something solid well after this modeling thing is over for me."

"I think so, too. You can't draw at all, though. You need to ask my man Two to get you right real quick."

Laughing, I said, "I was thinking the same thing."

"This is dope, though, pretty. I'm proud of ya."

My cheeks warmed, and just like that, a new emotion was unlocked. His praise made me feel a different sense of satisfaction than I had ever experienced before. Making him proud seemed to make me happy, and I wanted to do it more often.

With my smile still intact, I turned around and headed back toward the hallway.

***

"Let's go, Unc!"

I glanced at David, who was standing between Two and Julian. Both of them held his little hand as he bounced up and down with the cutest grin.

We had purchased wristbands for the day and were now standing just inside the entrance of the amusement park, and I believed the sounds of laughter and excitement were getting to him. My baby was ready to have fun. Julian asked Kendrick to come with us so he could focus on enjoying our nephews and not worry about my safety. I honestly felt like it was overkill. The stalker knew where I lived, but I hadn't been there in weeks, so I doubted he had been able to track me down as of late. I didn't voice my opinion because Julian was going to do what he wanted anyway. I was just glad to finally have a day out of the house.

"Aight, my man, let's go," Julian said, grinning at David. We entered the park, and the smell of funnel cake caught my attention immediately. I hadn't been to an amusement park in a while, but rollercoasters and funnel cakes were two of my favorite things.

Since I was now with child, I would probably stick to the kid-friendly rides with David while Two and Julian handled the real rollercoasters. That didn't mean I wouldn't eat to my heart's content.

"Let's make a plan, y'all," I said, glancing at the kids before focusing on Julian and Kendrick. "Let's hit the rides first, then we can grab some lunch."

"Sounds good to me, Auntie," Two said, and I had to clear my throat so I wouldn't let out a tear. His little deep, raspy voice was sounding a little too *manly* for me. The fact that he was the most mature nine-year-old I had ever met didn't help either. My baby was growing up, and it was a hard pill to swallow.

"Aight, cool. Let's see what we can get on all together first, then me and my boy Two leavin' y'all for some real roller coasters."

David frowned immediately. "Don't leave, Unc."

Julian laughed and scooped David into his arms. "My bad, D. I ain't goin' nowhere," he said and kissed his cheek. Seeing him interact with the kids made my insides warm. He was so good with them.

As if he felt my eyes on him, Julian looked at me. He wasn't smiling, but there was a hint of something in his eyes that put me at ease. The tension between us had been thinning out more each day since the day we played the video game. There was still some there, likely because we had yet to really talk, but it felt a lot lighter.

As we made our way through the park, Two walked ahead of us a little, pointing out every ride he wanted to get on before the day was done.

"Let me down, Unc," David said, patting Julian's chest. Julian obliged, and David ran to catch up to his big brother, who immediately grabbed his hand.

"They 'bout to wear our asses out, ain't they?" Julian asked, moving closer to me.

I chuckled. "They always do, but it's all good. They'll be knocked out as soon as we get back in the car."

He didn't respond, so I looked up at him. Of course, he was already staring at me with an expression I couldn't read.

"What?" I asked, unable to take it.

"Nothin', Jet. Come on."

We continued through the park and stopped in front of a family-friendly ride. The line wasn't long at all, so we waited until it stopped, and the operator allowed us all to climb on.

David was having the time of his life, screaming and giggling as we swayed back and forth, while Two looked ready to get on something more exciting. I leaned over and whispered in Julian's ear. "Once we get off of this one, Kendrick and I can take David to the kiddie area for a minute. I want Two to have some time to do what he wants to do."

He took a minute to reply, and I assumed it was because he didn't want to separate. I rolled my eyes.

"Kendrick's here, Ali. We'll be fine."

He sighed but nodded. "Aight, cool."

Once the ride stopped, we followed through with our plan, and David was reluctant until we made it to our destination. All the colors and characters in the area were right up his alley.

"Ooo! That one, TiTi!" he said, pointing at the alligator ride.

"Good choice, D. Come on."

I knew he was about to tire me out, but it was all good. I put a smile on my face and prepared to vibe out with my nephew.

***

Tate

"Y'all want some ice cream?" Jess asked the boys.

David jumped up from his seat and yelled, "Yes, ma'am!"

We all laughed and stood. I threw away our plates from the lunch we had just had, and we headed back into the bustle of the park to get to the ice cream stand we had peeped earlier.

We had chosen a good day to come to the park because it wasn't crowded at all. We got their ice cream quickly and easily found another place to sit and enjoy it. David chose to sit in Jessica's lap, while Two and I sat across from them. She set D up with a makeshift bib made of napkins, but as soon as he started on his waffle cone, he put his nose in it.

With a smile, Jess wiped it immediately, then showed him an easier way to eat the ice cream without messing up his face. I had been watching her all day, and while I knew she was good with the boys, seeing her with them today hit differently.

"Aye," I said, watching as she kissed David's forehead.

She looked up at me with raised eyebrows. "Yeah?"

"We might be aight at this parenting thing."

She smiled and asked, "You think so?"

"I do. I think we made a dope team today. We could have a house full if we wanted to."

I paused. I didn't know where that came from—or maybe I did—but I needed to chill.

I cleared my throat, and Jess looked away for a moment before smiling again and saying, "Maybe. Let's focus on the one we have for now, though."

"Y'all got a baby?"

I froze at Two's question and immediately looked at Jess. Her eyes were wide and glued to me. I figured Davi and Joseph hadn't told the kids what was up yet, and I hadn't even thought about how to break the news to them.

I wasn't sure how Two would take either of us having a child of our own. He was used to both of our undivided attention when we spent time together, and he was wise enough to know a baby would change that. He was also protective of his auntie, and I didn't think he was feeling Jess and me pursuing a relationship.

"Auntie... is that what you just said? That you and Unc got a baby?" Two asked again.

I was low-key relieved that he directed the question to Jess because I didn't want to be the one to answer him.

"Uh... yeah Two-Two. Well, the baby isn't here yet, but your Uncle Tate and I are going to have a baby in a few months."

We both observed him quietly as he processed. His eyes were squinted, and his head tilted to the side, just like his father did when he was deep in thought or frustrated. David, on the other hand, was happily eating his ice cream, oblivious to the fact that his grown aunt and uncle were low-key scared about his brother's next words.

"So the baby is in your belly right now?" he eventually asked.

David laughed at that and started rubbing his own stomach.

Jess nodded. "That's right, baby," she said slowly.

Two turned his focus to me then. "That's why y'all live together now? Because you gon' be a family?"

"Yeah, nephew. That's why we're living together now."

"You gon' marry my auntie, Unc?"

I chuckled. He wasn't letting up. How was I supposed to answer that?

I decided to answer truthfully. Joseph and I both instilled the importance of being a man and keeping it real to Two, and I didn't want to be a hypocrite.

"I don't know, man, but I would love for that to happen."

I heard Jess gasp, and I glanced at her. When our eyes met, I saw the questions dancing in hers. She wanted to know if I meant what I just said, and I hoped the look I gave her communicated the answer—I was dead ass. If Jess ever actually stopped running from us, I'd wife her in a heartbeat.

Two was quiet again. After several seconds passed, he nodded.

"So you good with this, nep?" I asked with raised brows. I couldn't even lie. I wanted my lil man's blessing.

He took a spoonful of his ice cream and nodded.

"I'm cool wit' it. You just can't be mean to her no more."

I laughed and raised my fist, extending it toward him.

"That's a promise, man."

He must have been satisfied with our answers because he ceased his interrogation after that. We settled into a comfortable silence, and I admired the three of them as they ate their ice cream. Spending the day with Jessica—and the kids—just felt *right*. The same way playing the game with her the other day did.

Jess and I had years in of knowing and spending time with each other. Our bond was always undeniable but short-lived. She had a long history of cutting our quality time off whenever we were really getting somewhere, but she had yet to go there today.

Something with us was shifting, and it made me feel like we were actually building this time. I hoped it was true because our connection had forever potential. She just had to let us make it there.

I Read, Too

♥

Jess

The steamy water was just the right temperature as I slipped into my bath. As I sank deeper into my bubbles, I let out a sigh. *I needed this.*

The day before had been a long one. I enjoyed our time with my nephews, but all the walking definitely had taken a toll on my body. I hadn't exercised since I moved into Julian's home, so my legs weren't used to all the work we put in at the park.

I sighed again as my mind wandered. As comfortable as I felt at that moment. My bubbles were the furthest thing from my mind. All I could think about was the fact that the water was enveloping me the way I wanted Julian to.

We had been spending a lot of our days together lately, and memories of our time together flooded my brain whenever we were apart. At that moment, I remembered how well he had been with the boys the day before and how much he seemed to enjoy it. His eyes shined every time one of them hugged him or engaged him in conversation.

He was going to be the best daddy ever, and I couldn't wait to witness it.

On the rides we all rode together, there were times when his large hands would brush against my skin. The warmth of that connection had me on edge most of the day, and it took real effort to remain in the moment.

I allowed my fingers to graze my skin lazily, and water trickled down my body. I felt as though I couldn't help how my body responded to that man. The friction that had been present between us since I told him about the baby seemed to be morphing into something else—something *more*—and I sensed he felt it, too.

I bit my lip as I thought about how his abs and muscular arms refused to be overshadowed by the designer tee he wore. The shirt wasn't tight at all, but the definition of his body couldn't be missed. He was so handsome.

I also didn't miss how he looked at me the rest of the day after Two gave us the third degree about having a baby together. He told our nephew he wanted to marry me, and the confidence in his eyes when he said it made me believe him. Those eyes on me were engrained in my memory, and it almost felt as if they were on me at that very moment.

My fingers started to wander, and the steady movement of the water against the contours of my body heightened everything I was feeling. As I continued to explore my anatomy, I allowed the last couple of days with Julian Tate to play in my mind like a montage.

Those recent memories began to fuse with older—more intimate—ones, and before long, I had been envisioning him with me in the bathtub. Lately, he touched my belly when he wanted to connect with our child or brushed his fingers against me in passing, but...

I missed his other touch. We had never shared a bath together, but I could only imagine how gently yet intensely he would handle me here. I ran a hand down my neck, then my chest, as I imagined him trailing kisses there. With the other hand, I applied more pressure to my center. I massaged myself sensually, wishing they were *him*.

"Mmph."

I tucked my lip between my teeth and completely gave in to my fantasy. I arched my back as I surrendered myself to the pleasure I was delivering to myself. All that mattered in that moment was the warmth of the water, the rhythm of my movements, and my thoughts of Julian Ali Tate.

My breathing intensified as I used two fingers to enter my folds. Stiffening my fingers, I quickened my pace and began winding my hips to intensify my movements. As the water splashed around me, I melted into a state of pure bliss and transcended into a world where Julian and I were really together and shared moments like this often. My movements became erratic as my breaths were shallower, and everything inside me began to tingle.

As I climaxed, I placed the back of my free hand over my mouth and bit down as I released an elongated moan.

Several seconds passed before my body returned to a state of normalcy. When I felt I could exit the tub without falling on wobbly legs, I stood and stepped out, immediately walking over to the shower and turning it on.

Damn, I thought as I stepped inside. I shook my head and cleaned my body thoroughly. As much as I felt like I needed that, it did little to curb my yearning for the real thing. I wanted *Julian*.

***

Wrapping a towel around my body, I stepped out of the bathroom with a sigh. My body and I had gotten well acquainted over the last year, so pleasuring myself wasn't usually such a chore.

The fact that I was leaving my shower just as sexually frustrated as I entered it had me ready to throw something. I didn't know if it was the baby, the fact that Julian and I were in close quarters, or both, but I was *horny*.

We had been doing well for the last month or so, but he hadn't acted even remotely interested in a physical relationship with me. If I was honest, it wasn't surprising. Before my birthday, Julian had managed to deny me of him for a year. When he decided to cut me off altogether, he stood on it, and now it seemed that he wanted to stand on having a healthy, co-parenting relationship *only*.

I knew he didn't trust me in the relationship department, but I wanted to earn that from him.

I was in love with him, and I knew it. We just made sense, and it showed every time we shared space. Unless he was actively ignoring me—which he hadn't done since my doctor's appointment—our conversations flowed naturally.

There was never a dull or uncomfortable moment where we were concerned, and I loved how in tune he was with my body language. I rarely had to vocalize my needs because Julian made it a point to just *know*. If we were on the sofa watching television, and I moved a certain way, he would pick up on it and get another pillow to support my back.

If I picked up my phone at a certain hour, he would automatically ask what I wanted to eat. He was a man in every sense of the word, and it was way past time for me to make him mine.

Once I felt like I had air-dried well enough, I lathered my body in lotion and coconut oil, then dressed in yoga pants and a tank top. Once

I left the bedroom, I passed the floor-length mirror in the hall and took a moment to admire myself.

Turning to the side, I smiled. I was so pregnant.

I wasn't showing too much, but I officially had a little pudge. In the formfitting top I wore, you could definitely see it, and I was excited to enter my baby belly era.

As I continued to examine myself, my smile faded. I needed to tell my parents that I was having a baby. I talked to them all the time, just like I did when I lived in New York, but I hadn't visited them since I took those tests.

I had been telling them I was out of town for work, and understandably, they bought the lie. Since I began my modeling career, I've spent most of my months in a different city or country, so as long as I checked in, they weren't suspicious. I hated lying to them, though, so it was about time I bit the bullet.

Shaking my head, I turned and headed for the main area of the large home. It was extremely quiet, which had me curious about Julian's whereabouts. He usually made it a point to wake me up for breakfast by now, but I hadn't seen him all morning. On a mission to find my baby daddy, I powerwalked through the hallway. My search was short-lived because when I entered the living room, I was greeted with a heavenly sight.

He was shirtless and lying on one of his sofas. His right hand lazily caressed his abs while the left held a book slightly above his face. I squinted slightly, trying to read the title of his book.

Murder on the Calais Coach

I lifted my brows in surprise. I had read that mystery and several others by the same author. I loved reading, but was surprised Tate did. I mean, he was a low-key nerd, so I knew he had to read some things, but not *fiction*.

I stood there admiring him in silence. He hadn't seemed to notice me, and I wasn't in a rush to make my presence known. I was enjoying the view.

As he lay there, he readjusted his body slightly. He placed his fingers just under the waistband of his pants, and I let out a moan that I intended to keep in. An arrogant smirk spread on his face, but he said nothing. He didn't even look at me.

Realizing I had officially been caught creeping, I spoke up.

"You didn't wake me up."

"Mornin', pretty." He hadn't looked at me yet, and I couldn't lie I wanted his attention. I kissed my teeth and placed my fists on my hips.

"How do you *know* I'm pretty, Ali? You haven't even looked at me."

I felt myself pout while Julian chuckled and finally looked up from his book. Licking his lips as he gave me a thorough once-over, he said, "My bad. Good morning, gorgeous."

It was times like this that I thanked the Lord twice for my chocolate skin. Without it, this man would see me blushing from a mile away.

"Good morning."

"I came to wake you, but you were already in the shower. I bought breakfast for you. It's in the kitchen."

"Thanks," I said and cleared my throat.

He didn't look at me again or say anything else, but I stayed where I was. I wanted to be in his presence. We usually didn't do that unless we were doing something together and *pretending* to get on each other's nerves, but right now, I couldn't think of one smart thing to say to him, so... I just stood there.

After a while, he looked at me again. I expected a smirk or a smart remark about me staring, but with soft eyes, he asked, "You need something, Jet?"

I dropped my gaze briefly.

"No, I just... uh... I have a book too," I said, immediately rolling my eyes. I was so thirsty for my baby daddy that I was out here volunteering unnecessary information.

He chuckled. "Consumed by unLYSHed, right?"

I frowned.

"How did you know?" I learned a long time ago that Julian watched my live streams and had learned a lot about me from them, but I never advertised how much I loved to read. It wasn't really fitting for my public image, so I kept it to myself.

"I noticed it peekin' out of your purse. Looked it up." I chuckled.

"You don't miss much, huh?"

He shook his head. "Nah, not when it comes to you."

There was silence until he finally gave me his eyes again.

Licking his bottom lip, he said, "Go eat. Then grab your book and come read wit' me, pretty."

His smirk was arrogant, and if I wasn't feeling as giddy as I was about him inviting me into his space, I would have had something to say about it.

Instead, I turned on my heels and marched to the kitchen to eat breakfast.

No Time Like the Present

♥

Tate

I glanced up from my book and smirked.

The visual was one I could get used to. Jess was sitting across from me, her back on the opposite sofa arm and her book in her hand. I didn't know how much time had passed, but I knew we had been there reading for a minute.

It was the first time we shared a chill morning like that, but I felt it fasho. I hadn't encountered one activity I couldn't enjoy with Jessica, and that had me feeling a way. We could have a dope life together, and I think we both knew it. Living with her for the last month or so had been dope. I got a glimpse into the settled down life and wanted it for us in the long term.

Jessica didn't seem to have a problem with it, either. I knew she was used to new scenery every other week, but she seemed to enjoy being a homebody too. When I went to work, I came home to a good-ass meal she cooked.

I learned that she was even more of a neat freak than I was. My house never had a speck of dust between the two of us. We just *worked*, and as far as I was concerned, there was no reason for us to change this living situation once the baby was born, stalker be damned.

That made me think about her parents. Mine knew what was up and were excited about their grandchild. Jess talked to my momma at least once a week, and they seemed to be vibing, which only made me want to lock her down even more. I couldn't even consider that until I met her parents, though.

I knew she was close with them because she had always talked about them for as long as I'd known her, but in the two months she had been at my crib, she hadn't mentioned visiting them. Jess was four months pregnant, and I hadn't met them... That didn't sit right with me because she had a father who loved her.

I knew I would be pissed if a man got my daughter pregnant and didn't have the respect to even meet me, so I had plans to correct that ASAP. I planned a dinner for later that night but had yet to tell Jess about it. I felt like giving her too much of a heads-up would give her ample opportunity to try and shut it down. If her parents genuinely couldn't make it, that was one thing, but I didn't need her trying to make up fake excuses.

I closed my book.

"Your parents know you're pregnant?"

Her eyebrows shot in the air, and her eyes widened. *I'll take that as a no.*

"Um, I haven't had a chance to mention it," she said, chewing on her bottom lip.

"Mention it? Jet, you be on the phone wit' your momma all the time, and she don't know you havin' a baby?"

Jess sighed and closed her book. She dropped her eyes to her hands and began wringing them together.

"My parents think I'm in Milan," she finally said.

Huh?

"Why they think that?"

She slid both her hands down her face. "Because it's what I told them."

I cut my eyes at her. She knew damn well that part was obvious. "*Why*, Jessica?"

"Because, *Julian*. I'm pregnant and unmarried, and that ain't an easy thing for a daddy's girl like me to come out and say. I know I have to tell them. I just needed some time."

I chuckled. Maybe I could understand where she was coming from, but I still wasn't feeling it. This was the one thing about Jessica Brielle that got on my nerves.

Her response to tough conversations was to avoid them altogether. Instead of just facing it, she chose to hide stuff, just like she did with telling me about the baby. Her father was going to be more pissed because she lied, and I didn't want to play a part in keeping him in the dark. It was time to rectify that.

"Well, ain't no time like the present, baby momma. Tomorrow is Mother's Day, so you need to see your momma anyway. Call your parents, and let's all have dinner tonight."

I stood and headed down the hall, with Jess calling my name behind me. I ignored her because I wasn't about to argue about things that weren't changing. We were telling her parents about the baby... tonight.

Parents, I'm Preggo!

♥

Jess

My heart hadn't beat steadily since Tate made me call my parents and schedule a dinner. Now that we were actually pulling up to *Legendary*, I felt like it was about to leap out of my chest.

"You good?" I looked up at Tate standing over me. I hadn't even noticed that he had gotten out of the car, much less opened the door for me.

"I'm fine," I said, placing my hand in his. He helped me out of the car and placed a hand on the small part of my back as he led me into the restaurant.

"Hi, guys. Welcome back," Sarah said from her spot at the hostess booth.

Since Demi's husband Ace owned *Legendary*, we all found ourselves there for dinner several times in the last couple of years. We were both familiar with their staff.

"Tate, the room is ready, just as you requested."

"'Preciate that," he said, and I frowned. "I know I didn't give y'all much notice at all." *What was he up to?*

"Y'all family, so it's all good," Ace said, approaching us. He dapped Julian up before pulling me in for a hug.

"I hear congratulations are in order," he said with a smile.

I smiled and nodded. "Yep. Thanks, Ace."

"No doubt. Lemme show y'all to the room." He turned and led us to the back of the restaurant. He opened a door and led us inside, and I gasped. The private dining area had two large bouquets and white balloons all around. When we made it to the table, I realized the tea light candles on it spelled out Happy Mother's Day.

"Happy early Mother's Day, baby momma," Julian whispered in my ear.

I felt myself tear up as I glanced at Julian. "This is so sweet."

He smirked but squeezed my hand a little. "Crybaby ass."

Ace chuckled. "Aye, I'ma get outta y'all's way. My staff already knows to give y'all the works, but if you need somethin', holla at me."

"'Preciate that," Julian replied as Ace left the room.

He led me to the other side of the table and pulled out a chair for me before he sat beside me.

The fact that he had done this in such a short amount of time stunned me.

"How did you make this happen in a matter of hours?" He kissed his teeth.

"Girl, I made this happen days ago. Quit tryin' me."

Ugh, I hated how perfect he was.

"Uh, when my parents get here, can we..." I took a deep breath. I felt silly for asking, but I needed to get it out before they walked through the door. It was something I needed to get through the evening, and I was hoping he'd be willing to give it to me.

"Can we what, pretty?"

"Can we pretend to be a couple? Like, can you tell them you're my boyfriend?"

I just didn't feel good about dropping this news on my parents without having a legitimate connection to my baby's father. Pretending to be married would only piss my daddy off about not being asked for my hand, so I felt like a boyfriend would be acceptable.

He eyed me silently with the most serious expression. I chewed on my lip and waited for his response. Julian wasn't as okay with embellishing the truth as I was, so there was no telling what his answer would be.

"You want me to *pretend* to be ya man, when all I've been tryna do for the last four years is *be* your man?" He chuckled. "I got you, Jet. It's your world."

I frowned. *Was that a yes, or...*

I realized he wasn't feeling my proposition, but I really did need to know if he was willing to accept it. Before I could ask for clarification, the door opened, and my mother entered. My father followed closely behind, and I swallowed. *Here goes nothin'.*

Julian stood from his seat before pulling my chair out and helping me up.

"Baby! This is so nice!" my mother said, walking over to us. I smiled and opened my arms wide.

"Hey, Momma. Happy Mother's Day." We stayed in that embrace for quite some time until my daddy cleared his throat.

"You ain't seen your daddy in a minute either. Can I get a hug too? Mother's Day ain't 'til tomorrow anyway."

I laughed and shook my head as I pulled away from my mother. My daddy was always a spoiled brat when it came to my momma's and my attention. He always wanted *all* of it.

"My bad. Hey, Daddy. Missed you too."

"Uh-huh, I bet," he said, wrapping me in his arms.

When we finally released each other, he looked past me. "Who is this, baby girl?" my dad asked, eyeing Julian.

I inhaled before releasing it slowly.

"Momma, Daddy, this is—"

"I'm Julian. Julian Tate. It's a pleasure to meet you both," Julian said, interrupting me. He stepped forward and extended a hand to my father. He never broke eye contact with him, and after looking at his hand for a few seconds, my dad finally shook it.

"Hezekiah Westin. Jessica's father." I chuckled because my dad's voice was firm and authoritative, completely unlike when he was just talking to me.

"I'm Chanelle Westin, her momma. It's nice to meet you too, young man," my mother said, swatting my dad's hand out of the way and pulling Julian in for a hug.

After introductions, my parents sat on the opposite side of the table. Shortly after that, a waitress arrived and got our drink and appetizer orders. When I only ordered water, my mother frowned at me. "You not gon' have a cocktail with your momma, girl? That's not like us," she said with a smirk. I laughed because it was true. One thing Chanelle Westin and I loved to do was dress up and get a cute drink together.

"Not today, Momma. I cut out drinking for a while."

"So, what is this?" my father asked, waving a hand in Julian's and my direction. *Right to it, then.*

I could tell by the look on my father's face that he wasn't interested in small talk. He wanted to know why this man was sitting by his baby girl.

Julian cleared his throat. "This is a relationship, sir." I sighed in relief before looking at my father and cosigning Julian's statement.

"He's my boyfriend, Daddy."

My dad chuckled. "Boyfriend, huh? What you want wit' my baby girl, Mr. Tate?"

Without missing a beat, Julian answered. "I want forever with her. I met your daughter about five years ago when her best friend married mine." Julian glanced at me before continuing.

"We've had a dope friendship all this time, but I'll be honest. I knew I wanted more from the moment I met her. She's beautiful, intelligent, and has a personality that's always made my days better.

"I've loved her for a long time, and I'm grateful she's finally allowing me to shower her with that love daily."

My mother looked at me. "This is *that* Julian?" I smiled and nodded.

"Yeah, it's him, Momma."

My mother was fully aware of my feelings for the man beside me and knew why I had run away from a relationship with him.

Her brows raised, and she straightened her posture.

"So this is *the* Julian, he's now your *boyfriend*, *and* you ain't ordering a drink. You sure you ain't got more to say?" she asked with a knowing look. Just when my heartbeat calmed down a bit, my mother had to go and put me on the spot. This was precisely why I avoided them all this time. I could never hide things from her. It just wasn't possible.

"Yes, I do. Momma, Daddy, I'm... I'm havin' a baby." My mother jumped out of her seat and rounded the table quickly. She pulled me from my seat and wrapped her arms around me. Tears fell from my eyes as I felt droplets of hers on my shoulders.

"I told you, sweetheart. I told you God had the final say. Oh, thank You, God. Thank You, thank You, thank You, Jesus," she said repeatedly.

In my mother's arms, I sobbed. I had cried several times during this journey, but this release was different. This was my *momma*.

Nobody in the world loved me like this woman. She carried me in her womb and felt all my feelings times ten. My father knew about my fibroids and how they had supposedly affected my fertility, so I knew he felt this moment, too, but my mother really walked this journey with me.

From the moment I learned about the fibroids, she made it a point to attend every doctor's visit. Our prayer sessions were extensive, and I didn't hold back any of my feelings about it from her. She knew *everything*.

She knew my desire for children of my own, and her heart ached when we were told it would never happen for me.

Closing my eyes, I wrapped my arms around her and cried some more. I thought I had finally accepted that I was going to be a mother after my first doctor's visit, but at this moment, it felt really *real*. I was giving my mother a grandbaby. It was really happening.

My eyes opened when I heard another chair scoot back. My father stood slowly, then rounded the table as well. His eyes were misty with unshed tears, and wordlessly, he scooped my mother and me into his arms. We remained that way until the waitress brought in our appetizers. Wiping our faces, we all sat down and began eating silently.

"When did you find out?" my mother finally asked.

I felt a sharp pain in my chest as I sighed. Looking into her eyes now, I hated that I ever kept it from her. From either of them.

"A couple of months ago." I saw the hurt in my mother's eyes and had to close mine momentarily.

"I'm so sorry I didn't tell y'all sooner. I was just afraid of how you might react since I'm not married," I said, looking between them. I felt like a little girl as I waited for their replies.

Her eyes softened, and she nodded slightly, but my father beat her to a response.

"I know not tellin' us is more about me than it is your mother, so let me say this. You're my daughter, Jessica Brielle. My baby girl. I don't care about none of that other shit more than I care about *you*. As long as you're happy and healthy, I'm good."

"I second that," my mother said softly.

"Are you happy?" my dad asked.

I glanced at Julian, who had been silent since the news dropped. I saw nothing but concern in his expression as his eyes searched my face. I smiled and nodded.

"I'm really happy, Daddy."

"I'ma take your word for it, baby girl," he said, eyeing Julian.

The door opened again, and the waitress made it back in. She looked at our appetizers and frowned.

"Was there something wrong with the appetizers?"

I shook my head and smiled at her. "No, everything is great. We need a little more time before we order if that's okay."

She smiled. "No problem. I'll give you some time." With that, she left, and Julian sat up slightly.

"There is one more thing, though," he said, glancing at me before focusing on my father. *Where is he going with this?*

"A little over a month ago, Jessica received a letter from someone she thought was a fan." *Oh my God.*

He was about to tell them about the stalker. I already knew this wouldn't go well. My father had been my protector all my life and was definitely going to have a problem with not being my first call.

"Apparently, this same guy has been sending flowers to her New York office every year on her birthday, but this time, he made a home delivery, and the letter implied that he intends to confront Jessica at some point."

"Why in the world wouldn't you say something, Jessica?" my dad asked, anger in his eyes. My mother looked more worried than anything.

I opened my mouth to speak, but Julian spoke up again.

"That may be my fault. The day I found out about the letter was the same day I found out about the baby. I was determined to protect them both and took matters into my own hands.

"I work as an FBI agent, and my home is off the grid for protection. I also have a top-tier security system, so I felt like it made sense for her to stay there. If I'm honest, I didn't give her much of a choice about that, and I apologize that y'all are just finding out, but I wouldn't be the man my father raised if I didn't do everything in my power to protect the woman I love and my unborn child."

"Is that right?" my father asked, his face still tight.

"Daddy, he isn't the reason I didn't tell y'all. The truth is, I knew the second I told you about all this, you would want to see me, and I'd have to tell you about the baby. That's on me, and again, I'm sorry for holding all this from both of you."

The table was silent for a moment.

"Have you figured out who this person is?" my father asked Julian. He sighed and shook his head.

"No, sir. I'm treating this like an active case and made it clear to my unit chief that finding this guy is my priority. I have the full support of my unit with this, and I will find him. I promise you that."

"And in the meantime... how are you protecting my daughter and grandchild?"

"I don't let her outta my sight unless I'm at work, and when I am, I hired a fully vetted bodyguard who she never leaves the house without. I'm not gon' let anything happen to her, sir."

My father went quiet again. "You say you love my daughter?"

Julian nodded. "Yes, sir."

"You think you love her more than I do?"

My eyes stretched slightly as I peeked at Julian. He didn't look the least bit intimidated, but I expected nothing less from him. Neither he nor my dad lacked confidence or arrogance, so I knew they could easily clash. I was just hoping they wouldn't.

"She's your daughter. I know how my parents feel about me, so I'd never try to take any credibility from your love for her. Maybe not more, but I know I love her at least just as much, and that love increases daily.

"I'm all in with your daughter, Mr. Westin. I'm in love with her and will protect her life with mine. None of this happened in the order I would have preferred. If it was up to me, I would have met you four years ago, changed Jessica's last name six months after that, and given you your first grandchild nine months later. Life happens, though, and I'm glad that regardless of where life has taken us, we ended up here, sitting at this table together. I'd like to have moments like this for many years to come."

Everyone at the table—including me—was stunned into silence. The fact that my father had nothing to say to that was a statement in itself. Julian had made his feelings for me clear and did it effortlessly. As his eyes penetrated mine, I knew he meant them too.

"I'ma hold you to all that, son," my father said eventually.

"I'd expect nothing less," Julian replied.

My father gave him a nod, and my mother smiled.

"Whew. Now that you've done your overprotective daddy routine, can we celebrate the fact that our baby is having a baby?" my mother said, playfully rolling her eyes at my father.

Daddy chuckled and nodded. "Yeah, we can do that."

***

"It's only a couple of hours," I told myself.

I kept repeating that as I started my car and backed out of Julian's driveway.

I had scheduled a mini photo shoot at my house for today; it was set to start in about thirty minutes.

Kendrick let me know he had a family emergency that popped up, so he would be a little late. Any other time, I'd just wait on him before leaving the house, but Shay had hired a stylist for the shoot, and she was at my house already, along with the rest of my team. I hated wasting people's time.

I was just going to head there now, and when Kendrick finished handling his business, I'd tell him to meet me there. Julian would be at work until later that night, and I wouldn't be without Kendrick for more than an hour.

It'll work out fine.

It only took me about fifteen minutes to get to my house, and four cars were already outside. Quickly, I parked and headed inside. When I reached the living area, I smiled. Music was already playing softly in the background as the stylist hung outfit options on a clothing rack. I hadn't been in this type of environment in a while, and I kind of missed it. Posing for pictures was one of my favorite things, so I was happy to return to it.

"Jess, hey!" Shay said, running over to me. She hugged me tightly and gasped moments later. I wore loose-fitting clothes, but it was impossible for her to miss my baby bump when our bodies touched.

"Are you..."

I bit my lip and smiled before nodding.

Speaking in a low tone, she said, "Oh my God! Congratulations, Jess. That's why you told me to have the stylist pull loose-fitting pieces."

She hugged me again, tighter this time.

"Yeah. I wanted to tell y'all when I found out, but it's just been a lot going on. I guess I need to break the news to the team," I said, releasing her. We both stepped further into the room, and Margo and Valerie smiled.

"Hey, y'all. Can we turn the music off for a second? I gotta tell you somethin'."

Valerie grabbed her phone and tapped it a couple of times before the music stopped.

"What is it, sis?" Margo asked, turning on the ring light in front of her makeup chair.

Exhaling deeply, I just spit it out.

"I'm pregnant."

For a moment, the four of them just stared at me, stunned. The stylist and I didn't know each other, but she smiled and spoke up first.

"Congrats!"

"Thanks," I said with a chuckle. I then focused on Valerie and Margo. Both of them looked surprised, and Valerie had tears in her eyes. After a minute passed, they both came and hugged me.

"Congratulations, sis," Margo said and gave me an extra squeeze.

Val was next. "You definitely threw us for a loop with this one," she said. When she released me, I sighed and nodded.

"I know. It's been a whirlwind of events since I found out, but I'm glad y'all finally know. I hated keeping the secret."

"I bet. That's a big one, girl. I can't believe I'm going to be an aunt!" Shay said excitedly, and I laughed.

"You shole is. All of you are," I said, looking at each of them.

"Anyway, turn the music back on. I missed y'all."

Val turned on the music. "Alright, let's get to work unless you have another major bomb to drop on us this morning," Val said.

"Nah, that's all I got. Come on, Margo. I'm so ready for you to beat my face. I haven't worn makeup in forever."

You're so Selfish

♥

Tate

"There's been another missing person's report, guys." I looked up from my phone just as the detective was handing J and me a file.

I contemplated checking on Jess because she hadn't been answering the phone, but it looked like that wasn't about to happen.

"Who is he?" Joseph asked, opening his folder.

"This time, it's a *she*." He gave both of us a knowing look before leaving the conference room.

"A woman this time?" J asked, flipping through the pages. I opened my folder and shook my head. Yeah, that was completely different. Maybe this would be the abduction to finally close it for us. These people have been missing for months, so it was time to bring their families some closure.

I read through the woman's file. She was a twenty-nine-year-old white woman who moved to Atlanta eight years ago. I flipped through the file, and there were only photos of her and her driver's license. I studied each photograph, committing the details to memory as I did every time we received new information about a case.

The file didn't have much, so I called Moreu.

"What's up, Tate?"

"Hey, we got another abduction down here. A woman named Claudia Leslie Butler."

I listened as Moreu began typing furiously. She was the best technical analyst in the bureau, and everyone in our unit was happy to have her on our team.

"It looks like her record is squeaky clean, just like our other missing people. She moved to Atlanta to attend college at Georgia State, made a life there, and never returned to her hometown, Birmingham, Alabama."

"Where does she work?" J asked.

"Nowhere. It looks like the last job she held was six years ago at… oh wait," she said, and I sat up.

"Wassup, M?"

"Her last job was Norman Wells Consulting, which is—"

"Which is our second victim's company. She didn't come up when we did the deep dive of his company?" I pulled the file out again and went through the photos. I stopped at one of the abduction sites. A brand-new Mercedes was left behind.

That was a nice car for a woman with no job.

"No, because you said only go back the last five years."

"Can you go through her bank statements?"

"You thinkin' somethin' shady happened?" Joseph asked.

"I think it ain't a coincidence that her last job was at this dude's company, and both of their asses are missin'. Somethin' ain't right about that."

After about a solid minute of not saying anything, Moreu yelled.

"Ha! Sorry, y'all, I got excited. Claudia Leslie Butler doesn't have to work because she's received a deposit of fifteen thousand dollars every month for the last six years. The deposits come from a trust named The Henderson Group. I dug deeper, and that trust belongs to none other than Norman Wells, our second victim."

She sounded like she was smiling, and I couldn't help but crack one too. I could officially see the light at the end of this tunnel.

"So he's payin' her off. It's likely she ain't the only one," J said, and I nodded.

"Aye, Moreu, get a list of any other employees who left the company abruptly and what their bank accounts look like," I said.

"I'm on it. I'll get back to you soon."

With that, she hung up, and I immediately dialed Jessica again. I had a feeling somethin' was about to pop off at work, so I wanted to check in, at least, in case I couldn't later.

"That's kind of surprising. The CEO didn't have any kind of record, and his business looks legit."

I nodded. "True, but you know how it goes sometimes. He's rich, man. If he had a record, it could be expunged, or this Claudia woman might just be one of many women who was paid off for somethin' foul he did. If you take care of the problem before it makes it to court, you don't need anything expunged."

Jessica's phone went to voicemail again.

"Man..."

"What's wrong, Tate?" I looked up from my phone and saw Joseph sitting across from me, wearing a frown.

"Jessica is ignoring my calls. I know she ain't sleep."

"Call Kendrick. Ain't he at the house?"

"Nah, he had an emergency, so she's over there by herself this morning."

I called again and again. It rang a couple of times before going to voicemail.

"Is she at the house?" Joseph asked.

"Shid, she better be," I said, but still pulling up my location app. We shared locations with each other, but I rarely checked the app because we always communicated when I wasn't with her. I was sure she was at the house because Kendrick wasn't supposed to show up until the afternoon.

When I checked her location, I realized just how wrong I was. I stood immediately. "I gotta go, J."

He stood, too.

"What's up?"

"She's at her house. I'on know what's up with that, but I'ma find out."

"Let's go," he said, and I didn't even debate it. If something was potentially going down in his world, I'd be right there, too, so I guess our jobs would just have to wait.

We headed out of the precinct without so much as a word to anyone around us, and minutes later, we were in his car on the highway, on the way to Jessica's house.

My mind raced as I rode. I was almost certain no one had gotten her from my house. It was like Fort Knox, because I spent a lot of money to make sure it was more than secure. That meant she left—without Kendrick and without me. What pissed me off the most was that she didn't call and say anything.

It was likely because I would have made her wait on me or Kendrick to leave the house, but so? That was what she needed to do, and we had already had that discussion. Did she think this was a game? Was she no longer taking this seriously? Had she lost her mind?

I hopped out of J's car before it came to a complete stop. The sight of all the cars in her yard had my blood boiling. *What was she on today?*

Before going into the house, I scanned her car. I ran my hands along all sides of it, and once J was with me, he began doing the same. I glanced at him and realized he had a bug detector in his hand.

I wasn't surprised he had one in his car because J was even more paranoid than me. Today, I was glad about it because it would make this process much easier.

Seconds later, I heard a loud beeping noise, and he was holding something up.

"It was on the bottom," he said.

"Fuck!"

Someone had put a tracker on her car, and I was sure they did it while she had been at her house. Joseph and I did a complete car sweep before I brought it to my crib, and it was clean then. Her car hadn't moved from my house since she moved in with me because she hadn't had to drive.

Now, the one time she's back at her crib without protection, there was a tracking device on it? The stalker was probably waiting on the day she popped back up.

I had no plans of her returning to her crib until all this was figured out, so I didn't think to get my security guy to put cameras on her house. If I had, I would know who put the tracker on the car.

Punching the door of her car, I yelled out. I was *pissed*.

"I'ma keep checkin' the car and make sure that's the only one. We need to get these to the lab ASAP," Joseph said, and I nodded. I was glad he was here because he was thinking clearly while I was only seeing red.

He kept sweeping the car while I went straight to her front door. The fact that the door was unlocked pissed me off further. I stepped inside, and my temple pulsed. Music was playing, and Jessica stood in front of a white backdrop, posing for the camera.

"Let's go, Jessica," I said, my tone controlled but loud enough for her to hear over the music.

Her eyes moved to me instantly, and she just stood there staring like a deer in headlights. She didn't move, and neither did anyone else in the room. I chuckled and crossed the room. Picking her up, I moved back through the house, saying, "I need all y'all to get out, now."

I looked around and saw her keys on the coffee table, so I grabbed them.

"Wait, Julian, I can walk. Put me down. Just let me explain."

"Jessica, shut up. I turned around and looked at the four women, who had yet to move a muscle. I took in everything about their appearances and made a mental note to study the files Moreu gave me on them more thoroughly.

"Y'all can't hear? Get the fuck out. Now!" I yelled, making the one I knew to be her assistant jump. That seemed to have done the trick because they started scattering like roaches after that. I tried to remain patient as they packed up, and after ten minutes, they were all gone. A lot of things got left behind, but I didn't care. They could never get their shit back for all I cared.

I carried Jessica outside to the door. When we made it outside of it, I put her down. Her eyes were wet with tears, and her lip was trembling. I looked away briefly, knowing her tears could break me down.

"Go to the car."

Still shaking, she did as I asked. I locked her house up before descending the steps. J was standing by her car.

"It's clean, so you can drive it. I'ma take this tracker to the lab."

I nodded. "'Preciate it, dawg. I'll get up wit' you once I get her situated."

"Aight." I watched as he headed to his car. It wasn't until he drove away that I finally went to Jessica's car. I climbed into the driver's seat and pulled off immediately.

"Ali, I—"

"Don't say anything to me, Jessica. Let's just get to the house."

With that, I turned the radio on and drove off.

***

I held the front door open and waited until Jess entered the house.

I heard her footsteps retreat as I locked up the house. I stood there for a minute, trying to calm down before I went to find her. The ride home did nothing for my mood. Every time I looked at her, I thought about what could have happened if I hadn't left work, and that made me mad all over again.

Just two weeks ago, I was promising her father that I'd never let anything happen to her, and this morning, I was close to breaking my word. I didn't know how to cope with that. Torn between wanting to ignore her and needing to make sure she was good, I stood in that spot a little longer.

I knew my mood wouldn't help hers, and I didn't need her blood pressure high because I hurt her feelings. With a deep sigh, I went to find her. I'd do my best to maintain my anger, but a conversation needed to be had.

I walked through the foyer and into the living room, where I found her sitting on the sofa, staring at the black television screen. When she sensed my presence, she stood and turned toward me but made no moves to come closer.

"Julian..." Her voice was shaky. The way she said my name sounded like she had more to say, but she paused. I assumed she was trying to gauge whether or not I planned to let her speak, so I folded my arms and tilted my head, silently telling her to say what she needed to.

"I was wrong for leaving without telling you, and I apologize for that. I really do. My assistant planned the photo shoot yesterday, and by the time we realized Kendrick would be a little late today, people were already at my house.

"I couldn't cancel at that point, and I figured Kendrick could just meet me there. I wasn't going to go anywhere but my house, and I had a trusted group of people around me, so I knew I would be okay until he got there. I swear I was doing the shoot and coming straight back here," she finished.

I remained silent as I examined her. She was breathing hard, and she wouldn't leave her hands alone. I chuckled and shook my head when I realized that was her big speech.

"That's it?"

She scrunched her eyebrows but nodded slowly. "Yes."

I shook my head again.

"You're so selfish."

Her eyes snapped to mine, and there was a fire in them. That made me laugh.

"What? You ain't like that? Me tellin' the truth makes you mad, Jessica? You can join the got damn club with that 'cause I'm fuckin' pissed."

"I upheld an obligation, Ali. I had a job to do. You go to work every day, so you can appreciate that, so how am I selfish?" she asked, her voice elevated.

"Aye, you sound dumb. Lower your voice."

She stomped toward me with folded arms. "You ain't gon' keep talkin' to me crazy because you're mad, *Julian*. I said I was wrong for not callin' you, but I don't regret going to the shoot. I was safe, and I'm back here in one piece. I trust my team, and—"

"Fuck your team!"

She jumped back slightly at the sound of my voice. I didn't even mean to be yelling, but Jessica and her mouth was asking for that.

"You're the most selfish muhfucka I know," I said, getting in her face. I lowered my voice but made sure we were only inches apart. I wanted her to hear every word I had to say.

"Every move you make is about you, and it's been that way since I met you.

"You want me, and you *know* I need you, but you refuse to let me have you. You find out we're having a baby and keep it to yourself until somebody else makes you tell me.

"You're so willing to carry your ass outside to get snatched by whoever is gunnin' for you without thinkin' about how it would affect the niggas who care about you."

I laughed, even though there was nothing funny about what I was saying. "I told your father he could trust me to protect you. What the hell am I supposed to tell him when somethin' happens because you don't care 'bout anybody but yourself?

"How you think I'ma react if something *actually* happens to you, Jessica? I'ma be outta the FBI and prolly in jail behind your selfish ass, but you don't care about that. All you care 'bout is the next thing on your got damn to-do list. If that ain't selfish, I'on know what is, man."

I swiped a hand across my head and inhaled slowly. I needed to calm down. I needed to distance myself from the current source of my anger for my child's sake. I took a step back, but Jess took two toward me.

"Back up," I said in a low tone.

"You need me?" she asked, all the attitude gone from her tone and face. Out of everything I had just said, that was what she was stuck on. That wasn't even important at this point. Her safety was, and that was where her focus needed to be. Still, she took another step into my personal space.

I chuckled. "Get out my face, Jessica. Real shit."

She shook her head, and I dropped my head for a second. I wasn't about to do this with her.

"No," she finally answered.

Gripping my shirt with one hand, she rested the other on my cheek and moved closer. I sucked in a breath and shook my head.

I was mad, but I wasn't dead. There wasn't a world that existed where I could be *this* close to the love of my life and not have a physical reaction to her. She was playing with fire, but she knew that.

"I apologize," she said softly. I watched as she lifted on her toes and licked her lips. She still wasn't tall enough to reach my lips, and I tried my best not to give in to her, so she settled for my neck.

"Jessica, move," I said, mumbling.

Again, she shook her head. She placed both her hands under my shirt and slid them upward, lifting my shirt with them. She then lowered herself and began kissing my abs.

The air in the room was thick with all our unresolved problems, and this woman was turning to sex as the answer. The sad part about it was that I was going to let her.

Frustrated, I let out a groan and lifted her into my arms effortlessly. Turning around, I tossed her on the sofa behind us and quickly removed my shirt and pants before I covered her body with my own, careful not to put my weight on her. She lifted her head and kissed my chest again, and as much as I wanted to ignore her affection, it only made it harden more.

Reaching under myself with one hand, I pulled her pants and panties down before releasing myself from my boxers. I observed her expression as my manhood grazed her opening and almost lost it right there. It was crazy how drawn to her I was. How obsessed with her I was.

No matter how messed up our situation was, this right here would always be where we could connect. I'd never be able to deny her, and as pathetic as that was, it was a fact.

I had yet to enter her, and she must have been getting impatient because her eyes fluttered open, and she frowned. Shaking my head, I placed one arm above her head and gripped the arm of the sofa, then slid into her slowly. Never taking my eyes off hers, I continued to plummet until every inch of me was buried deep inside her warmth. I froze there.

We had done this so many times over the years, but I had never fully acclimated to this feeling. Entering Jess was always an otherworldly experience. Every single time, her insides stripped me of every guard I set up to keep her out of my heart and soul. It's like she demanded my vulnerability in these moments, and my body was always willing to hand it over.

She gasped, then let out a moan that had me devouring her mouth with my own. Showing her real affection wasn't my plan. My only intention was to deliver dick, then ignore her for a few days, but damn...

How could I *not* kiss every inch of her pretty face and her soft body? She was too perfect. Holding back was an impossibility when it came to Jessica.

Jessica's breath stroked my chest when she whispered, "Come on, baby."

She kissed me in that same spot, which was all I needed to start moving again. I pulled out before thrusting into her continually. I tried to make every stroke deeper than the last one, and I felt the familiar fire that came with lying with Jess centering in my core.

I kept my eyes on her as I pounded her, and she bent her knees before locking her legs around me. That gave me access to go deeper, so I gripped the sofa on either side of her and straightened my arms, locking them at my elbows. Slowly, I inched out of her. She felt so good that my dick twitched as it passed every inch of her tight, warm walls.

Jessica's mouth hung open, but she was silent as her eyes pierced mine. Her chest was heaving at that point, and her eyes began to water.

"Stop teasin' me, Ali. Just give me the—"

Just as the tip was about to exit her, I switched gears and plunged back in—hard, deep. Her smart mouth was open even wider then, but I didn't think she was breathing anymore. She gripped my biceps and squeezed tightly as I pounded into her repeatedly, showing no mercy.

I wasn't letting up, and because she wasn't one to go out without a fight, Jess sucked in a deep breath before lifting her hips to match my thrusts. She began to wind them under me, and the sensation her movements had me experiencing had me about to shed a tear of my own.

"Got damn, Jet."

"Oh my... *shit*, Ali!" She screamed as she began to shake uncontrollably. The visual alone sent me over the edge, and I continued to thrust as I released everything I had into her. It took both of us a minute to catch our breath, but as we came down from our high, I scooped her in my arms and switched our positions so my back was on the sofa.

I rested there momentarily, and she laid her head on my chest. It felt so right, but I regretted what had just happened with every second that passed.

"Sit up, Jet," I said, tapping her on her side. She sat up with a frown, and I stood, looking for my clothes on the floor.

"What's wrong?" she asked, still on the sofa.

"We ain't ever had a problem in the bedroom. It's everything about a relationship we don't align on, and instead of standin' there and talkin' through some shit with me, you did the same thing you've always done.

"I've never been able to deny you when you're in my presence, and that prolly won't change, but I cut you off when I did for a reason, Jessica. Sex ain't ever been the solution, but it's always *your* answer.

"I made my feelings for you clear a long time ago. Now, I've laid 'em out for your pops, and you're still runnin'. My feelings can get hurt, too, Jet, and I'm tired of you stompin' on 'em. I ain't mean to take it here with you, but I promise this is the last time. If you can't get over yaself so we can be as happy as I know I can make you, we have nothing to talk about outside of our child."

My work phone rang, and I grabbed my pants to fish it out of the pocket.

"Wassup, Moreu?"

"I finished the search for ex-employees. Several of them were paid lump sums before they left, and all of them were women. There is one incident that I found interesting."

"What is it?" I asked, moving down the hallway. When I reached my bedroom, I placed the phone on speaker and entered my closet.

"A woman named Leslie Dade was working there around the same time as Claudia. She quit shortly before Claudia did but only received payments for a year. She uh... she committed suicide one month before the first abduction."

"Fuck." That hit me hard for more reasons than one.

"Yeah. She's survived by her mother, Harriet Jones-Dade. I'm sending you their information now."

"'Preciate that, Moreu."

I hung up and went to the shower. By the time I got out, hopefully, there would be some addresses for me to hit up. I needed to get out of this house anyway. Being able to put this case to bed was the perfect reason.

I showered and dressed quickly, then headed to the front of the house. Just as I was passing Jessica, my phone dinged. Moreu had sent me the address of Leslie's mother and sister. Jess was still on the sofa and with red eyes and a tear-streaked face.

I looked away and continued through the house, but she followed me.

"Can we talk?" she asked. Her tone was just as vulnerable as the night she told me about the baby.

"Nah," I said and glanced at her. Her red, puffy eyes were doing a number on me, but I couldn't even worry about it. Not right now, anyway. Before opening the front door, I made one request and hoped that she actually listened. "Stay in this house 'til Kendrick pulls up, Jessica."

With that, I was out the door with thoughts of the case and my baby momma on my mind.

***

"Davi will be back in an hour. As soon as she's back, I can meet you."

I pulled up at the stoplight before responding to J.

"Aight, cool. All I'm 'bout to do is talk to the mother to see what she knows. It shouldn't be that serious."

When I called J with the news about Leslie's family, he let me know he had to go home once he dropped off the trackers. David was running a fever, and Davi had a shoot scheduled that she couldn't cancel. Since David couldn't roll with her, my boy took off for the rest of the day.

I didn't expect more than a standard interview when I visited this family. We had both done plenty of these solo, so him not coming wasn't too big of a deal.

"Aight, bruh, but if somethin' pops off, call me."

Pulling up to the address, I parallel parked on the side of the road and turned off my engine.

"I got you, dawg. Take care of my lil man."

We hung up, and I got out of the car, anxious to get a clearer picture of what had happened with Leslie. People didn't commit suicide because all was right in their world. I knew better than most how suffering in silence could cause a person to do the unthinkable. I was almost certain our second victim had something to do with Leslie's decision, but I was going into that house with an open mind. I didn't need my emotions surrounding the subject to cloud my judgment. I also didn't need to stray from the main goal, which was to find four missing people.

The home was in a middle-class neighborhood with average-sized houses. The first thing I noticed about the one I was visiting was the grass. While the other yards were freshly mowed, this one was unkempt with tall weeds. Neighborhoods like that usually offered maintenance for a monthly fee. The fact that this homeowner likely refused the services told me that she didn't want people in her space.

I climbed the steps and knocked twice. I was still coming down from my argument with Jessica, so I had to work hard to put a smile on my face. I wanted to come off as understanding and empathetic to whoever opened the door, or they'd likely not let me in.

After a couple of minutes, the door opened slowly. I saw yellowed eyes peeking out at me, but the home was dark, and whoever was there had only cracked the door.

"Good afternoon, I'm Supervisory Special Agent Julian Tate. I was hoping I could speak with you briefly."

"Regarding what?" The voice that answered me surprised me. Moreu hadn't said how old Leslie's mother was, but her eyes looked older than her voice sounded. She couldn't have been past her fifties.

I needed to play this carefully because I didn't have a search warrant. She had to agree to let me into the home, or I'd have to wait until later tomorrow. After a minor observation of my surroundings, I was eighty percent certain that this woman could offer me some helpful information. I just needed to finesse a little bit so that I could get it.

"During a case we've been working on, we've come across information about a Leslie Dade—"

"My daughter," she interrupted me to say.

"Yes, ma'am. First, let me tell you how sorry I am for your loss."

She opened her door wide, and I examined her thoroughly. She was extremely skinny; I was sure that was a new development. The way her skin sagged indicated that she had recently been starved—or starving herself. The white T-shirt she wore was dirty, and her jeans had two holes in the knees that didn't look like they were made that way.

"Sorry? You're *sorry?* Is that really what you came to my doorstep to say? Nobody's sorry but *me*. I'm the only one hurting behind this loss while the world moves on like nothing happened. You couldn't even begin to understand what I'm going through, so keep your sorry," she said with venom in her tone.

This woman was clearly hurting, and it looked like she had no one left. Grieving was a harrowing task, but doing it alone had soul-breaking potential. My heart went out to her. I swallowed a lump in my throat and dropped my head for a second before meeting her glare once again.

"Uh, you're right. I can't imagine or take away your pain," I began, and her eyes softened. "But if there was a way to bring closure to what happened with your daughter, would you be willing to talk with us about that?"

"No," she said softly and fixed her clothes.

I followed her movements and froze. I wasn't sure how I missed it before, but now that I noticed the bracelet she wore and the reddish-brown spot on her T-shirt, I couldn't focus on anything else.

Realizing she had said something to me, I snapped out of my thoughts and looked into her eyes. While I spoke, they were soft with understanding, but now, they were defensive.

"Ma'am? My apologies, but I missed what you said."

"I said, with all due respect, unless you have a warrant, I do not wish to participate in whatever you're working on. It won't bring her back, so please leave now."

I took a step back.

"Yes, ma'am, I understand. I'm sorry I wasted your time." With that, I descended her steps and headed to my car. I started it and immediately drove off, with the woman watching the entire time.

Instead of heading for the interstate, I circled the neighborhood and scanned the area. When I found a good place to park my car without the woman detecting me, I stopped and sat up in my seat, not taking my eyes off her front door.

I was good at my job because I was observant. I rarely guessed, but when I did, it was because I was at least 99 percent sure I was right.

The bracelet that the woman wore was the same one I noticed on Claudia's wrist in most of the pictures from her file. I had been around enough blood to know what it looked like when it dried on clothing, and that was exactly what I noticed on her shirt. Those were facts.

I guessed that she was the one who had abducted those people, and her sensors went off as soon as I knocked on her door. There was no way she was holding them in her home because her neighborhood was buzzing. Someone would have noticed something by now.

Nah, she was keeping them somewhere, and that was why no bodies had been discovered. Her latest victim was abducted that day, so I had a feeling she would be leaving her house sooner than later. Me at her door had probably sped up her timeline to carry out whatever her plan was, and I was going to sit there as long as it took to close this case.

I dialed Moreu.

"What's up?"

"Leslie's mother. Does she have any property other than her home?" I asked, getting straight to the point.

"One second."

She silently typed for a while before saying, "No."

"What about anybody else in her family?"

As soon as I asked that, the woman stepped out of her front door. I grabbed the binoculars from my dashboard and put them over my eyes. She looked up and down the street. I held my breath for a minute, but I was pretty sure the tree I parked behind shielded me from her view.

Once she was done with her scan of the street, she hurried down her steps and got into her car. I pressed the start button on my car, and my engine came to life silently.

"Her late husband owned a used car lot. It looks like it went out of business two years ago. I just sent you the address for it."

"'Preciate you, Moreu."

"No problem."

I plugged the car lot's address into my navigation system before slowly pulling off. When I did a lap of the neighborhood, I realized there were two ways to exit that would take you to the main street, so I left in the opposite direction of her but sped up a little.

I hoped she was respecting the residential area's speed limits because I didn't want to lose her. Luckily, when I reached the neighborhood's exit, I noticed her pulling into the street. I did the same but was sure to leave enough space between her car and mine.

We were only driving briefly when I realized she was taking the same turns my navigation system was directing me to make. Knowing we were headed to the lot, I quickly sent the address to J. I wasn't sure if Davi had made it back yet, but he asked me to keep him updated, so I just wanted to keep my word.

Seconds later, he was calling.

"What's that address?" he asked.

"It's where I'm headed now. I went to the mother's house, and she wore Claudia's bracelet. She had blood on her shirt, too, so I stayed outside her house to see what her next move would be. Shole 'nough, she left the house in a hurry. I'm tailing her, but I'm sure we're headed to the address I sent you."

"Aight, but don't go in. Davi's on the way home now, so wait 'til I get there."

I knew he would ask that of me, and as long as there wasn't an immediate threat, I would do that.

"Aight."

"I'm serious, Tate."

"Me too. I gotta go, though. She's pullin' in."

I hung up and watched as she turned into the abandoned lot. It was gated, but I could tell it wasn't very secure. There were a few old cars in the lot and a nice-sized warehouse. I stopped a little way down from the gate's entrance and waited.

Quickly, she hopped out of her car. She went to the trunk and pulled out some gardening scissors and a tarp. She also had a crossbody bag on. It was small, but the bulky item hanging slightly from it gave me a bad feeling.

Just that quickly, I knew I wouldn't be able to keep my word to Joseph. If somebody was alive in that warehouse, I wasn't willing to risk their life by waiting on my partner. If he had gotten here first, he wouldn't either.

She slammed the trunk shut, then rushed into the building. I was low-key thanking God she didn't lock the gate behind her. After unlocking my door, I contemplated my next move. If no one was in there and I went inside, I knew I'd be sitting in front of internal affairs.

I'm not wrong, though.

I trusted my gut, and it was telling me that I could save lives by going in. There was a loud noise inside, and I left my car immediately.

Fuck it.

With my gun in hand, I rushed inside, and unfortunately for me, I stepped on something that sounded off upon my entry. Seconds later, the noise stopped, but I was sure Harriet knew she was no longer alone.

It was dark, so I used the flashlight attached to my piece to look around. It was dead silent, but she had to be in there somewhere. The warehouse smelled terrible, and I saw there was trash everywhere.

It wasn't too big, but I wanted to scan each area thoroughly. Once I shined the light on one side of the room and didn't see anyone, I checked the other. As soon as I did, I aimed my gun.

"Don't shoot, Harriet," I said calmly. Her hands were shaking, but the gun was directed toward me. My bright light revealed her location to me, and behind her were the four missing people. Each body was attached to wooden poles firmly planted in the ground. Their hands were tied above their heads, and their mouths were gagged and taped. I recognized each of their faces immediately. Claudia had only been there for a few hours, so she was in the best shape physically. Her face was streaked with tears as she looked at me with pleading eyes.

The business owner, doctor, and judge had all been there for over a month, so they looked significantly worse, but from what I could tell, they were alive also.

Thank God.

Knowing I couldn't help any of them until I disarmed Harriet, I focused on her. With as much empathy as I could muster, I said, "Miss Harriet, I get it—"

"You don't!" she yelled, cutting me off.

I took a step closer to her, and I noticed her fingers wrap around her gun tighter.

"Stay back! I'll shoot you and all these conniving people. I swear, I'll do it!" Tears fell from her eyes, and she sniffled but didn't bother wiping them.

"Don't tell me you *get* it. Do you know what they did? That pathetic excuse for a man who raped my daughter and poisoned her with alcohol to try and make her forget it. This lying bitch saw the whole thing happen and lied to authorities about it.

"Thurgood Taylor should never be allowed to practice medicine again. Do you know why? Because he altered his initial medical report of what happened to my Leslie and said the sex was consensual. I knew it was a lie, and we tried to fight it, but the judge handling my lawsuit was paid off. They all deserved to suffer for as long as they did, and now they deserve the same fate that met my Leslie."

I kept my eyes on her and the gun, but I'd be lying if I said her story didn't make me wanna lock up the individuals behind her. Each of them, in their own way, contributed to her daughter's suffering.

"My baby girl never bounced back from that night. Never! Do you know what she said to me in her suicide note? She said she was sorry that she couldn't be stronger for *me*. She said the pain of the memories of that night was too much to bear, and she would just rather not be here anymore. Until you have to read a letter like that from someone you love, *Agent Tate*, don't try to tell me you get it."

I inhaled before releasing it slowly.

"I already have, ma'am. A few years ago, I, uh, I endured a similar loss."

I felt tears build behind my eyes. This wasn't something I wanted to discuss with a stranger, but I was hoping my story would disarm her.

She said nothing, but I noticed her shoulders relax. She dropped her hand from the door and ticked her lips between her teeth. I felt like she was giving me the green light to continue, so I did.

"Growing up, I had a cousin I was very close to. Kaia and I did everything together, and when it was time to figure out life after high school, that didn't change."

I cleared my throat. Talking about this was a lot easier said than done, so I was going to abbreviate this story so that I could get through it without crying.

"To make a long story short, we went to college, and I kinda got into my own things. You know, basketball, I joined a fraternity… stuff like that. Kaia remained the introvert she always had been, and I was too busy to notice that she was suffering in silence. Kaia committed suicide at the beginning of our junior year of college.

"I was the one who found her in her apartment. In her letter, she apologized for letting me down. She went on to talk about a night I never knew happened. Somethin' real bad happened to her, and I was too busy with my own life to notice. She said the weight was too much, and she thought it would be better to get out of everyone's way—out of *my* way. She asked me not to blame myself, but I can't help it. I'll prolly never forgive myself for not noticing the signs, and I gotta live with that."

My vision was slightly blurred because of the tears in my eyes, but I kept my gun steady. I could still see Harriet and noticed her shoulders sag.

In a gentler tone than she had before, she said, "So you do get it. You understand why I have to do this."

"Harriet, I understand that you think hurting the people who wronged your daughter is going to make things better somehow, but I'm here to tell you, it's not. I tried that, and it didn't work. Please don't ruin your life by doing something that I know for a fact won't take your pain away."

She was silent momentarily, and her fingers relaxed a little around the gun. She dropped the gun a little.

"This isn't the answer, I promise. Give me the gun, Harriet." She took a step toward me and dropped it a little more. When I thought she was about to surrender herself, she said, "My life was ruined the day my Leslie ended hers."

Her fingers tightened around her piece, and she raised it again. I fired my weapon and watched her fall to the ground. I aimed for her shoulder so I knew she'd live.

I tried to walk forward so that I could get the gun from her reach, but I stumbled back a little.

"Shit," I said and placed a hand on my lower stomach. Harriet and I must have fired at the same time because I was hit, and it hurt like a *bitch*. I felt around the wound and realized it wasn't too deep. I should be aight. I tried to walk toward her again but fell to my knees instead.

Oh, damn.

I allowed my body to drop, then looked at my fingers. I was losing way too much blood for such a shallow wound. All I could do at that point was try to stay conscious long enough for my boy to get here and pray that would happen before Harriet could stand. That prayer was answered fairly quickly because minutes later, the door opened, and I heard my boy's voice, along with a bunch of other people.

It only took them a minute to come into my line of sight, and I watched as the officers untied the victims. Another went to check on Harriet while J kneeled over me.

"She's alive," the officer beside Harriet said.

I looked up at J and smiled. "Wassup, dawg?" My voice sounded much weaker than I wanted it to, making me wonder whether I was actually smiling.

He kissed his teeth, but I saw the relief wash over him.

"Stupid ass nigga ain't even got on a vest. I told you to wait."

"My bad." I turned my head to the side, and the sudden motion made me extremely dizzy. Noticing black spots in my vision, I tried to speak quickly, knowing I was about to pass out.

"Aye, Officer. When y'all get the suspect in custody, don't leave her unattended. She needs to be placed on suicide watch." Her last words sounded too similar to the way I felt in the months following my cousin's passing. Without my parents supporting me through it, I could have gone a different route, and as much wrong as Harriet had done in the last few months, I didn't want her story to end up like that.

He nodded, and I turned to J. Again, a wave of dizziness hit me. My vision was hazy at best, but I wasn't out yet, so I continued to run my mouth.

"Aye, call Jet, dawg. Make sure you sound worried and shit. Tell her I'm down bad. She gon' eat that shit up. You know she been arguin' wit' me today? Tell her she betta come runnin' in the hospital yellin' at everybody. I want her threatening everybody and tellin' 'em they better take her to her baby daddy." I chuckled at my own words, and that was a bad move because I started fading fast.

"Nigga you *are* down bad, and it ain't funny. Now shut the hell up and save your strength. They're 'bout to get you up on this stretcher, and the transition ain't gon' tickle."

I took his advice and shut up, and at that exact moment, everything went black.

Who You Talkin' To?

♥

Jess

"Your best friend is here, Miss Westin," Kendrick said. His voice was muffled, so he must have been outside my bedroom door. I lifted my head from the pillow it was buried in. My head was throbbing, likely from all the crying I did before I fell asleep.

"I'll be there in a minute," I called.

"She, uh," he said, then paused. "She asked that you get dressed."

I frowned. I had already called Davi and told her about my disaster of a morning with Julian, so there was no way she thought I was going *anywhere*. The last thing he asked me to do was stay home, and I was not in the market to have him more pissed at me.

"I can't, Kendrick. Tell her—"

My door bursting open cut my response short. It was Davi.

"Get up and get dressed, now," she said, her tone more serious than I'd ever heard it.

Her red cheeks and the tears in her eyes had me jumping out of bed and rushing to her.

"What's wrong, Vi?" I asked, my heart racing. I hadn't seen her cry in years. She was the one who always pointed out the positive things in a bad situation and convinced you that everything would be alright.

Something was wrong, and because she was so worked up about it, I knew it was bad.

She exasperatedly sighed before wiping her eyes and pushing past me. She marched straight to my closet, and I followed. I watched as she found a pair of black leggings and a matching crop top in my labeled drawers. She tossed them toward me, and I caught them before she went to the opposite side of my closet and grabbed a warm-up jacket.

Because she had me scared that something had happened to someone in her family—my family—I began dressing in what she had picked out for me, but I repeated my question.

"What's wrong, Vi?"

She waited until I was completely dressed before she let out a shaky breath and said, "Tate's been shot."

***

Tate's been shot.

Davi's words had been playing in my head since she'd spoken them twenty minutes earlier. Everything after that had been a blur, but somehow, I managed to get in the back seat of Kendrick's SUV. I was now cradled in Vi's arms while she stroked the top of my head.

"What if it's too late?" I asked in a whisper.

Vi adjusted her body a little. "What did you say, Jess?" Her voice was as solemn as I felt, and I wanted to cry again. I sat up and looked at her.

"What if it's too late—I'm too late?" My heart ached as I repeated myself. "Vi, we argued *bad* today. I did a dumb thing, and he was pissed about it. Then, when we got home, I made it worse. He left the house so angry and…" I let out a shaky breath. "I never got to tell him that I meant it when I said I loved him. I let my pride cheat me out of time with him, and now it could be too late."

I dropped my face in my hands and cried silently.

I felt Vi's arms wrap around me once again. "It's not too late, Jess, I promise. Tate is a fighter, and I refuse to believe he's going to let one little bullet take him out. He knows there are too many people here who still love and need him." Her voice cracked, so she cleared her throat before continuing. "He knows you're one of those people, Jess, and I know he's fighting to pull through for you and y'all's child. He's going to be okay."

Instead of responding, I just rested my head on her shoulder and rode the rest of the way to the hospital with my eyes closed.

***

"We're looking for Julian Tate. He would have gotten here almost an hour ago."

I bounced my leg rapidly as Davi talked with the attendant. The woman frowned, and so did I. She was taking too long to point us in the right direction, and now she was looking clueless. If she didn't know where he was, she needed to call someone who did.

She began typing on her computer, but then someone else wearing scrubs went behind the desk to get her attention. I folded my arms and looked at her pointedly, waiting for her to tell her co-worker she was busy and would get back to them after she helped us, but this bitch had the nerve to turn away from the computer completely.

I chuckled as the two conversed like Vi hadn't just asked her a question. *I don't have time for this.*

Davi rolled her eyes and cleared her throat. I knew she was about to check the rude bitch, but I beat her to it.

"I know you just heard her ask you something. Y'all kill me at these hospitals, always acting like you got something better to do than help the person in front of you. Whatever y'all got to talk about can wait because somebody we care about just got shot, and we're trying to locate him." I forced a smile and lowered my voice before finishing with, "Ms. Beverly, get ya ass back on that computer and tell me where I need to go to get to Julian Ali Tate."

Rearing her head back at me with an attitude written all over her face, she opened her mouth. Luckily, the guy who interrupted her search in the first place spoke up first.

"I was a part of the team that brought Mr. Tate in. The doctor is in with him now but should be coming to Waiting Area B to update the family soon. I can show you there now." He cleared his throat and went from behind the desk before walking toward the hallway to the right of us.

"Rude," the woman still behind the desk said, mumbling.

I chuckled but kept walking, not about to let her get me kicked out of this hospital for punching her in the throat.

A couple of minutes later, we were at the proper waiting area, and Joseph was already there, pacing the floor. He looked up almost immediately and crossed the room in a few short steps.

"Where are the kids?" he asked, looking at Vi.

"I dropped them off at my mom's house."

I bit my lip as he kissed Davi. He looked stressed; I didn't consider that a good sign. Joseph hugged me next and held it for a minute. "He's aight, Jess," he said in a low tone.

When he released me, he gestured toward a row of unoccupied seats, and we followed him.

"What happened?" Vi asked as she sat down. I remained standing.

Joseph's jaw tightened. "He don't listen. He got a lead on our case, which led him to a warehouse. He called me, and I told his stupid ass to wait on me. He didn't listen, and he got himself shot. This man didn't even put on a bulletproof vest before goin' in."

My chest tightened, and I grabbed it. Joseph looked at me, and his expression softened.

"The doctor hasn't come out yet, but it was only a graze wound, Jess."

"If that's the case, what's taking so long?" I asked.

Joseph sighed. "The bullet didn't go all the way through, but it got lodged in his torso at sort of an angle, so he lost a good amount of blood in a short time. He blacked out before we got him in the ambulance, but—"

"Oh my God," I said as more tears fell. I figured Joseph was trying to reassure me, but hearing about Julian's blood loss and becoming unconscious only heightened my anxiety.

What if it was too late?

"Jessica!" I turned and saw Julian's parents approaching us. They both had red-rimmed eyes and looked understandably worried. Celeste brought me in for a hug, and when she released me, Senior followed.

"Thanks for callin' us, young man. Has there been any word yet?" Senior asked, glancing at Joseph.

"No, sir. We should hear something any minute now."

Celeste grabbed my hand and led me to a seat. She sat in the one beside Davi and patted the other, gesturing for me to sit also. I honestly didn't know if I could sit still, but I also felt the need to be strong for her and Senior. I loved Julian—I was *in love* with him—but he was their only son. I could only imagine what was going through their heads at that moment.

Celeste greeted Davi, and I realized they must have met before. She then turned to me. My hand was still in hers, and she rubbed it gently. "He's gon' be okay, baby. He ain't got a choice," she said with a chuckle.

Swallowing a lump in my throat, I said, "Yes, ma'am."

We all remained together silently for the next few minutes. A doctor approached me when I was about to excuse myself and go to the restroom.

"Family of Julian Tate?" he asked, and we all stood.

He made his way to us, and I studied his expression. It was serious but not solemn, and that had some hope blooming in my core.

"Good afternoon. Because of the angle in which the gun that hit Julian was fired, it only fully penetrated the top layer of his skin."

"Oh, thank ya, Lord," his mother said, lifting her hands in the air. The look on the doctor's face had me holding in my praise a little longer. He continued.

"The bullet did touch a blood vessel in the dermis, but the lack of penetration suggests that Mister Tate moved out of the way at a crucial moment. This caused all the initial bleeding, but we've since been able to stop it.

"Although the medicine we administered should have kept him out for the better part of the day, he woke shortly after we cleaned the wound. While I'm sure he is in a lot of pain, he will be okay."

Finally, the words I needed to hear to consume oxygen were spoken, and I inhaled deeply. I hugged Celeste, then Senior, as everyone began to vocalize their relief. The doctor waited for us all to calm down before he spoke again.

"We tried to give him something for the pain, but he insisted he speak to a Jessica Westin before that happens." I felt my face warm as the doctor looked between each of us.

He wanted to see me.

That made me giddy and nervous at the same time. I was excited because he requested my presence but nervous because of the way we left things. I was almost sure I was the last person he wanted to see.

"I'm Jessica," I said, stepping forward.

The doctor gestured behind him. "I'll show you to him now. He is allowed visitors, but no more than three at a time," he said, looking at everyone else. Celeste spoke up. "You go see him first, honey; we'll be right here." I nodded and followed the doctor to the back.

His eyes were on me as soon as I opened the door. I felt fresh tears forming as I scanned every inch of his body. He looked as he always did, except for the IV attached to his body and the large, covered area below his abs.

"You just gon' stare, or you gon' act like you happy I ain't die?" he asked with a smirk.

He winced but tried to mask it. Because I knew he didn't want a pity party, I ignored his obvious pain for the moment. Stepping entirely into the room, I rolled my eyes.

"Don't make jokes because nothin' 'bout this is funny. Where is your medical gown? I know they put one on you."

Julian kissed his teeth. "I took that off as soon as I woke up. You knew better than that."

I shook my head before making my way to his bed. As soon as I got there, I hit him in the shoulder.

He tightened his face and glared at me.

"I know they told you I was shot. The hell you hittin' me for?"

"Why would you ever go in that building alone and without a vest? Joseph told you to wait, but you just had to be a hero, I guess. And you wanna call me selfish? Look at you... You weren't thinking about your unborn child or about leaving me to be a single mother when you did that stupid shit. And what about your parents? What about—"

"Aye, let's rewind a lil bit," he said, cutting me off. I frowned.

"What are you talkin' about, Julian?" I asked, annoyed that he wasn't taking this seriously.

"You said I wasn't thinkin' 'bout leavin' you to be a single mother. You're not already 'bout to be a single mother, Jet? I gotta be missin' something." He smirked, and I let out an exasperated sigh.

"Ugh, you get on my nerves. You seriously risked your life today, and now you wanna play? I swear, if you ever scare me like this again, I'll kill you myself," I said, grilling him.

His smirk transitioned into a full-blown grin. "Get me right if I'm wrong, baby mama, but it sounds like you might care about a nigga."

Rolling my eyes again, I crossed my arms. "Nigga..." I allowed my voice to trail off because I honestly had nothing to say that would contradict his statement.

I more than cared—I *loved* him.

He raised a brow and asked, "What nigga you talkin' to, Jet? *Whose* nigga are you talkin' to?"

After exhaling, I answered him straight. "Mine... *nigga.*"

Now, he was flashing me his pearly whites, and I couldn't help but smile at his handsome face.

"Bet. That's what the fuck you shoulda been on a few hours ago instead of usin' me for my body and makin' me cuss yo' ass out. Come here."

As bad as I wanted to hold in my laugh, I couldn't. This man was insane. To my surprise, though, in the midst of all my cackling, tears fell.

Julian shook his head. "Uh-uh. We ain't doin' that cryin' up in here, pretty. I'm good. Come here," he said again."

Wiping my eyes, I frowned.

"You're in pain, Ali. I am not about to lie in the small bed with you and make it worse."

He kissed his teeth. "I'm straight. Now, come here."

"You're actually not."

"Jessica Brielle... come here." I stared at him a minute longer, trying to decide if I was going to listen. Knowing he'd likely hurt himself trying to get up if I didn't, I did as he asked, careful not to touch his wound.

Slowly, Julian lifted an arm and wrapped it around my waist before kissing my forehead.

"I told J to make sure you came in here ten toes behind 'bout ya man. You better have flipped a table over or somethin' 'bout me."

I laughed loudly. "Nah, no tables. Me and the homegirl at the desk were definitely 'bout to tussle, though. I let her make it 'cause I didn't wanna get kicked out before they let me see you."

He chuckled. "I guess that'll do. So you done playin' with me? You gon' let us happen now?"

I nodded. "I'ma let us happen. I love you, Ali. I always have," I admitted, lifting my head so I could look into his eyes. I lowered my face and brushed my lips against his before kissing him softly.

"I already knew that, pretty. I love you too."

I kissed him again and smiled. Jessica Westin officially had her man. *Finally.*

"Your parents are here," I said, sitting up a little. As much as I would love to lock the two of us in this room together for the rest of the night, I knew everyone wanted to see him alive and well as much as I did.

"Gone and tell 'em to come in here, then get the doctor for that medicine. This is hurtin' like a bitch."

Stickin' Beside 'Em

♥

Tate

"Somebody's at the door, pretty," I said and smirked.

"Who is it? Kendrick's off today," she said, her voice drawing nearer. Her fresh scent invaded my nostrils before her hands wrapped around my neck from behind. I was chilling on the living room sofa, and she stood behind it.

I held my phone up for her to see as she kissed my neck. That simple gesture made me rethink what I had planned for our evening.

I didn't even have to turn my head to know she was smiling. The security footage on my phone showed our friends standing outside the house holding various aluminum tins.

"You told them to bring food? I was just about to cook," Jess said, kissing the same spot again. Tilting my head back, I reached up and brought her face to mine for a kiss.

"Keep your lips off my neck before I have their asses waitin' out there while we handle some shit."

She laughed and shook her head. "Nah, the doctor said none of that for at least three weeks. It's only been two, so we're not takin' it there."

I kissed my teeth as the doorbell rang again. I pressed a button in the security app and unlocked the front door before kissing her again.

"Girl, please. I been over that, and we're gettin' right tonight. Believe that." The front door opened, and my house was filled with noise shortly after. I expected everyone to enter the living room first, but it sounded like they were headed toward the kitchen.

"You've been cookin', cleanin', and bein' my nurse for the last two weeks without lettin' up. I figured you could use a break, so I told all these friends we got to cook for us tonight. We shoulda *been* put 'em to work."

Jess stood and rounded the sofa and sat next to me. Immediately, I draped an arm around her shoulders and brought her closer.

"I like doin' all those things for you."

All the noise I had heard minutes ago was approaching the living room.

"Ahem."

I smirked when I heard Davi clear her throat.

"Wassup, Sunshine," I said, not bothering to turn around. Doing it hurt too much, so everybody needed to come into my line of sight if we were going to communicate.

"Are we interrupting something?" she asked as tiny feet came running toward me. Two jumped on the sofa beside me, and David wasn't too far behind. I got a lil nervous because it looked like he was headed straight for my lap, but my woman intercepted him.

"Hey, lil man," she said, scooping him up and tickling him.

"Wassup, Unc? You straight?" Two asked, extending a hand toward me. I chuckled as I met it with mine and dapped him up. Two was my main man. So many of his characteristics mirrored J's and mine, and

I loved watching him grow into the young man he was becoming. I couldn't wait to do the same with my kid.

"Yeah, I'm straight, my boy, just a lil sore."

He smirked. "So that means you got an excuse for when I beat you in *2K*?"

I threw my head back and laughed loudly. He definitely got his confidence from the men in his life.

"Nah, I ain't *that* sore, partna. Fire it up," I said, and he rose from the sofa and jogged over to the television.

"So y'all ignorin' me?" Davi asked, plopping down on the loveseat adjacent to us.

"Girl, the better question is, why are you askin' in the first place? You know damn well you were interruptin' somethin'," Jess said and kissed David on the cheek.

I chuckled but said nothing. Davi and Jess argued like cats and dogs, but there was nothing but love there.

Davi rolled her eyes. "Just rude."

"Where's everybody else?" Jess asked.

Davi slumped in her seat and closed her eyes.

"In the kitchen, organizing the food. I cooked it, so it's the least they could do."

I laughed and said, "We appreciate you, sis."

"Hey, y'all!" Demi's greeting was followed by Crissy's. They entered the room with Joseph, Air, Ace, and his kids following closely behind. Everyone made themselves comfortable, and we settled into casual conversation.

"Ooo, Crissy, girl. You're about to pop! When are we getting this nursery together?" Jess asked.

"That's exactly what I was just asking her," Demi said, rolling her eyes.

As the women took over the conversation with baby shower talk, I looked over and admired mine. It had been a minute since we all linked up, and although Jess had been doing her thing, taking care of the home front, I knew she missed being outside. I figured a fun night with our closest people would do her some good. Judging by the smile on her face, I'd say I did the right thing.

"Here, Unc," Two said, tossing me a game controller. I grabbed it.

"'Preciate that, nep."

"Unc!" David yelled, making everyone laugh. I leaned over and kissed his forehead. He wiped it off but grinned.

"David, let's go play!" Aris, Ace's daughter, said. Ace's twins and David were all four, so they always vibed when they were together.

David looked at me with raised brows. "Can we?"

"Go ahead, my boy." David, Aris, and Deuce hopped up and ran to the back of the house. Both David and Two had bedrooms at my house because of how often we chilled together. I loved being their godfather and took my role in their lives seriously.

Ten minutes into Two starting our game, Davi stood and told everyone to make dinner plates. Two and I stayed put because the game we were in the middle of was too crucial, but I knew his mama wouldn't like that.

"Two, Tate, get y'all's butts off that game and wash your hands."

I pressed pause and flashed puppy dog eyes at Davi. "Come on, Sunshine. We just started. Give us like twenty minutes, aight?"

Two glanced at me before giving his mother the same look. She stared us down but eventually rolled her eyes and left the living room. With a smirk, I pressed play, and we were back at it.

The next hour or so went that way, with my godson and I yelling at the television screen and talking trash to each other while everyone vibed around us. It was a lit family night, for sure.

> **You look good.**

I sent the message before lowering my phone and gazing at the recipient. Her phone must have been on vibrate because seconds later, she lifted it from her lap. I watched as her eyes scanned the screen. She stole a glance at me, smiled, then began typing. My phone dinged shortly after.

> **Pretty: You look better.**

> **I'm ready for them to leave. I want you to myself.**

She shook her head and grinned as she composed her reply.

> **Pretty: Lol, you're the one who asked them to come.**

> **And now, I wanna make you come.**

Her eyes widened, but she bit her bottom lip. She looked around at everyone before focusing on her phone again.

We were all sitting around my backyard patio area with music playing. After we ate, we played a few games, and everybody who wasn't pregnant had a drink. The kids were asleep, except for Two, who was inside playing video games. We had had a good time with our people, but it was time to wrap this up, and we both knew it. She had yet to text me back, so I sent her another one.

> **Since I got 'em here, you gotta make 'em leave.**

She gasped, and her mouth hung open as she typed quickly.

"Um, are y'all's fast asses sexting while we're all sitting right here?" Demi asked with a smirk.

Ace glanced at me then Jess before looking at his wife and kissing her cheek. "Mind your business, D."

"We were not," Jess said, glaring at Demi.

"Liar. Y'all's nasty asses want us outta here, and I'ma let y'all have it because it's late anyway. I'm sleepy," Crissy said, rubbing her belly.

"It is late. We gon' head out too," Joseph said, standing.

Jess kissed her teeth. "As long as y'all know you're leaving because you *want to*. It has nothing to do with me or Ali."

Joseph chuckled and kissed her cheek before helping Davi up.

"Tell yourself what you need to, sis."

Everyone stood, and we hugged and dapped each other up before they went into the house to get their children and belongings. After we all talked outside the front door for another ten minutes, they were all gone.

I wrapped my arms around Jess from behind as they drove away. She was twenty-three weeks along, and her belly was kind of out there. She wasn't as big as she would be by the end of it, but I was loving being a witness to the journey.

Kissing her neck, I whispered, "Come on."

We entered the house and headed straight for my master bathroom. She turned on the shower, then undressed silently before turning to me. Because of where my wound was, doing things like lifting my hands above my head still kind of hurt, so she helped me undress.

Jess and I had gotten into a routine of showering together in the last two weeks because she didn't believe I could clean myself without worsening the injury. I wasn't complaining, though. I never would where her touch was concerned.

Once my clothes were off, I stood there and watched as she inspected the dressing on my wound.

"Come on," she said, grabbing a clean washcloth. We entered the shower, and she took her spot closest to the stream of water. Lifting the washcloth to the water, she wet it and put some of my bodywash on it before turning to me.

With a focused gaze, she washed my body thoroughly, careful to follow the instructions the doctor gave when nearing that part of my body. I loved witnessing her love on me like this.

I had endured so many years of the Jess who shut her feelings for me off so easily that it was hard to accept this version of her at first. She had been so attentive to my needs and well-being since we made it official, and now, I couldn't get enough of it.

Her touch had my member rising, and in seconds, it was at full attention and grazing her stomach. She acted as if she didn't notice, but I sensed the change in her breathing. Determined to make love to her that evening, I took matters into my own hands.

Reaching around her, I grabbed her loofah and bodywash and made a lather before rubbing it into her body. She sucked in a sharp breath but said nothing. I smirked. I knew she was just as turned on as I was, but she was trying to respect the doctor's orders. I, on the other hand, no longer gave a fuck about them.

I continued to rub her body but set the loofah down and allowed my hands to do the job solo. Jess cleared her throat but still ignored me, so I lowered a hand and allowed it to caress her bottom lips.

"Ali," she finally said, her voice cracking.

"Wassup, baby?" I asked, smirking.

"Sto-stop doing that, please. We can't go there."

I continued to stroke between her folds. "Why can't we?"

Almost whining, she replied, "Because the doctor said so, Julian. You're still recovering."

"I'm straight." To prove it to her, I bent down and kissed her neck. Granted, bending my body that much hurt like hell, but I didn't care. I wanted my woman, and I was about to have her.

I kissed the other side of her neck before moving to her mouth and devouring it with mine. She moaned against my lips and broke away. The conflicted look on her face had me laughing.

Using my index and middle fingers, I entered her, and she tilted her head back.

"This is happenin' pretty, so stop worryin' yourself wit' whether you should feel bad about it. I'm good, and I'm gon' prove that to you in a minute.

Letting out a groan mixed with lust and frustration, she finally wrapped her fingers around me.

I missed this something serious.

The last time we were together, I was upset and didn't allow myself to enjoy it fully, but I was making up for it tonight.

Sighing, she began stroking me slowly.

"This is so not right," Jess said. With one hand holding the bottom of her belly, she lowered herself to her knees.

I groaned. I wasn't sure there was a better feeling in the world than her soft hands massaging my hardness until she replaced them with her lips.

I groaned. "It feels 'bout right to me."

This woman of mine opened her mouth wide and put my length deep inside it in one motion. Her warm, wet tongue slid against the bottom, forcing me to brace myself by placing both my hands on the shower wall.

A second ago, Jess was against taking it there with me, but now she was pulling no punches. She sucked, bobbing her head up and down, and after a few seconds, she added her hand into the mix. With her fist wrapped around me, she began stroking with a twisting movement so that every part of my dick had her attention at all times.

I felt the tension building up within me, and I groaned in frustration. It wasn't my plan at all, but I knew I wouldn't last long if she kept this up.

"Move baby. I'm tryna feel you." I needed to be inside her, but when her sneaky ass smiled, I knew she had other plans.

She shook her head and looked up at me, and I watched as she puckered her lips around me even more. Her cheeks sunk inward, and her mouth became a vacuum as she sucked even harder. My entire body heated at that point, and there was nothing I could do but surrender to the pleasure my woman was delivering. She quickened her pace, and I felt my orgasm in my damn toes. I tried to exit her mouth, but she held me in place and continued her oral assault as I released long and hard.

I closed my eyes and leaned forward as I struggled to catch my breath. The sound of her laughter caught my attention, and I snapped my eyes open as she stood. Gazing into my eyes with a smile playing in hers, she said, "Tired?"

I chuckled as she turned around in front of me. I was sure she thought she had just wiped me of all my energy, but I was just warming up. I could never be drained of my desire for her. That was replenished the second her ass grazed my groin when she shut the showerhead off.

"Nah, I'm good. Come on," I said, scooping her into my arms. I felt some pain but ignored it. I carried her out of the shower and grabbed a towel for both of us on my way out of the bathroom. Once we were back in my bedroom, I set her down and wrapped one of the towels around her before doing the same for myself.

We dried off silently, and I started to reharden as I watched her caress her own body as she dried it. Once I felt I was dry enough, I tossed the towel to the side and approached her. Her eyes went straight to my manhood, which was standing at full attention. Her eyes widened, and she shook her head.

Taking a step back, she tightened her grip on her towel and said, "Julian, no. We've already done too much, and I know carrying me in here hurt. I heard you strugglin'."

I laughed and snatched the towel away from her. Closing her in my embrace, I kissed her neck softly.

"It ain't hurt. You worried 'bout the wrong thing anyway. Focus on *him*," I said, pressing my torso into her. She rolled her eyes, but a moan escaped her lips, and I smiled as I grabbed her hand.

"It's aight, baby. Just let it happen."

I led her to the bed and gently pushed her down on it. I was about to cover her body with mine, but she shook her head and held her hand up to stop me.

"Uh-uh. We shouldn't be, *but* if we actually doin' this, then I'm the one puttin' in work. Have a seat," she said and licked her lips. I smirked but obliged. I just needed to be inside her. I didn't care what position we were in. Once my back was against the headboard, she crawled to the top of the bed then positioned herself so that her knees were on either side of me.

With her hands on my chest, she leaned forward and pressed her mouth against mine softly. I gripped her chin as she licked my lips, then slipped her tongue between them. She continued to kiss me deeply as she lifted off her knees and planted both her feet on the bed.

She closed her lips slightly as she began sucking my tongue gently, and I felt as though I could have come right then. I wasn't going out like that, though. My next release would happen inside her. We must have been on the same page with that because a second later, I felt her lower lips graze the head of my dick.

Slowly, she lowered herself until I was inside. She threw her head back and moaned.

"I missed this," she said breathlessly.

She continued to slide down further while I placed one hand on her belly and the other on her breast.

Opening her eyes, she looked down at me as she started to rotate her hips. She moved against me slowly as she wound her lower body in circles. Every time her hips pushed back, she lifted herself up, and when they twirled forward, she plunged down with precision.

"I missed this shit, too, pretty."

I didn't know if it was possible, but the longer she kept me buried in her, the wetter she seemed to become. Feeling her warmth, watching her love faces, and hearing her sexy moan was sensory fucking overload. She was accommodating my yearning for her in every way possible, and it was driving me insane.

I began to massage her breasts, just to have something else to focus on so that I wouldn't bust so quickly. Jessica was perfection and handled my body as if she knew it better than I did.

Everything she was doing felt amazing, but her slow movements were like a sweet torture that I wasn't sure I could take anymore. Deciding to take control of the situation, I gripped her ass and lifted her slightly before bringing her down hard. I did it again before holding her in place above me. Without warning, I began to ground my pelvis into her, thrusting upward fast and hard.

Jess yelled out and dropped from her feet to her knees. She moved her hands from my thighs to her breasts, gripping them as they bounced up and down with the rest of her. I knew I had caught her off guard, and it was intentional.

Jess and I had a history of being competitive in the bedroom, and my injury didn't erase that. I was tired of her running the show, and it was time to remind her of who I was. I continued to plow into her, and for a minute, she just held on as I worked her over. Once she regained her footing, she began matching my thrusts and rocking her hips even faster than the pace I had set.

She smirked as she eyed me, and I kissed my teeth.

"You don't run nothin', Jessica Brielle."

She raised a brow. "You sure?"

I chuckled and said, "Positive," before I gripped both her thighs tightly. In one swift motion, I flipped her on her back and pressed her knees toward her ears before delivering a series of hard thrusts that had both of us in here yelling.

"Jet!"

"Wait, Ali, wait! I'm about to—"

Cries replaced her words, and I felt her clenching around me. It was all I needed. Seconds later, I was unloading in her for the second time today. I wrapped my arms around her and pulled her to me as I collapsed beside her on the bed. We lay in silence with our eyes closed until she wiggled out of my embrace. I didn't open my eyes until I heard her speak.

"Oh my God. This is bad," Jess said, sitting up. I lifted my head and followed her gaze. The dressing that was on my wound was soaked in blood, and it was halfway off.

Now that we had come down from our high, my abs felt like they were on fire.

"Damn," I said, laughing a little.

Jess kissed her teeth and glared at me before getting off the bed. She was back a minute later with everything she needed to fix me up.

She started cleaning the wound, and we were silent while she worked. After a couple of minutes, though, she rolled her eyes and kissed her teeth again.

"I'm straight, Jet. I'm good, I'm good," she said in a deep voice and rolled her eyes. "Lyin' ass."

I burst out laughing. "Aye, don't do that voice again 'cause you don't sound nothin' like me. I am straight. We just got a lil carried away. We won't go as hard next time."

She froze and lifted her eyes to meet mine slowly. "Next time? Boy, bye. Tomorrow, you're going back to the doctor to make sure we didn't mess anything up, and we ain't doing that again until a month *after* he clears you."

"Girl, bye," I said, using her phrase on her. "You don't even believe what you're sayin' right now."

"Hmph, we'll see," she said, finishing up.

Instead of debating things I already knew the outcome of, I said to her, "Come here."

"Hold on."

She cleaned up the supplies and took them back into the bathroom before turning the lights off and joining me on the bed.

She sat with her back propped against the headboard and let out a deep sigh. I immediately rested my head on her lap and my right hand on her stomach.

Rubbing her belly gently, I lifted my head and kissed her stomach.

"Hey, Baby Tate," I said, my mouth touching her skin. "Are you a boy or a girl? Ya momma wants to wait to find out, but you can tell me. It'll be our first secret."

Jess snickered, but I ignored her and kissed her belly again.

I continued to massage it, and she laughed again. "My baby doesn't keep secrets from me," she said. I could hear the smile in her voice.

"I bet you—"

A soft push against my hand shut me up quickly. Jess gasped. She felt it, too.

Say somethin' else, baby," Jess said with wide eyes. She placed her hand beside mine while I continued talking to our baby, and sure enough, there was more pushing.

"Oh my God." I looked up at Jess and chuckled. Of course, she was crying. I couldn't front, though. Feeling my baby kick for the first time had me a little choked up myself. We stayed like that for the next several minutes, talking and rubbing, but no more kicks came. After a while, I figured Baby Tate was over us for the night.

"Lay down, pretty."

I moved my head from her lap, and she slid down in the bed. She pulled the comforter over us both and rested her head on my chest, careful not to let her lower body make contact with mine.

"Girl, if you don't put that leg over here, I'ma know somethin'."

"No, Ali."

Not saying anything else, I reached under the cover and grabbed her thigh before draping it over my body. I wasn't about to let her worryin' about my injury cheat me out of any more nights of closeness with her. I was over that.

We lay in silence before something I hadn't thought about in a few days entered my mind.

"Aye," I said.

"Hmm?"

"We need to talk about the other situation we're dealin' wit' right now."

Her body tensed, so I knew she understood what I meant.

"Relax. I ain't bringin' it up to stress you or nothin', but we haven't talked about how you need to handle yourself if somethin' actually pops off."

My chest tightened when I said it, but the conversation needed to be had. If the day I got shot didn't teach me anything else, it taught me that I couldn't control everything all the time—as much as I wanted to.

I didn't plan on letting it happen, but if this stalker ever got to Jessica, I needed her to know how to protect herself.

"Okay," she said slowly, her voice tight.

"You scared me the other week, but you made me realize that sometimes, stuff happens. I've been outta commission for the last couple of weeks, but I'm back now. I'm gon' find this person, but the reality is that he's still out there right now.

"I need you to be prepared on the off chance that this dude is actually able to get to you."

I paused and waited for her to respond. I felt her adjust to a sitting position, and I sighed.

"Lay down, girl."

Ignoring me, she said, "If that happens, I'ma tell him straight up. My man is a killer, so you better let me go!" I couldn't see her face, but her white teeth glowed in the darkness, and I heard the smile in her voice.

I chuckled and shook my head. She lay on my chest again before I continued.

"I'm serious, Jessica Brielle. If that ever happens, you gotta play it smart. I'on know what this guy is capable of, but the fact that he was able to follow you to Atlanta and is still here is a red flag.

"It means he has enough resources to uproot his life and move quickly. People like that have no problem flyin' under the radar, and that can pose a problem one day."

"I hear you."

"Keep hearing me, 'cause I ain't done. *If* that ever happens and you end up alone with him, you can't be poppin' off like that. You gotta play into it."

She sat up again.

"Whatchu mean play into it?"

"I mean, make him feel like you're happy to be together finally. He thinks he's in a relationship with you. He's in love with you, and if he thinks for one second that you don't feel the same way, things could go wrong."

"I'm not an actress, Ali," she said softly.

"We can practice, then. Listen, I'ma do everything in my power to make sure you never have to go through that, but I want you ready just in case. If you ever find yourself in that situation, I need you to know this: I'm already on the way to get you. Just focus on self-preservation 'til I pull up, aight?"

She kissed my chest, then lay down again.

"Aight."

It's You.

♥

Jess

"I don't care how much you like white and gold, Brielle. This baby's nursery is gon' have some color in it. Now keep lookin'," my momma said, not even bothering to give me her eyes.

I laughed but kept quiet. She and Julian were on the same team with that, so I knew I was going to end up losing that argument. If I *had* to include some color in my baby's room, it would still be subtle, and I wouldn't be budging on the overall aesthetic.

"What about this?" I asked and pointed to the pale pink Sherpa rocking chair I found online. I handed her my tablet, and she examined it closer before smiling.

"Cute. I don't think I would like it in blue, though."

I shook my head. "Me either, but I think I'm havin' a girl, Ma."

She laughed. "You might be right, but just don't get so sold on the idea of a girl that you're overly disappointed if it's a boy."

"I guess." I took my tablet back and continued my search for nursery items. I was twenty-six weeks pregnant, and Julian and I would be finding out the gender of our baby in only a few days. I was beyond excited; unfortunately, my mother's advice came a month too late. I was already sold on my baby girl. I had a strong feeling that I was carrying our princess and would be beyond shocked if it was a boy.

My mother had come over to hang out with me, and we'd been on the sofa, looking at baby stuff for the last few hours. She was just as excited to be a grandmother as I was to be a mommy.

"How was the appointment?" she asked.

I smiled. "Great. Doctor P brought in a perinatologist."

My mom frowned. "They're for high-risk pregnancies, right? I thought the doctor said you were all good."

"She did. She already had the gynecologist who specialized in fibroid care check me out, but she wanted to bring in Doctor Osoff for a third opinion. He said all my stats point to a normal pregnancy, just like Doctor P said. He checked my placenta and everything. He said it was hard to believe I had had a fibroid issue and agreed that I could have a natural birth."

My mom smiled wide as she clasped her hands together.

"That's amazing news, sweetheart. I know how you were feeling about possibly having to have a C-section."

I sighed. "I know. Honestly, everything about this entire pregnancy process has been a blessing and a miracle. I'm in awe of it all."

She reached over and hugged me tightly. "Me too, baby, and I'm so happy for you,"

"Aight, pretty ladies, Kendrick just pulled up, so I'm 'bout to head to work," Julian said, entering the living room. My chest tightened at the mention of him going to work. He had officially returned to work three weeks ago, and I wasn't excited about it.

I always knew his job could be dangerous, but him actually getting shot was a big reality check. I wanted him to change career paths. Either way, he loved what he did, and he assured me that he and Joseph were sticking to their interviews and wouldn't have another case for a while. I really had no choice but to accept it.

Julian kissed my mother's cheek, then did the same to me. "Y'all need anything before I go?"

I smirked and shook my head before holding up the credit card he handed me an hour ago when he noticed us baby-shopping.

"Nah, this will do."

Grinning, he shook his head before kissing me again. "Yeah, I bet. I'll see you later, Ma." She smiled brightly at him, and I rolled my eyes. Chanelle loved her some Julian Tate, and he ate it right up. When she first got to the house that day, they hugged like they were long-lost family members and talked for half an hour like I wasn't even there. I was over them.

"See ya later, baby," she said.

I shook my head, and Julian glanced at me. "Don't be a hater all your life, pretty. I'ma see you later too." He winked at me, then left the room. Seconds later, I heard the alarm set and the front door closed.

My mother closed the catalog she was looking through and turned her body toward mine. I glanced at her and realized she was postured for a *talk*. I flipped my tablet over and gave her my undivided attention.

"I really like him for you," she said, smiling.

I chuckled. "I like him for me too, Ma."

"He's strong, protective, and loving, all the characteristics I want to see in your future husband."

"Is that right?" I asked sarcastically.

"It *is* right. He's gon' make a great daddy too."

I frowned when she said that. I agreed, but that thought had me a little on edge lately.

"What's wrong, sweetheart? You disagree?"

I shook my head. "No, I agree, I just..." I paused, unsure if I wanted to go there with her.

"Girl, what is it?" she asked, folding her arms.

I laughed because she knew me too well.

"It's really nothin', Ma. You know how my thoughts run wild sometimes."

"Tell me about these thoughts so I can help you reel 'em back in."

I sighed. "Julian is excited about the baby. He's always on me about my vitamins, getting rest, and all that. I think it's sweet, but I've been wondering lately if it's me *and* the baby he wants or... just the baby." I felt myself tear up as I finally said the words out loud.

I hated that these insecurities were plaguing my mind. I felt like the enemy was trying to steal my happiness, but I couldn't deny they were there.

"He loves *you,* Jessica, trust me. The problem is that you *never* really thought you were enough for him. You've run away from love with that young man all this time because you thought you needed a baby to keep him.

"Now you're having one and still thinking that same thing. I see the way he looks at you and the way he treats you. Shoot, look at the way he treats *me*. All that tenderness is out of love for you, baby. The baby is such a sweet bonus, but *you* make him happy. *You* are more than enough, and it's time for you to start believing that yourself. Okay?"

"Okay."

"You're happy with him, right?"

"Very," I admitted.

"Then focus on that because this thing you're worried about isn't even a thing. Not for him. If I thought he wasn't your one, I would have said it long ago, and so would your father. If you don't trust nothin' else, I know you trust our judgment, and we're right about him, baby."

A tear fell as I nodded. "Yes, ma'am."

She hugged me, and we remained that way for quite some time.

I am enough.

***

"Aw, look at that sweet face! Heyy, Amina Denise Legend. It's your auntie Jess, baby girl," I said, cooing as I gazed at the beautiful face through the screen.

Crissy had given birth only hours ago, and her little one was *flawless.*

"Crissy, you did so good, boo! She's perfect," I said, smiling from ear to ear. Kendrick opened the back car door and helped me out.

"She is. Thanks, sis," Crissy said softly. She had a lazy smile, and I knew she was tired.

"I'ma let you go, boo. Get some rest. You know Davi and I will be up there first thing tomorrow. Congratulations again." Crissy and Air had a big family, and I knew everyone would be excited to see their new addition. Instead of intruding on their family moment, we decided to visit the next day.

"Okay. Love you guys," she said.

"Love you too, boo."

I hung up the phone and sighed. It had been a long day, and the last thing I felt like doing was washing off the makeup Vi insisted putting on me an hour earlier.

I spent most of the day chilling with her and the kids, and she randomly stated that she wanted to practice her makeup skills. Vi was great at doing makeup, so I didn't understand why she felt the need to practice, but she insisted I be her guinea pig, so now I had a beat face and nowhere to show it off.

Kendrick unlocked the front door, and I stepped inside. Because Julian's car was outside, once I made it in, Kendrick said, "I'ma head home, Ms. Jessica. I'll see you tomorrow."

I smiled. "Alright, be safe."

I continued into the house and frowned as I locked up after myself. It was unusually quiet.

Since they closed their last case, Julian hadn't been working too late. He and Joseph went to the prison to conduct their interviews during the day, and he spent a couple of hours transcribing them afterward. All his time after that was usually spent with me. I'd be surprised if he was working, but I decided to check his office anyway because it was too quiet for him to be in the living room.

When I turned and entered the living room, I gasped.

"What the hell?" I asked under my breath.

The sofas, the loveseat, and the armchairs had been removed from the room. In their places were four large photography box lights, a white draped backdrop, and a rack of women's clothes. I walked toward them, and as I observed what was on the shelf, I realized they were the clothes I purchased days before when Julian took me shopping.

He said he wanted me to ball out on his dime, and I did that. I turned and saw two high-end cameras sitting on the coffee table, which was now moved out of the way.

"Nosy."

I jumped at the sound of Julian's voice then turned toward it.

"How am I nosy? I walked into all this," I said, waving toward the setup.

He kissed his teeth as he headed toward me.

"You're nosy because you walkin' through lookin' at everything instead of waitin' for me to reveal my own surprise." He wrapped me in his arms and kissed me slowly. Once he lifted his head, he kissed me again quickly but didn't let me go.

"What *is* the surprise?"

"You been MIA on your social media platforms, and I realize you were tryna get some content to post the day you went to your crib. Well, I still ain't willin' to let strangers in my house, but I want you to have pictures if you want them." He kissed me again before finishing with, "So, I'ma take 'em."

I laughed, but he didn't crack a smile. I frowned a little. "You're serious?"

"Yeah, I'm serious. What kinda question is that?"

I lifted on my toes and puckered my lips. Because I still wasn't high enough to reach his lips, he had to meet me halfway, and after being stubborn for a few seconds, he did.

"I apologize. I'm just surprised, that's all. I didn't know you could even operate a professional camera, but it looks like you *own* two of them," I said, glancing at the coffee table.

"Girl, I bought them last week. I been doin' my research, though, and I got this. If you think about it, I'm the best person to take ya pictures anyway."

I raised a brow and asked, "Why is that?"

He smirked. "I done seen you in every way and from all angles. I know your body better than *you* do, so I know how to capture it best."

I couldn't help but blush. I glanced up at him again. He was now giving me a thorough once-over.

"You look good," he said before kissing my lips softly.

I smiled. "Thanks. Is this why Davi insisted on doing my makeup today?" I asked, nodding my head toward the photo shoot setup.

"Maybe. Come on, though. Pick out your first look and shit."

I laughed, allowing him to grab my hand and lead me to the clothes rack. Beside it was a table with accessories laid out carefully, and they all matched the clothes I purchased the other day—I was more than certain Davi helped him with this, but the effort he put in to make this happen had me on the verge of tears.

Trying to hold them back, I perused clothing items and grabbed a pair of loose-fitting boyfriend jeans ripped at the knees, followed by a pink top. Well, it was more like a bralette, but it was covered in faux fur, and it would be cute with the denim and a pair of white sneakers.

I turned to show my man what I had picked out, and he raised his brows and grinned.

"That's how you feelin'? That outfit is low-key a pregnancy announcement."

He was right about that. I was well past the point of wearing clothes that hid my belly, but this top would basically be putting it on display.

I shrugged. "I'm ready for people to know. We're not hiding it, right?"

"Hell nah, we ain't. Gone and get dressed." He smacked my butt hard, then jogged away quickly. Shaking my head, I dropped my clothes and changed right there. Once I had the outfit on, I picked a pair of sunglasses that matched the top perfectly. They were a pale pink, and the lenses were the same color but transparent.

Because he had apparently thought of everything, there was a full-length mirror next to the clothes area, and I checked myself out. I was cute.

"I'm ready," I called loudly, unsure where he went.

Seconds later, he was back in the room, picking up one of his cameras. He licked his lips as he observed me from head to toe.

"You look good."

My cheeks warmed, and I dropped my gaze for a moment. Julian spoke those three words to me often, and it wasn't so much what he said but *how* he said it. He never haphazardly admired me. His examinations were always thorough, and I could hear and feel the appreciation in his voice every time he complimented me.

Ugh.

I just loved him.

"You told me that a few minutes ago."

Walking toward me, he said, "I meant it then too."

He placed his free hand on my protruding belly, and we both stared at it for a moment.

Without warning, he lifted the camera and hovered over where we were currently connected. There was a flash and a shutter sound before he lowered it and studied the screen. He tapped a few buttons before moving beside me and allowing me to see. The picture he took of his hand on my belly was perfect, and I could see it framed somewhere in this house in the next few days.

I glanced at him. "You might be a natural," I said, giving him his props for capturing the moment nicely.

He smirked. "Told you. Gone over there. Let me show you what else I can do."

Laughing, I did as I was told and headed to the backdrop. Julian grabbed his phone, and after a few seconds passed, one of my favorite songs flowed through the room. He placed the other camera he bought on a tripod and positioned it slightly behind him, but based on how he angled it, I figured he was trying to capture both of us in that frame.

When he lifted the other camera and placed it in front of his face, I began moving around in front of the backdrop. Julian snapped several photos as I fell into different poses, and when he bent down and continued, I didn't even try to hold in my laugh. He was taking this photo shoot seriously, and I loved him for that.

I had more fun than I had in a while, dancing and posing while my baby's daddy photographed me.

Once the song ended, I went to him, and he showed me some photos. I couldn't lie; they looked good. The angles in which he captured me were professional and flattering. I knew Val would be proud.

I lifted a hand in his direction, and he met it with mine in a high-five before he kissed me.

"I did my thing, huh, pretty?"

"You did! You need to start charging people for your services, Ali. We could be rich."

Laughing, he shook his head. "Nah, my talent is too sacred to be snappin' pics for just anybody. You two are the only people I'll ever put this work in for," he said, placing his hand on my belly.

I sighed and frowned. "You love tryna make me cry. We gotta get through the pictures, remember?"

"Girl, ain't my fault your ass is overly emotional. Tap into that real nigga Jet that existed before I put my baby in you, and boss up."

I rolled my eyes. "And just that quickly, you killed the moment."

I turned around to choose a second look. Before I left his personal space, he pulled me back to him quickly. Wrapping his arms around me, he kissed my neck softly.

"Don't do that. I love your simp ass, so it's all good, pretty."

He kissed the other side of my neck, then my chin, and I shuddered as my body heated. Just that quickly, I was over my fake attitude and ready to end the photo shoot so that he could bend me over something.

Julian pulled back a little and chuckled. "Nah. We're finishin' what we started, so get ya fast tail over there and pick another outfit."

I sighed and headed toward the clothes rack.

***

"Wassup, family."

Julian knocked on the open door before leading me inside the hospital room.

Amina Legend was three days old, and we both had been itching to meet her.

"Wassup, y'all," Air said as we fully entered. The room was dimly lit, and Air was sitting in a chair pulled close to the bed Crissy lay in. She had the baby cradled in her arms and was cooing at her but looked up when she realized we were there.

Smiling, she said, "Hey, family."

I rushed over to them, grinning widely. "Hey, sis! How is it that you're still glowin' after putting all that work in to get baby girl here?"

Chuckling, Air said, "That's the same shit I said." He hugged me before heading toward Julian.

I kissed Crissy's cheek, and she blew me one back before moving the blanket Amina was wrapped in away from her face so that I could see her clearly. I gasped immediately.

"Oh my God, Crissy. She's even more perfect in person."

"Ain't she, though?" Crissy said with a laugh. "You wanna hold her?"

I kissed my teeth. "You know I do." I headed to the sink on the other side of the room and washed my hands before hurrying back. I gently took the baby from her mother, making sure to support her head during the transition. She had yet to open her tiny little eyes, but there was no denying how adorable she was.

I gasped again and pouted when I realized she was wearing one of the custom onesies I had made for her.

Glancing at Crissy, I grinned. "I love her outfit, sis."

Smiling softly, Crissy replied, "Thanks, girl. Her supermodel auntie bought her custom and designer everything."

I swayed gently from side to side, nestling the precious bundle of joy while soft conversation buzzed around me.

"How you feelin', man?" I heard Julian ask.

Air let out a sigh. "Complete, man. These two right here got me feelin' good; I can't lie."

I glanced at Crissy, and as I suspected, her light-bright ass was blushing at her man's words.

"I feel that. I'm happy for y'all, dawg. I really am." Julian's voice got closer as he passed me, but I didn't look to see where he was going. Baby Amina had my undivided attention. The faucet began running for a minute, then it shut off, and seconds later, Julian was standing beside me, requesting the baby.

I rolled my eyes. "I just got her, goofy. Move."

He kissed his teeth. "You done had her for ten minutes, pretty. Gimme."

Crissy and Air laughed as I rolled my eyes again. "Fine."

I extended my arms slightly, and he wrapped Amina in his arms. "Be careful," I said, my eyes still on the baby.

"Girl, I got this."

I observed him as he cradled her and realized he *did* have it. My man was looking like a pro as he rocked her back and forth.

"Hey, sweetheart," he said in a low tone. His voice was laced with a tenderness I had never heard before as he talked to the newborn. She stirred a little as he continued to coo at her before she curled into his chest.

Crissy nudged me and whispered, "He's a natural, girl."

I chuckled and glanced at Julian again. He really was, and as beautiful as the visual was, I felt my chest tighten as I gazed at him. He looked to be in complete awe of Amina, and that was, unfortunately, serving as a reminder of my fears.

Pretty soon, he would be able to bond with our baby like this, and I was excited about it, but... that thought I had been working to dismiss began to trickle back into my mind as I watched him now.

If you weren't pregnant, he wouldn't be with you.

I wanted him to love our baby. I wanted him and our child to have the best, most healthy relationship ever, but I wanted to be a part of the equation. I wanted to be confident that I was a part of the equation because he wanted *me*. Not just because I happened to have gotten pregnant or because we were forced together due to a stalker.

"You see how tiny she is, pretty? This 'bout to be us soon."

Trying to force my thoughts to the back burner, I smiled. "It sure is."

"I can't fuckin' wait. Aw, shit, I'm sorry, Amina. I ain't mean to curse," he said, eliciting a laugh from all of us.

We stayed and chilled with Crissy and Air for a couple of hours before heading out with promises to check on them soon. We left the hospital hand in hand, and on our ride home, Julian spoke excitedly about Amina and our unborn child. Little did he know, his words were both comforting and unnerving for me.

I thought about just talking to him about it, but if I was imagining all of this, I wasn't trying to cause a rift between us because of my insecurities. We were doing so well, and I wanted us to stay in a good space.

I sighed and looked out of the window. I needed to work through this sooner than later.

***

"I'm so obsessed with this little face," I said in a low tone as I gazed down at Amina.

She was officially two weeks old and had been home for five days. It was Friday night, and the guys decided to go to *Ace on Air*. Davi, Demi, Paul, and I were having our own little function at Crissy's house. Paul was Ace's assistant, who became Demi and Crissy's best friend. Vi and I had also grown closer with him in the last couple of years. We were all in her woman cave while the kids chilled in the next room.

"I'm obsessed with these glasses," Crissy said, putting on another pair. I finally got the prototypes and brought them to get the girls' opinions. I had designed four pairs, and I was in love with each of them. I thoroughly enjoyed the creation process.

"Yeah, me too. Every pair is *fire*. The girls are gon' love 'em," Demi said, and I smiled.

"Thanks, y'all," I said, glancing at Amina again as I rocked her. She was sound asleep.

"When are you thinking about launching? I wanna plan the party," Vi said, smiling brightly.

Paul cleared his throat and spoke up. "*We* wanna plan the party." They both *lived* to plan a get-together.

I laughed. "Y'all are gonna have to share that task with Shay, I'm sure. I won't officially launch until my baby's born, though. My next steps are hiring models and scheduling a photo shoot for the website and product launch, which brings me to my next question..."

I allowed my voice to trail off as I looked at each of them with a wide grin.

"Will y'all be my models?"

Paul hopped up. "Yes, ma'am! I have always wanted to be a model girl. My pictures are gon' sell you out!" He started dramatically strutting toward the door, and I had to stop looking at him to avoid laughing loudly and waking the baby in my arms.

"Okay, so that's a yes from Paul. What about y'all?"

"Girl, bye. You know we're down," Crissy said with a soft smile.

"Cool." Since the stalker was still not found, I didn't think Julian would be a fan of me conducting a full-scale photo shoot with hired strangers. Each of my friends was beautiful, and Julian was low-key a professional photographer, so I was confident in our ability to pull this off together.

"You look mighty comfy over there with Amina, Jess. You're next, boo," Crissy said, her smile growing.

I smiled at the thought. I was twenty-eight weeks along, and the time until I met my baby was winding down. I was beyond ready. Julian hadn't been talking about anything other than our baby for the last few weeks, and his excitement radiated off him. I knew he would be the best daddy, and I was looking forward to watching him love on our blessing.

"What's wrong?"

I lifted my gaze to Vi and frowned. "What you mean?"

"You're frowning, and there are tears in your eyes, girl. What's wrong?" she asked again, sitting up.

It wasn't until she mentioned tears that one actually fell. I swiped it away quickly and readjusted Amina in my arms.

"Nothing's *wrong*, really. I just... I don't know."

"Uh-uh, don't do that. Spill, Jess," Demi said, looking serious.

I chuckled and rubbed my lips together, unsure whether I wanted to say it. My mother had already told me I was overthinking things, and I didn't want to keep harping on the same issue, especially when it wasn't *actually* an issue.

Knowing that my friends wouldn't let me go without telling them what was up, I just said exactly what was on my mind.

"Do y'all think Julian is gon' get tired of me after the baby's born?"

The three of them turned their lips up almost simultaneously.

"Why would you think that?" Paul asked.

I sighed. "I'on know. I see how excited he is for the baby, and I get to thinkin' about the fact that we wouldn't be together right now if it weren't for this baby. If the baby is the only reason we're together, that's not the best foundation for a relationship," I said, getting choked up toward the end.

Vi stood and walked over to me. She took the baby from my arms and handed her to Crissy before approaching me again and kneeling before me. I rolled my eyes because I sensed she was about to say something that would have me crying even more than I already was. One thing I was looking forward to was my hormones getting back in order once my baby was born.

"Jessica Brielle Westin, if you think the *only* reason Tate is with you is because of the baby you're carrying, then you're delusional. If y'all's relationship had been up to him, y'all would have been together years ago. He loves you so much, and a blind man can see that. I mean, girl, look at you. That man has single-handedly picked you up and placed you in your soft-girl era. Little miss I-can-do-everything-myself never lifts a finger anymore because her man makes all her desires a reality. It's because he loves you, best friend. I know you love him too. I need you to cling to what's true and not let these lies trying to infiltrate your mind get the best of you.

"The *truth* is Tate is your one, and after all this time, that hasn't changed. After all these years, God blessed y'all with a baby and a space where you could finally admit and explore your feelings for him.

"Have the last few months with him been anything less than wonderful?"

I shook my head.

"Has he done one thing that would lead you to believe that he isn't crazy in love with you?"

More tears fell, and I shook my head.

"That's because he is. Baby or no baby, Tate wants *you*, best friend. That's one thing I know for sure, so if you can't believe what your heart is telling you, believe *me*, because you know how I'm comin' about you. You and Tate are the real deal; this happiness you've been experiencing with him is just a taste of the rest of your life. Okay?"

I laughed through my tears. "Girl, have you been talkin' to my mama? She said almost that exact same thing."

Vi smirked. "That's because we both know what's up. Believe us."

I nodded. "Okay." I knew she was right and needed to get out of my head, but it was easier said than done. I didn't understand why it was so hard for me to accept that I finally had my happily ever after, but it was difficult. Julian's and my relationship had been a push-and-pull match for so long that I was almost expecting something to go wrong that would pull us apart once again. I needed to figure out how to let go and be happy. *Soon.*

***

"Yeah, if we can finish up with Riley, we might be able to chill a lil bit."

I stood at Julian's office door, watching as he spoke. His eyes were glued to his computer screen, and I noticed his earphones were in, so I was sure he had no clue I was standing there. We hadn't talked that day, so I at least wanted to tell him good night before I went to bed.

If I was honest, we hadn't talked in about a week. I told Vi I was going to let the negative thoughts about our relationship go, but they seemed to have multiplied since then. It had been hard for me to be around him, so I spent a lot of time talking to the girls on the phone, working on my sunglasses line launch, or pretending to sleep. I hated how awkward I had been acting, but I found it hard to act normal when my mind was actively sabotaging my relationship.

Finally, Julian looked at me.

"Hol' on, J," he said before removing one of his earphones.

"My bad, pretty, I ain't hear you. Wassup?" he asked, giving me a once-over. He smiled briefly, but his face grew serious seconds later.

"Nothing. I was just coming to say good night." I entered the room entirely. I steadied myself by placing a hand on my belly before leaning over and softly kissing his lips. Once I pulled away, I stood there for a minute.

He put his hand on my stomach, and he stared at it. I felt myself tear up as he smiled. I felt like I was hating on my own baby, but I didn't know if I could help it. I knew Julian loved our baby, and I wanted to be just as sure about his feelings for me. Only... I wasn't.

"Good night, Julian," I said, a disappointed look crossing her face.

His brows creased as he frowned and looked up at me.

"What's wrong, Jet?"

I shook my head and smiled softly before taking a step back. "Nothing. I'm just tired."

We stared at each other for a minute. I silently tried to convince him I was okay, but I could tell he didn't believe me. Instead of calling me the liar I was, he eventually said, "Aight. I'll be in there in a minute."

I nodded and left the room. As I walked toward our bedroom, I wrestled with my thoughts. A part of me felt like it was just my hormones getting the best of me, while the other part was really believing what my subconscious had been saying.

It wasn't fair for me to treat Julian the way I had been without even telling him why.

We said that we would give this a real shot, and I wasn't holding up my end of the bargain because I was keeping my true feelings away from him, and it was driving me insane. I needed to let him in and allow him to put my mind at ease. I loved Julian and needed to give him the chance to say it.

Taking a deep breath, I turned on my heels and headed for his office again. However, the words he spoke as I neared the door stopped me in my tracks.

"I mean, come on, dawg. I'on even know if we would be together right now if it weren't for the baby, J."

My heart broke as the words left his lips.

I was just going to ask him if he wanted me or if our relationship was more about the baby. I wanted my mother and Davi to be right, but I needed confirmation. Without it, my doubts were never going to leave me.

I didn't even have to ask, though. He delivered the answer without any prompting from me.

He didn't know if we'd be together if it weren't for the baby.
He didn't *know*?

Those words confirmed my worst fears were valid and proved that I wasn't just making things up in my mind.

Weeks ago, Julian ensured my house was as secure as his, and Kendrick could pick me up from anywhere. If he didn't know why we were together, what in the world was I doing here?

Delaying my heartbreak.

I chuckled. I had avoided taking it there with Tate because I knew I wouldn't recover if we didn't make it, but now, it looked like I would have to try. His yelling jolted me out of my thoughts and kicked me into gear.

I hurried back to our bedroom—*his* bedroom—and pulled on a pair of sweatpants. Tears blurred my vision as I grabbed my purse and tiptoed through his home. I didn't want him to hear me leave because I didn't want to have a conversation about what I was choosing to do.

I didn't see the point because there was no mistaking what I had just heard. Whenever he decided to leave his office, he would notice I left. He would call, and I'd assure him I was locked up safely in the house he so graciously secured. I knew he'd be pissed, but as long as I was safe, he needed to give me the space I required at the moment.

We were two months away from meeting our baby, so I needed time away from him to figure out how to co-parent with the love of my life.

Hoping he couldn't hear the security system when it announced the door was open, I grabbed the keys to his SUV, because it was the only car not in the garage, and left out. I wasted no time starting the car and pulling off.

***

I parked the car and hopped out, wiping my eyes as I locked it. My plan was to go straight into the house and lock up, but headlights flashing behind me delayed that.

I rolled my eyes, realizing Julian must have realized I was gone much sooner than anticipated. Now, here he was to drag me back to his house.

Well, I wasn't going. I needed space to figure out my next move, and he would have to give me that. The car stopped behind the one I drove, and when the driver got out, I was pleasantly surprised.

"Hey, Jess! I was headed over to Margo's house and saw a car in your yard," Valerie said, standing by her car door. Margo did buy a house in my neighborhood, and although I felt a little jealous that they had clearly been hanging out without me, I understood. I had been MIA and couldn't expect their lives to stop because of mine.

"Val! Hey, girl, I'm glad you stopped by. I miss you guys."

She finally made her way to me, and we hugged. She wore a hood on her head, prompting me to look at her entire outfit. She was in an all-black hoodie set, which I found odd because Val was the type to dress up to go to the grocery store. I didn't even know she owned sweats.

"We missed you too. We never see you anymore," she said as we released each other.

I sighed. "I know, but I'm going to do better, I promise. What were you and Margo about to do?"

I wasn't going to Margo's house because I didn't want Julian to worry. If they came to hang out with me at mine, however, he'd be able to see that I was okay using the security cameras he had installed.

"Just watch movies and chill, you know. Where have you been, anyway?" she asked.

I tried to contain my eye roll as I replied.

"Girl, it's a long story, but basically, the person who used to send me those notes and flowers on my birthday actually was a stalker."

She frowned. "What happened to them just being a superfan?"

I sighed. "That was before they moved with me to Atlanta and left a note at my house."

"That's kind of sweet, though. They must really love you," she said with a small smile.

I shook my head and casually looked toward my front door as I replied, "I can do without that kind of love."

Val got quiet, so I glanced at her. She was no longer smiling. Instead, her lip was turned up as her eyes penetrated mine. I stopped rubbing my tummy.

"What's wrong, Val?"

"That's such a rude thing to say, Jessica," she replied. Her voice shook as she spoke, and my skin tingled as I continued to observe her.

Her cold eyes were scaring me, and all types of alarms began to go off in my mind. I glanced toward one of the security cameras, praying Julian had noticed I was gone and had already checked the footage.

I straightened my posture, trying to prepare myself if she jumped wrong. Val was my friend, and I was hoping she wouldn't try to put her hands on me—at least not while I was carrying a baby—but the look in her eyes had me squaring up just in case.

I noticed something shiny in her hand, so I looked down, and my eyes widened as I lifted them to hers once again.

"Val, wait, you don't—"

"I can't believe I ever loved you," she said, lifting the syringe.

I shook my head as tears fell. I took a step back, but she was quicker. She stuck the syringe in my stomach, and I winced from the pain of the puncture. Whatever it was didn't affect me immediately, but she quickly stuck another one I hadn't noticed in my neck.

As I faded out of consciousness, I silently prayed that Julian was on his way to me.

MAC.

♥

Tate

"We're good on that, though, and the prison is on lockdown tomorrow, so we got an off day," Joseph said. At the same moment, I noticed Jessica at my office door.

When I observed her face, I realized she must have been there for a minute. I had my wireless earphones on as I talked to J because I was transcribing notes from our interview and discussing them.

"Hol' on, J," I said before removing one of my earphones.

"My bad, pretty, I ain't hear you. Wassup?" I asked, giving her a once-over. She had on one of my T-shirts and a pair of my boxers, which made me smile, but it didn't last long because thoughts of how she had been acting the last couple of days filled my mind.

Something was going on with her, and as clearly as I tried to make it so that she could talk to me about anything, she refused to open up—to me, at least.

When I picked her up from Crissy's house the other day, I walked in on her laughing and talking, looking like *my* Jess. As soon as she saw me, though, she got quiet, like she had been for the last week.

I felt like we were doing good, but she just switched up out of nowhere and was low-key avoiding me. Once I got off the phone with J, I planned to get to the bottom of what her problem was that night.

"Nothing," she said softly. "I was just coming to say good night." She entered the room entirely and touched her belly before leaning slightly and connecting her lips with mine. Once she pulled away, I placed my hand on her belly and smiled. I'd be meeting my baby in a little over two months, and I was hype about it.

"Good night, Julian," she said, a disappointed look crossing her face.

I frowned in confusion.

"What's wrong, Jet?"

She shook her head and smiled softly before taking a step back. "Nothing. I'm just tired."

I stared at her for a minute, not believing anything coming out of her mouth. It was all good, though. We wouldn't be going another night with this tension between us. For now, I would let her fake sleep while I finished working.

"Aight. I'll be in there in a minute."

I watched as she left the room and waited a little longer before putting my earbuds back in and addressing J again.

"My bad, dawg."

"You straight. Wassup? Jess, okay?"

"Shid, I'on know. Ask Sunshine. She prolly knows better than me."

"Are *you* straight?" was his next question.

I exhaled. I had yet to voice my concerns, but now was as good a time as any. J's advice was always rooted in wisdom, so maybe he could give me some clarity before I went to talk to Jess.

"Nah, not really. Jess been actin' different lately. We went from talkin' twenty-four seven to her avoidin' me. I'on know what caused the shift, but there is one, and I'm just about over it."

"I'm sure it's nothin'. Women get hella emotional when that due date gets closer. It's prolly her hormones, bruh."

I chuckled. "Well, her hormones only got her actin' funny with my ass. She got all the words and laughter in the world for Davi and them, but when she looks at me, it's like she don't want no parts of me."

Was that it? Was she over me?

My chest tightened at the thought. Now that it had entered my mind, though, it seemed like a logical response to the way she had been doing me.

"Jess loves you, Tate. That's a fact."

I laughed arrogantly. "Does she, though? Or is that what I been tellin' myself so that this didn't feel as one-sided as it always has been? I mean, dawg..." I allowed my voice to trail off before voicing a truth I had been avoiding for a minute now.

"I'on even know if we would be together right now if it weren't for the baby, J."

He sighed. "Don't say that, Tate. You know it ain't true."

"Ain't it, though? I've been in love with Jessica since we met, and she's been playin' me to the left for the same amount of time. I ain't gon' lie. The way she's been actin' got my mind on some shit, like, what if she don't fuck with me for real? I feel like I low-key bullied her into a relationship."

J laughed at that. "Nah, you ain't bully her into a relationship. You bullied her into letting you protect her, and the time y'all have been spending together pushed her to stop denying what she feels for you. I believe Jess is really in it with you, but you need to let her in on your concerns. Until you do, all they'll ever be is concerns, and that will drive you crazy. Talk to your girl, man. We can finish this tomorrow."

I was silent for a moment as I processed his words. He was right. I wasn't going to feel any better about it until I talked to her, so I needed to go and handle that.

"Aight. I'll check you tomorrow."

"Cool."

I lifted my phone to hang up, and once I did, I noticed an alert that had me out of my seat immediately. My phone was on silent mode, so it didn't sound off when the front door opened, but apparently, it had fifteen minutes ago, and the alarm had been set. That meant someone left, and the only people here were Jess and me.

Not wasting anytime looking through the house, I went straight to the security feed on my phone and rewound it a few minutes. Sure enough, she was getting into one of my cars and driving out of the garage.

"What the fuck, Jessica!" I yelled and took a deep breath immediately after. I couldn't go off the deep end. Not until after she was back home safely. Right now, though, I needed to find her. She had her phone with her, and it was at her house, so I immediately headed out of my office.

Luckily, I had a pair of sneakers at my front door, so I stepped into them before leaving. An uneasy feeling washed over me as I drove to her house, and I called J.

"Yeah?" he answered immediately.

"Jess left the house. She's at her crib, according to her phone, but I got a bad feelin'."

"I'll meet you there," he said and hung up. I tossed my phone in my passenger seat and punched the steering wheel. I hoped I was wrong, but my gut was tellin' me somethin' wasn't right. I pressed the gas harder and sped the rest of the way to her house.

Why, Jessica?

***

J and I pulled up at the same time. I went straight for the front door and used my fingerprint to unlock it. As soon as I stepped inside, I knew something was up. All the lights were off, and it was too quiet for someone to be here.

My suspicions were confirmed when J walked into the house, holding Jessica's phone.

"It was in the yard, near the car."

"Aagh!" I yelled and threw my phone.

"Calm down, bruh, 'cause we can't do nothin' right now but figure it out. You got her a security system installed after that photo shoot thing, right?"

I nodded. That was how I was able to enter the house with my fingerprint. After the bug was put on her car, I decided not to take any more chances. Her home was just as secure as mine.

"Aight, so how do we check the camera feeds?"

I walked over to my phone and picked it up off the floor. Luckily, there was only one crack on it, so I'd be able to see the footage clearly.

I accessed her camera feed and went to the last time motion was detected outside her home before we got there. J and I watched as Jess pulled up and exited the car in a T-shirt and sweatpants. She was wiping away tears just as a car I didn't recognize drove in behind her. The porch lights were on, but they didn't shine far enough for me to get the make or model of the other car. However, when the driver got out, I noticed Jess looking up and smiling. That had me frowning.

The feed had no audio, but as she and the person talked, Jess seemed very familiar with them. The other person had yet to step into the light, but if they were who had taken my woman, I knew they would eventually. I quickly fast-forwarded the footage and stopped when the person moved closer to Jess.

Whoever it was must have been aware that there were cameras because their face was shielded from view. The person had a slim build. They were probably five-eight and no more than one hundred fifty pounds.

It was a woman. Jess had to look up to talk to her, and while it was clear she had been crying, she seemed comfortable as she spoke and rubbed her belly casually. I watched intently, not willing to miss anything. It wasn't until a few minutes into their conversation that I noticed Jess's demeanor shift. She frowned and stopped rubbing her stomach. She said something, squared her shoulders, and was now defensive.

I clenched my fists as Jessica glanced down. When her eyes again met the other person's, she no longer looked defensive. She was afraid. She shook her head rapidly as she said something, but her pleas must have fallen on deaf ears because a second later, the person lifted their hand toward Jess's belly.

"Fuck," I heard J say beside me. *Fuck* was right. The woman had a syringe in her hand, and we could do nothing but look in horror as she injected an unknown substance into Jess's belly. I felt tears fall from my eyes as she stuck another syringe in her neck. Jess was slumped into the woman's arms in seconds, and she struggled to wrap her arms around her. She got rid of Jessica's phone, dragged her to her car, and drove off silently.

LET IT HAPPEN

"Who is that?" J asked.

I couldn't even respond. I rewound the footage to the point where she stuck Jessica's stomach. I paused it there because her arm was the only visible part of her body.

I wasn't sure what I expected to find by examining her hand, but it was all I had, so I clung to it. She had no nail polish, and her nails looked like they were chewed off. The woman wore a gold bracelet and three rings on her left hand.

I frowned.

"Wait," I said, mumbling.

I zoomed in, grateful that I purchased high-definition cameras. *Those rings.*

I had seen them before—twice. Once at Jessica's birthday party and again on the day of her photo shoot. Her photographer wore them, and as I continued to think about it, I remembered thinking she had some fucked up fingernails.

If I wasn't mistaken, her name was Val or something close to it.

I swiped out of the security app and went to my email. Moreu sent me information about everyone Jess worked with a while ago. I found the file on Valerie and opened it up.

Valerie MacKenzie Stuart.

Her middle name was where she got her MAC. Jess's photographer was the stalker. "How did I miss that?"

"Look. There's an address. Let's go and hope that's where she took Jess," J said, pointing to the address under her date of birth and social security number.

We bolted out of the house, and I hopped into his car's passenger seat. Wasting no time, J put the address in his navigation system and took off in the corresponding direction. As he drove, I prayed like I never had in my entire life.

Let them be okay, Lord. Please, let them be okay.

***

I glanced at the GPS and realized we were only minutes from our destination.

"What's our plan?" J asked as he drove. I glanced at him. He spoke calmly, but his jaw was tight, and that vein that only appeared when he was upset was protruding from his forehead.

I kissed my teeth. "I ain't playin' with this bitch. She injected somethin' in Jessica twice. I'm shootin' the lock off her apartment door. Then I'm shootin' her ass before I get my woman. The only positive in this whole situation is that she lives by the hospital. She better be here," I said, my voice elevating.

"Aight then," J said. We didn't speak again, and seconds later, he screeched to a halt at Valerie's apartment complex. I hopped out and ran straight to the door with her apartment number on it.

The door looked poorly made, so instead of immediately shooting the lock, I stepped back slightly and kicked it. The door opened easily, and I lifted my gun as I rushed into the apartment, with Joseph following closely behind.

What I saw had me about to lose my sanity. Jess was lying on the sofa, clearly unconscious. The left side of her head was swelling, and Valerie was kneeling in front of Jess, crying with her head resting on Jessica's stomach. She didn't even flinch at the commotion we caused when we burst into her home.

Before I could get my hands on her, J rushed ahead of me and yanked the woman up. She began wailing at that point.

"She won't wake up! I didn't mean to hurt her. I love her. Oh, God. Please, wake up, Jess," she cried.

Her words constricted my breathing, and I went straight to Jessica and lifted her into my arms. I checked her pulse, and she was still breathing, but she was out. I rushed to the door but realized I didn't drive. J, who had Valerie in handcuffs, tossed me his keys.

Take my car and go straight to the hospital. I'm callin' the police, and I'll wait here 'til they pick her up. Davi and I will be at the hospital ASAP. Nodding, I rushed outside and carefully laid Jessica in the back seat. I tried to drive carefully, but that was hard. All I could think about was getting her to the hospital so that they could get whatever Valerie gave her out of her system.

I needed her to be straight.

Open + Honest

Jess

*O*uch.

I shut my eyes almost as soon as I opened them and grabbed my head. It was extremely bright, and my head felt like a ton of bricks rested on it.

Moving both hands to cover my eyes, I inhaled deeply before letting it out. I repeated this several times as I tried to assuage the excruciating headache.

What was going on?

I continued my deep breathing as I lay with my eyes closed, trying to recall how I ended up in bed with a headache. I remembered leaving Julian's house after overhearing him on the phone with Joseph. Once I got to my house, I ran into Val, then…

Oh my God.

My body stilled as I realized where I must have been. Val injected me with something, and that had to be the reason for my headache, and now I was sure I was at her house.

I messed up.

I trusted Val. I considered her my friend, but she had been the one stalking me all this time. *She* was the one who hurt that model so that I would get the *Bodii* gig, and now, she had hurt me—my *baby*. With my eyes still closed, I ran one hand down my body and touched my belly.

She injected me there first, and I had no clue what she had put in me. A tear ran down my cheek. If something had happened to our baby, Julian would never forgive me. I would never forgive myself.

I had to find a way out of here.

"Jessica, are you awake?"

I frowned at the friendly, unfamiliar voice. Taking another deep breath, I slowly opened my eyes and tried hard to adjust to the brightness in the room.

"Oh, I'm sorry. One second," the same voice said.

Moments later, the room was dimmer, and I could finally focus. I looked around and realized I was in a hospital room.

A woman in scrubs came into my line of sight, wearing scrubs and a soft smile that matched the kind voice I had heard a minute ago.

"Hi, Jessica. I'm Nurse Sophie. I'm glad to see you awake. Several people outside will be glad about it, too."

"What happened?"

Her smile faltered briefly. "If you'll give me a moment, I'll get the doctor, and he'll explain everything to you."

"Wait!" I winced because the loud volume of my voice ricocheted in my already throbbing head.

"Ma'am?" she asked.

"Julian Tate. Please get him before you send the doctor in. He needs to hear what the doctor has to say, also," I said, more tears falling from my eyes as I rubbed my belly. As much as I was trying to stay positive, I was already thinking the worst.

Her smile faded again. "Uh, I'm not so sure that's a good idea. The doctor will want to be the first to see you since you're awake now. Also... Mr. Tate is very upset. We almost had to have him removed from the floor, and I don't think his disposition is good for your current state."

I sighed. "I don't care how he's acting. I need him in here, and I need to see him *before* the doctor comes in. Please, get him," I requested, hoping my voice sounded firm through the weakness.

"Yes, ma'am," she said and nodded before leaving the room.

I closed my eyes again and tried not to settle my mind on any particular topic until I was no longer alone. It wasn't long before the door opened again.

I opened my eyes as Julian walked inside. His red eyes were all over me, and his jaw tightened when they made it back to my face. With one glance, I sensed every emotion he felt—relief, anger, concern, and *fear*.

"Are you okay to be alone with him, Jessica?" Nurse Sophie asked. Never looking away from him, I nodded.

"Yes."

"Yes, ma'am. The doctor is with another patient but will be in shortly."

As soon as she walked out, I spoke up. "Julian, I'm so sor—"

He lifted a hand and shook his head. "How are you feeling?" he asked.

I inhaled and let it out shakily. "Terrible." I placed a hand on my tummy again. Looking him in the eyes, I softly asked, "I messed up. I lost our baby, didn't I?"

A tear fell from his eyes, and he closed them briefly. When he opened them again, all those emotions were still there. He shook his head. "Why did you leave?"

I continued to cry as I prepared to be as open and honest as I should have been hours ago.

"I've been feeling... insecure lately. I can't tell you when the thought entered my mind, but since it has, it's refused to go anywhere."

His face unchanging, he asked, "What thought?"

I took another deep breath. "The thought that we're only actually together because I got pregnant. Julian, I haven't been running from you because I didn't want to settle down.

"I stayed away because I thought I'd never be able to make you truly happy."

He frowned. "Why would you—"

"Let me finish, please," I requested. He bit his bottom lip and nodded.

"Before I met you, I had fibroid surgery. It was complicated and didn't go as smoothly as the doctors had hoped. When it was all said and done, they told me I'd never be able to have children.

"Julian... I've watched you be the best uncle to our godchildren. I see the look in your eye when David runs into your arms or when Two says something you know he got from you. I've always known you would want children someday, and..."

"And because you thought you couldn't have any, you figured I wouldn't want you?" he asked, still frowning.

I nodded. "When I *did* get pregnant, I was excited, but somewhere down the line, I started to overthink things. I had gone all that time feeling like not having a child was the reason I couldn't be with you, that I convinced myself that the baby was the only reason you were with me. Then, earlier tonight, I heard you on the phone with Joseph.

You told him you didn't know if we'd be together without the baby. That's when I left."

Julian dropped his head briefly before crossing the room. He kneeled beside my bed so that we were face to face.

"I've clearly done a piss poor job of lettin' you know just how much I fuckin' love you, so let me be clear. Jessica Brielle, you do it for me. You and that smart mouth have always been my version of a happy ending. Ain't a thing on this Earth I want more than I want you, and if I would have known all that you just told me, I would have put all those thoughts to rest a long time ago.

"Havin' a baby with you is one hell of a bonus, and I thank God for that blessin' every day, but not before I thank Him for you. You've always been my dream, pretty. You and you alone. Know that."

I could no longer see because of how much I was crying, and my head was in a significant amount of pain, but at that point, I didn't care. I lifted a hand to Julian's face, and he leaned closer and kissed me softly.

"When I was talkin' to J earlier, I was tellin' him how much I loved you and that I was startin' to second guess whether or not you loved me just as much. He straight up told me to stop actin' like a bitch and to come to you about it."

He kissed me again. "It might be corny, Jet, but I need to hear you tell me how you feelin', too, because you not the only one who's been walkin' 'round here on some insecure shit. I need to know what's connecting us other than my feelings for you and our baby."

I nodded and wiped my eyes again.

"When I met you, I knew I could love you. Your good looks and slick mouth intrigued me, then your sense of humor drew me in even more. The second time we saw each other at Davi's house, that's when I knew I loved you. It was the first time we made love, but you were so sweet to me, and it was completely different from how I envisioned you would be.

"I mean, you're a man who has every reason to be arrogant, but you treated me like I was the prize from day one. You took the time out of your life to learn me and spoiled me with your attention to the little things. From making them spell my middle name right on my Starbucks cup to keeping my favorite soap stocked at your home in Virginia, you just never missed.

"I love the way you love your family and how fiercely you protect the people you care about. You have such a big heart, and I'm extremely blessed that you've given me a place in it. Julian, I could talk for days about how much I love you, but I'm giving you too much of my good stuff. I gotta save something for my wedding vows, hell," I said, rolling my eyes before wiping them again.

He laughed and kissed my forehead.

"That'll do for now, pretty," he said with a smirk.

"I have to find a new photographer," I said, frowning. My team had been together for so long, but it was still kind of hard to accept that Val was no longer a part of it. I didn't trust easily, so there was no telling how long it would take for me to find someone new.

Julian kissed his teeth. "Man, forget that. I'm your got damn photographer."

I couldn't hold in my laugh, but when I released it, my head throbbed immediately. I grabbed it and winced. Julian frowned.

"Are you in pain?"

I nodded. "I don't think they've given me any medicine. Probably because of the baby. That's a good sign, right?"

He kissed my forehead again, then stood. "It is, but I just need you to relax and not even worry about that right now. You're alive, Jessica, and that's a blessing. Let's just focus on that until we learn more. I'm 'bout to find this doctor," he said, turning.

Just as he made it to the door, it swung open. Julian moved to the other side of my bed. He stood beside me and grabbed my hand as the doctor approached us.

"Good evening. I'm Doctor George, and I was the one who examined Ms. Westin when she came in. Ms. Westin, do you consent to me sharing your personal health information with Mr. Tate present?"

I nodded. "Yes."

Doctor George nodded. "You were injected with eight grams of sodium oxybate, a prescription-only sedative used to treat narcoleptics. The substance was poorly administered in your stomach area and had little effect on your faculties, but the neck injection is what caused you to lose consciousness initially."

Julian squeezed my hand as the doctor continued.

"It looks like you bumped your head against a hard surface, likely when you were unconscious, and the attacker tried to move you. The great news is you don't have a concussion, and the substance is just about out of your system.

"What about—" I cleared my throat. "What about our baby?" I asked.

He smiled, and that eased some of the tension I felt.

"Your baby girl is just fine," he said, and I screamed, then grabbed my head again. Julian rested his free hand on my head and began rubbing gently. He refrained from yelling out, but I saw the shock in his expression.

He smiled wide and glanced at the doctor before gazing at me.

"We're havin' a girl, Doc?"

The doctor cleared his throat. "I apologize. I assumed because you were thirty weeks along, you knew. But yes, you are having a girl. Again, I'm so sorry for spoiling that surprise."

"It's okay," I said, smiling. Julian and I had been holding off on opening the envelope that revealed our baby's gender. We had planned to make a video and post it on my social media, but it was all good. I was just ecstatic to know that my baby girl was okay, and judging by the look on Julian's face, he felt the same way.

"Your head will probably be sore for the rest of today and maybe tomorrow. I can give you some mild headache medicine if you'd like. Because of the baby, I wanted to wait until you were awake to administer anything," the doctor said.

"Will it affect the baby?" I asked.

"Not at all."

I nodded. "I'll take it then. Thanks."

"I'll be right back." When he left the room, I gazed at Julian.

"I told you it was a girl," I said, grinning.

He chuckled and kissed my cheek. "Yeah, you did." He kissed me again before hopping up suddenly. This man started hitting the Dougie like his life depended on it, and I had to work overtime not to laugh since my head was still hurting.

"Baby, stop. My head hurts," I said, trying to suppress my laugh.

He stopped immediately and came to my side again. "My bad, pretty, but I'm hype right now. I'm 'bout to be the best girl-dad. Just wait."

I closed my eyes and nodded. "I know you are." Seconds later, I felt his lips on mine, and then he whispered, "I love you, girl."

***

"What do you want for dinner?" I asked, closing the book I was reading.

I looked at Julian and frowned. I was excited to start my new book and had been lying on the sofa wrapped up in it most of the day. I hadn't seen much of him until an hour ago when he silently lay on the sofa and rested his head on my tummy. I thought he was reading, too, but now that I was looking at him, I realized his focus wasn't even on his book.

He seemed to be staring into space, and the book rested lazily in one of his hands. It was almost closed.

"Baby," I said, touching the top of his head.

"Wassup?" he asked. His voice was monotone, and he didn't bother looking up.

"Look at me," I requested softly. Once he did, my frown deepened. His eyes were red-rimmed but dry, like he had been on the verge of crying, but the tears never came. Something wasn't right in his world, and I had been too caught up in my book to notice.

"What's wrong?" I asked.

He shook his head before opening his mouth, but I beat him to speaking up.

"Uh-uh. Don't say nothing because that's clearly not true. Baby, what's wrong with you?"

He closed his eyes briefly before raising his head. He then lifted my shirt above my belly and kissed it several times before looking at me again.

"Tomorrow is the anniversary of my cousin's death," he said, then rested his forehead on my stomach.

We sat in silence for a moment. I wondered if he was talking about his aunt Tracee's daughter. I remembered one of his cousins saying something about her daughter dying and it being Julian's fault. His reaction to seeing her that day and his response to his cousins let me know that there was a lot to that story, but I never asked him about it.

His strained expression and the tone of his voice told me he was carrying more than just grief surrounding his cousin's death, so I needed to know more so I could determine how to best support my man.

Taking a chance, I began rubbing his head as I asked, "Your aunt Tracee's daughter?"

He looked up at me again with furrowed brows, so I explained.

"I remember your cousins mentioning her daughter."

His jaws tensed, but he nodded.

"Yeah, her name was Kaia. We were the same age and close all our lives. I don't have one significant childhood memory that doesn't include Ky. We did everything together." He chuckled, then shifted his gaze to the blank television screen before continuing.

"The only school we applied to was Chaney State. We had been talkin' 'bout goin' there for years and were hype to move away from home when the time finally came.

"Our freshman year started off cool, but Ky was never that social. She talked to me, but she was an introvert at heart and had a hard time lettin' folks in. I uh—" Julian paused and sat up. I did the same, with my eyes glued to him. He cleared his throat, then ran a hand over his face. Inching closer to him, I circled my arms around his body. He immediately lifted an arm and threw it across my shoulders, and I rested my head on his side.

"You don't have to talk about it right now if you're not comfortable, Julian," I said, sensing his internal struggle.

"Nah, it's all good. I'ma get through it. I uh-I was the complete opposite. I never had a hard time connecting with others, and I was intent on enjoyin' college to the fullest. We kinda drifted apart that year."

He paused again, and I began rubbing his back. After a few moments of silence, he kept talking.

"We would meet up for lunch or something at least once a week, but other than that, I was always on the go. The rest of our freshman year went that way, and when I pledged our sophomore year, I only got busier. She hung herself in her apartment that year. I was the one who found her."

Tears began rolling down his face, and I bit down on my lip, trying my best to hold my own back.

"In her suicide note, she wrote about somethin' that happened to her while I was on line for my fraternity. She had apparently been tryna branch out and find her own path at school, and she made a friend. The girl invited her to a warehouse party, and they drank that night. They drank a lot, and to make a long story short, that friend set Ky up to be sexually abused by some niggas at the party."

Julian dropped his head and held his face in his hands as he began to sob. I could no longer hold my tears back at that point. The sadness in his cry had my heart breaking. I couldn't think of anything to say, but I knew no words would make it better anyway, so I just held him.

He swiped both hands down his face and shook his head.

"She never told anybody. She didn't tell *me*." His voice cracked as he spoke. "And I was too caught up in my own stuff to realize she was goin' through somethin' major. In the note, she tried to assure me it wasn't my fault. She said she knew I'd try to retaliate if I knew what happened, and she didn't want me to throw my future away for her. She asked me not to blame myself, but it's all I've been doin' since the day I found her. I know my family blames me too."

Julian leaned forward and rested his elbows on his knees as he continued to cry silently. I lowered myself to the floor and knelt before him. Taking his hands in mine, I asked him to look at me.

It took him a minute, but he eventually gave me his eyes, which were completely red.

"Baby, listen to me. I know it's a lot easier said than done—and I am *so* very sorry for your loss. You can't keep carrying the guilt or the blame for this tragedy. Your cousin—may God rest her soul—didn't want you blaming yourself because she didn't blame you.

"The way she chose to deal with her hurt is heartbreaking, and I can't imagine how painful it was for you to find her that way. But... the choice she made was hers alone. The people who matter know that, baby. I saw how her mother looked at you at your mom's birthday party. She loves you, and she misses you. I heard your mother tell you that everyone there loves you. *Believe her.*"

I lifted my body so that our faces were inches apart and continued.

"Your cousin loved you too, and that love is the reason she didn't tell you about what happened to her. It's not that you were too caught up in your own life, baby. It's that she was actively trying to protect you and your future. Focus on Kaia's love for you so that you can begin to accept that you are *not* to blame for this. I can't tell you how to grieve, but I am asking you to let me help you through it. Tell me what you need, and I got you. I love you."

I kissed his lips, and he instantly pulled me into his arms and set me on his lap, making the nightdress I wore raise over my hips. Grabbing his face, I wiped his tears as he dipped his tongue in and out of my mouth.

His hand moved under us, and I felt his hardness rest against my thigh. My man needed an escape, and I was going to provide him with just that. Silently, I lifted myself slightly and moved my panties to the side before lowering myself on him.

Because my belly was bigger, he had to move us on the sofa so that he could lie back. It was one of the only positions we could manage lately, but I had zero complaints about that. Caressing his chest, I rode his body just the way he liked, circling my hips as I rose and fell on his member.

His hands roamed my body before resting on my breasts as I worked to relieve him of some of the pain and tension he was feeling.

"I love you, girl," he said, his voice low.

I moaned. "Mmm, I know. I love you too, baby."

Wanting to feel him deeper, I lifted even more and moved to a squatting position so that my feet were planted on the sofa. I put my hands on my knees and bounced up and down, my eyes never leaving him.

As we moved together, I witnessed his worries fade, allowing him to fully immerse himself in this moment with me. I knew his euphoric state wouldn't last, but I was determined to make the most of it.

It wasn't long before my body began to tremble with pure pleasure. I rode my way through my orgasm and put all my focus on catering to my man. I leaned in and claimed his lips again as I guided him to ecstasy. His dick began to pulsate inside me, and I gave him a few more hard thrusts, beckoning his climax forward. In seconds, I felt him release as he peppered kisses across my collarbone.

Breathing heavily, I eventually lifted my body so that his softening member slipped out of me. I then climbed to the other side of the sofa and rested my back against its arm before reaching out to Julian.

"Come here," I said, and he immediately did as I asked.

Resting his head against my breasts, he kissed both of them before pressing his lips against mine briefly.

"My family holds a cookout in Kaia's honor every year. When I was in Virginia, it was easier to act like work got in the way of making it to the function, but I'm only an hour away now. I have no excuse, and my momma already called and said I better be there."

I kissed his forehead, and he looked up at me.

"Can you come wit' me?"

I kissed my teeth then smiled. "Boy, bye. That's a given. You're done carrying this alone, Julian. I love you, I'm here, and I got you. Forever."

He stared at me for the longest time until he finally kissed me again.

"Forever."

Just Try It

♥

Tate

"You good, baby?" Jess asked.

I glanced at her and grinned.

"I'm good, pretty." I was surprised at how true that statement was. We had been at my cousin's cookout for the last hour, and everything was smooth. I had been working hard to take my baby's advice and focus on the love Kaia had for me, and after walking around and looking at the different pictures of her that had been blown up and displayed throughout the yard, it got easier.

Many pictures had me in them because we had always been joined at the hip. I laughed as I reminisced on the good times and told Jess some funny stories from our childhood. For the first time in a minute, I allowed myself to enjoy time with my family instead of focusing on what they might think about me. It was good music, food, and vibes, and I was glad I came.

I turned and noticed Aunt Tracee sitting on a bench, laughing with my mother. She and I hugged when I first got here, but we hadn't talked much. Whenever I looked at her that day, I thought about what Jess had said the night before.

She loves you, and she misses you.

If I was honest, I missed her too. She had always been my favorite auntie, and I spent almost as much time at her house as I did my own as a kid. I loved her to death but found it hard to face her after Kaia died.

I felt like I had let her down because I failed to protect her daughter. We were all each other had in Chaney, and it was my job to make sure Kaia was good while we were away from home. None of that was an excuse for how I had been treating Auntie Tracee, though. She didn't deserve my distance, and it was past time for me to get over my issues and be there for her.

"I'ma go holla at my momma and them," I said to Jess. She looked around until her eyes found my mother. Her eyes widened when she realized who she was sitting with, but she smiled at me and nodded.

"I'm here if you need me," she said.

I kissed her cheek and stood. "I know."

I headed across the yard. My aunt was the first to notice me as I approached, and she smiled.

"Hi, baby," she said.

I kissed her cheek, then my mother's, before I sat between them on the bench. My mother kissed her teeth. "Boy, you didn't have to sit your big behind right here," she said and rolled her eyes before scooting over a little.

I chuckled. "My bad, Ma. But, um... can I talk to Auntie for a minute? Alone?"

My mother's eyebrows shot up, but she smiled. "Of course you can, baby. I need to go talk to my daughter-in-love about this baby shower, anyway," she said and stood. I watched as she walked over to Jess and observed them interact for a minute before I turned to my aunt.

"Auntie, I'm sorry," I said, getting straight to it.

She sighed and placed a hand on mine.

"Baby, you have nothin' to be sorry about."

I shook my head. "But I do, though. Kaia was my responsibility while we were away at school, and I dropped the ball." My chest tightened as I spoke. "I wasn't there for her like I should have been, and I gotta own that."

My auntie sat up and squared her shoulders. With a stern expression, she said, "You will *not* own that. You and your cousin loved each other, but you can't live, think, or act for someone else. Ky's choices were her own, Lee. Stop blaming yourself because I don't."

I wiped a lone tear from my eye and said, "I'on know if I can do that, Auntie."

"You can. You have to try, baby. I miss my baby—Lord knows I do," she said, and her eyes watered. "But I can't change what happened, just like I couldn't prevent what happened… just like *you* couldn't have prevented it. We didn't know about what happened to Ky at that party 'cause she didn't want us to know, baby, not because you weren't there for her.

"She hid her pain well because she thought that's what she needed to do to protect us. As much as I wish she would have said somethin', I know I can't make someone open up. Neither can you."

I dropped my head, and she placed a hand under my chin and lifted it. "My daughter's death is not on you, baby. It never has been, and I should have made that clear to you a long time ago."

"You don't blame me?" I asked, my voice cracking. She said she didn't, but I was struggling to accept that. I wanted—*needed*—to hear her say it again.

"I don't blame you because you *are not* to blame for this."

She removed her hand from my chin and wrapped it around me. I hugged her back, and we stayed like that for a minute as tears spilled from my eyes.

I wasn't to blame for this.

I cleared my throat, and we released each other as Floyd, Marcus, and Isaac were passing us. Floyd was a couple of years older than me, while the other two were one year younger. None of them had ever been outside of our hometown. Growing up, we were all pretty tight, but that changed once I went to college.

Floyd swore I thought I was better than them, so he started moving differently. Isaac and Marcus always followed their big brother's lead, so they joined his hate train, and I was too prideful to be the bigger person. Once Kaia died, they used that as another reason to hate me. Out of all our family members, those three never let me forget that I was to blame for my cousin's death. Floyd and I had come to blows a few times, but I knew this wasn't the place, so I kept my distance.

"That's another thing we gon' get right today. Flo, y'all come here."

Floyd turned his head toward us. He grilled me, then smiled at my aunt. As expected, his little brothers followed suit.

"Wassup, Auntie?" he asked.

"What's up is I'm tired of you treatin' Lee like this because he decided to do somethin' different with his life than you did. Y'all are cousins—*blood relatives*—and you walk around here like enemies. Life is too short to hold stupid grudges, so we're puttin' an end to this today. Floyd, tell Lee what your problem with him is, and be honest."

Floyd remained silent. He eyed me silently, and I kept mine on him. After a minute, he kissed his teeth.

"You switched up, bruh. You went to that fancy-ass school and forgot who your people were," he finally said.

LET IT HAPPEN

I chuckled. "I ain't ever forget who my people were, Flo. Be for real, nie. You started movin' different wit' me the minute I got the acceptance letter to Chaney. The first time we came to blows was the day before I went to college, and it was because *you* kept talkin' 'bout how I was abandonin' the hood. I hadn't even left yet, and you were already on that."

He laughed. "Aight, I'll own that, but look what happened. You *did* ditch the hood. Before Auntie's birthday party, when was the last time we saw you, Lee?"

I inhaled deeply before releasing it. My eyes scanned the yard until they found my woman. She was already looking at me with concern written all over her face. Her shoulders were squared, and she was bouncing her leg like it was killing her to sit still. I knew she was ready to jump bad on my behalf at any given moment, and seein' her little feisty ass in go-mode, calmed me down a little.

I looked at Floyd again. I stood and took a step toward him. He squared up immediately, but I wasn't about to take it there with him.

"Aye, you right about that; I have been MIA. After everything with Kaia happened, I blamed myself. Shid, I'm still workin' through that part. You blamed me, too, and you never let me forget that when I was comin' home, so eventually, I found it easier not to. That wasn't the right way to handle it, and I apologize for stayin' away, but it ain't because I forgot about y'all. It's because I couldn't face y'all. It hurt too much, and I ain't know how to deal wit' it."

He glared at me silently. His brothers had their eyes on him, no doubt, waiting to see how he would respond to what I said. Finally, he relaxed his stance and sighed.

Swiping a hand across his head, he said, "Aye, bruh. That ain't on you. Ky's death rocked all of us. You dealt wit' it by keepin' your distance, and I dealt wit' it by blamin' you. That wasn't cool, and that's my bad," he said, extending a hand toward me.

I knew that was his version of an apology, and I accepted that because Auntie Tracee was right—life was too short.

Grasping his hand, I pulled him into a brotherly hug, then did the same with Marcus and Isaac.

"We good, Lee," Floyd said as my mother and Jess approached us. I grabbed her hand immediately and pulled her toward me. Once her back was pressed against my chest, I kissed her cheek.

"Pretty, these are my cousins, Floyd, Marcus, and Isaac." I pointed at each of them as I introduced them. "This is my woman, Jessica."

Floyd grinned. "Last time we saw each other, she was ready to throw hands 'cause I was talkin' shit about you, Lee. You got a real one, fasho. Nice to officially meet you, Miss Jessica. Is it safe for me to shake your hand?" he asked, and everyone laughed.

I couldn't see Jessica's face, but I was sure she wore a smirk.

"As long as y'all are bein' nice to him, we're all good," she said, lifting a hand and placing it on my arm.

Floyd laughed. "We good, then."

I released Jess, and she hugged my cousins. I turned to give my aunt another hug.

"Thank you, Auntie. I love you, and I promise you gon' be seein' more of me from now on."

She smiled. "I better. I need to be number one on the babysitting list when my great-niece gets here."

Looping her arm around mine, Jess smiled and said, "I'm holdin' you to that, Auntie. Prepare to be sick of me."

Aunt Tracee laughed and stood before pulling Jessica into a hug. I grinned as I watched my girl interact with my family. She fit in like the missing puzzle piece, and that had me plotting a proposal. Floyd was right about the fact that I had a real one, and it was past time to make her a Tate.

***

"Baby, come here!"

I looked toward the bathroom from my spot on the bed and sighed. As soon as we got home from the cookout, Jess locked herself in the bathroom. I wanted nothing more than a shower and to crash, but she had been taking forever to wash her behind. The only reason I wasn't kicking the door down was because I was trying to be understanding of the mood swings my baby had her going through. There was no telling why she wasn't letting me in there.

I was contemplating going to a guest room to shower when she called me. I stood and headed to the bathroom. When I opened the door, she was standing beside the bathtub, wearing nothing but a smile. The tub was filled with water, bubbles, and rose petals, and lit candles surrounded it.

"What's this?" I asked, giving her a thorough once-over.

"A bath. Come on," she said, extending a hand toward me. I accepted it and moved closer to her. With her eyes locked on mine, she buried her hands under my shirt and placed them on my chest. I chuckled when she bit her lip and trailed her hands up my body slowly, bringing my shirt up with them.

I helped her out and lifted my arms slightly to completely remove my shirt. I tossed it to the side, and she made quick work of removing my pants and boxers. Once she had my hand in hers again, she led me to the tub and gestured for me to get in.

I chuckled. "I'on take baths, pretty."

"You are today. We can shower after," she said, rolling her eyes. I stared at her, silently smirking, and she waved her hands toward the tub again with a huff.

I kissed my teeth. "Crybaby ass."

Knowing she would have a fit if I didn't, I stepped into the warm water and lowered myself to a sitting position in the large tub. Letting out a heavy sigh, I closed my eyes and tilted my head back until it met with the wall. I couldn't lie; it felt nice.

Without looking at her, I said, "You better be gettin' in here wit' me, Jessica Brielle."

She laughed. "I guess I will since you're beggin'."

Seconds later, I felt her soft body pressed against mine. I bent one knee to give her more room to adjust herself between my legs. My hands found her belly instantly, and she sighed as she rested her head against my chest.

"Why you makin' me take a bath?" I asked, massaging her stomach gently.

She moaned. "Because today was a lot, and I wanted you to have a moment to relax. Tell me this water isn't doin' that for you."

I opened my eyes and glanced at her. She was already looking up at me, smirking.

"It's aight," was all I said.

"Yeah, I bet."

We fell into a comfortable silence, and I closed my eyes again. As I enjoyed the feel of the water and her smooth body, I relaxed, and memories of the day's events began to play in my mind's eye.

It had been a long day, but the outcome was for sure worth it. Finally, talking to my aunt about Kaia lifted a major weight off me, and I was breathing a little easier because of it. Even reconciling with Floyd removed some burdens I didn't even realize I was carrying. Overall, it was a good day, and I wouldn't have gotten through it without the woman in my arms.

"Thank you, Jet."

She shifted in my arms. "For what?"

"For bein' you. For bein' mine." I opened my eyes and lifted my head enough to kiss the top of hers.

"I've wanted you for a long time, but I swear, if I knew life could be this good, I woulda knocked you up a long time ago.

"It's crazy how perfect you are for me. You go as hard as my momma does for me, and that's really sayin' somethin'." I chuckled. "Wit' you, I feel fuckin' safe… safe to *let you* have my back. Safe to tell you when I ain't feelin' as strong as I'd like to. I can just *be* whoever and however I am at any given moment with you. I ain't ever had that before, and the fact that I have it with you ain't somethin' I take lightly. I'm so in love wit' you, pretty, and I—"

My eyes were still closed when she lifted her body off mine. I was about to go off about her leaving my arms while I was sharing my feelings and shit, but then I felt her small hands grab my dick.

I opened my eyes just in time to catch a glimpse of her fine ass sinking back into my lap as her lower lips swallowed me.

"*Fuck,* Jet. You just gon' cut me off like that?" I gripped her waist loosely, not wanting to guide her movements. Because my baby had grown so big inside her, Jess had become a pro at reverse cowgirl in the last few weeks. I wanted her to do her thing.

"Sorry," she said through a moan.

Leaning back, she placed her hands on my thighs, and she angled her pelvis just right before lifting herself slowly. I arched my torso beneath her so that when she slid back down, she felt it deep.

"Ahh!"

Her scream was passion-filled and sexy. I wanted to hear it again, so I repeated that movement, and my baby didn't disappoint.

Her head fell back, and her body arched as she moved above me. Jess's wetness was already abundant, but her natural juices, coupled with the bathwater that surrounded us, were a *problem*. It heightened every feeling for me, and I was in straight heaven.

She continued to roll her hips, and I began kissing her spine, encouraging her to speed up. When she did, I matched her movements, and before long, we had been bucking against each other in a heated frenzy. Our session was getting so hectic that water spilled out of the tub.

"I'm right there, Ali!" That was my cue to take her there, so I held her hips in place and pounded into her with precision and force. That took us both over the edge because, at the exact same time, we were calling each other's names loudly. I exploded in her while she pulsed around me uncontrollably.

We were doing this bath situation at least once a week from that point forward.

Jess lifted her body again, but this time, when she lowered it, I was no longer inside her. She turned to the side so that we were semi-facing each other and loosely wrapped her arms around my neck.

"I don't take your presence in my life for granted either, Ali. It's like God wrapped so many of the answers to my prayers into one amazing man I'm blessed to call mine. I love you, baby."

She pressed her lips against mine, initiating a deep, meaningful kiss. When she pulled away, I groaned.

"Damn, girl. Let's shower and get in the bed before you have me sliding up in you again."

Legendary Memories

♥

Jess

"Oh my God, Vi. Please tell me you're recording this," I said through tears.

I took deep breaths, trying to compose myself, but as soon as I focused on the guys again, I burst into another fit of laughter.

"Girl, I'm getting it all, trust me," Davi said through a giggle.

Davi, my mother, and Julian's mother worked together to throw the best baby shower I had ever attended. We were now watching all the men in the room struggle to get a blown-up balloon out of their shirts without using their hands.

Before the game started, Julian and Air talked the most trash about how quickly they would win, but they seemed to struggle the most, and it was hilarious. Or maybe it was the fact that they were trying the hardest that was so funny.

Air was in the middle of the floor, rolling his hips like he was hula-hooping, while Julian was a few feet away from him, wiggling like a worm. They had been at it for about five minutes, and while all the other men were beginning to give up and take their seats, those two were only going harder.

"You gotta switch your moves up, Ali. Hit 'em with the Dougie!" I said, and I almost fell out of my seat when he actually took my advice. To my surprise, the balloon really started to inch lower in his shirt as he moved his torso from left to right.

"Aye, there you go. Get it, baby!" I said, hyping my man up.

Crissy, who was holding her baby in her seat, handed Amina to her Aunt Laura before she stood and walked over to her husband.

"Get it together, Aaron. We're 'bout to lose! Do some jumping jacks or somethin'!" she said, laughing.

At that point, they were the only two standing, and while Air started hopping up and down as his wife suggested, Julian surprised everyone when he ran toward the stage I was sitting on. He gripped the end of the stage with both hands and leaned his upper body forward, putting him in kind of a vertical push-up position.

"Ali, what the..." My voice trailed off as I watched this man low-key hump the stage with his stomach. The balloon moved down even more, and the room erupted in loud laughter.

I heard Air kiss his teeth. "He cheatin', man," he said before joining Julian on the stage. The new method was working for both of them, but because Julian had a head start, his balloon fell out first.

Wiping my tears, I jumped out of my seat and clapped with everyone else. Julian hopped up on the stage and wrapped me in his arms. He kissed me and said, "Told you I was gon' win, pretty."

He then turned to Davi, who stood near us on stage and was still recording with her phone.

"What I win, Sunshine?"

She laughed. "You won a baby. She'll be here in a few weeks. Congratulations!"

He chuckled and shook his head. "I'll take it."

"Alright, y'all. Let's open some gifts. Babe, can you help me get them?" Vi asked, looking out into the crowd at Joseph, who hopped up immediately.

Julian sat beside me as they brought gift after gift to us. Our family and friends had outdone themselves, and I was sure we wouldn't need to buy anything for our baby girl for at least a year. She was spoiled rotten already.

After we opened the last gift, which was the exact car seat I wanted, Julian and I stood. He helped me down from the stage, and we made our rounds throughout the room, hugging everyone and thanking them for their love and support.

The day had been perfect, making me even more excited to meet my little one.

Julian kissed my cheek.

"I'm 'bout to go make us some to-go plates before everybody takes all the good stuff," he said in my ear. I laughed and nodded.

"Yeah, make a whole separate plate full of them rolls," I requested.

Ace's restaurant, *Legendary*, catered for our shower. While their chef made all the traditional baby shower foods like pasta salad, meatballs, and wings, he also prepared some *Legendary* favorites, like their crab-stuffed salmon, ribeye steak, and mac and cheese. I loved all of it, and they had the best bread on the planet, so I was glad Julian was beating the crowd to what was left.

I felt arms around my shoulders, and when I looked up, I realized it was my father.

"Hey, Daddy," I said, smiling.

"Hey, baby girl. You enjoyed today?"

I nodded. "I did."

He glanced at me. "You look happy."

My smile widened. "I am."

He kissed my cheek and nodded. "Then I'm good. I see ya boy is over there tryna steal all the food. Let me go make my plate before I have to fight his ass," my father said with a chuckle.

I shook my head as he walked away. Julian and my father had a great relationship, and I was grateful they connected as well as they did. My dad never thought anybody was good enough for me, but Julian made it a point to show him how much he loved me.

I was surprised my father hadn't made any slick comments about him marrying me because I knew how much he hated the idea of my shacking up. Something about Julian had him not pressing the issue, and I was just glad he approved of my guy.

"That ain't right, Sunshine. How you gon' do us like that?"

I turned my attention to Joseph, whose face was tight, while Davi stood in front of him with her arms folded and an indifferent expression.

"It *is* right, babe. We did the planning and setup, so y'all are going to clean up. We want to take Jess to the spa anyway, so that gives y'all a few uninterrupted hours to get everything done," Vi said, lifting her toes and kissing his cheek.

I laughed. I had no idea we were ditching the men for a spa date, but I wasn't against it. Just being up and moving around all day exhausted me, so the last thing I wanted to do was stay while the venue got cleaned up. Falling asleep while getting a facial or massage sounded a lot more appealing.

Vi left Joseph standing there and came over to me.

"Let's get out of here before all these men start complaining about having to clean up. Steph is going to take all of us to the spa," she said.

I sighed. "Let me at least tell Julian I'm leaving, Vi."

She shook her head. "Nope. His best friend can tell him because I had just relayed the message. Let's go, sis."

Shaking my head, I followed her and the rest of the women out of the building. I felt kind of bad about dumping the work on them, but I'd make it up to my man later.

Do it Now... I Did

♥

Tate

"How y'all let us get caught with the mess?" Air asked, throwing another plate in a trash bag.

Ace kissed his teeth. "What you mean *let* us? Apparently, we married some sneaky women 'cause I ain't even know they left."

I laughed and stacked another chair. "Speak for y'all selves. My woman ain't sneaky. She would have stayed with me if y'all's didn't force her outta here."

"Yeah, aight. Jess couldn't wait to get a break from you," J said, shaking his head. "How you feelin', though? It's 'bout that time."

I paused as I thought about it.

"I'm ready to meet my daughter, man... I just wish I woulda been a lil more proactive wit' marryin' her momma."

"What you mean?" Ace asked.

I sighed and sat in the chair I was about to stack. Air, Ace, and J pulled chairs up and sat around me, waiting for me to elaborate.

"I just feel like Jet and I wasted a lot of time. Our baby girl will be here in less than six weeks, and we goin' into parenthood as fuckin' boyfriend and girlfriend. Nothin' about that sits right wit' me."

"Then change it," Ace said with a shrug.

I kissed my teeth. "I'm gon' propose, of course. I already got somethin' planned for that, but ain't no way we can plan a weddin' in a month. Not one that Jet would want anyway."

"You can marry Jess *today* if you want to. I married Demi the day I found out she was pregnant. I told her to meet me at the courthouse, and we got it done."

Air laughed and said, "You damn shole did. Pressed ass."

Ace waved him off. "Whateva. Anyway, I still gave her the wedding she wanted after our twins were born, but we weren't having different last names on my babies' birth certificates. Everybody was gon' be a Legend. Fuck what you heard," he said with a chuckle.

Ace glanced at me with a serious expression. "So do it now... I did."

I remained quiet but nodded as they stood and continued cleaning the place. I stood, too, but Ace's advice still rang in my ears.

Marry her now.

I chuckled as I pulled out my phone to call Jessica's father. I was gon' do just that.

Da Coat House

♥

Jess

"I can't believe Demi didn't tell us she was dancing tonight! I wonder if Ace and them are here," I said loudly, leaning into Julian.

The night had finally come for the Unique concert. I asked my doctor if going to a concert during this stage of my pregnancy was safe, and she assured me the baby would be fine. I was happy to hear that because I had been wanting to experience Unique in concert for years.

He was on stage performing a new song he recently released with the singer Kelsie Lee. I assumed he brought her out that night because they were both from Atlanta, and she was killing it.

I knew Demi was one of Kelsie's main backup dancers, but she said nothing about tonight's performance. I was excited to cheer my girl on while she did her thing.

When the song finished, I hopped up and cheered loudly, hoping Demi could hear me. Ace had gotten us seats on the floor right in front of the large stage. They were the best seats in the house, and I knew they cost him an arm and a leg. This had been the best concert experience I'd ever had, hands down.

"Alright, y'all," Kelsie Lee said as the music faded out. "I got one more song I wanna sing. Is that alright, Atlanta?"

"Girl, you know that's alright wit' us!" I yelled. I loved Kelsie's music too.

Julian laughed and shook his head. He kissed my cheek and said, "You a mess, pretty."

"This is a throwback Kelsie Lee single, but my producer asked me to do this one for two people who mean a lot to him. Y'all know how I feel about Si, so I told Unique he had to help me make this happen."

That piqued my interest because Si, or Josiah, just so happened to be Joseph's father. We all lived in New York together at one point and had grown close during that time. He and Joseph's mother, JoAnna, attended our baby shower two days earlier, but I assumed they returned to New York after. If he was making song requests, that must have meant he was at the concert.

Before I could ask Julian whether he knew if they were in attendance, Kelsie said something that made me freeze.

"Tate, Jessica... this one is for you. Can you come up on stage and help me sing it?" The live band began playing softly in the background.

"Wait, *what*?" I turned to Julian, fully expecting him to be as confused and surprised as I was, but he was relaxed, with a hand stretched toward me.

"Come on, Jet. She needs our help."

"Julian!" I said, not moving. How was this even happening right now?

He smirked and mocked me. "Jessica! Bring ya butt on, nie."

Slowly, I placed my hand in his and allowed him to lead me to the stage. The security guard moved out of our way as we drew nearer, and once we were at the steps, I took a deep breath. There were more of them than I thought, and I knew I'd be tired once we made it to the top.

Reading my mind, Julian chuckled. "You can do it, baby. I promise it'll be worth it once we make it up there."

"When did you set this up? I can't believe I'm going on stage with my favorite rapper in the whole wide world."

He kissed my cheek before leading me up the steps.

"Don't worry 'bout when I set it up. Just know if he don't keep his eyes and hands to himself, he's gon' get slapped. He needs to focus on rappin'."

I laughed as I took the last step, and I squinted and immediately shielded my eyes with my hands. There were tens of thousands of people in the crowd, but now that I was on stage, I couldn't see anything but lights.

After a few seconds, my eyes adjusted to the brightness, and I was able to focus them on Kelsie Lee and Unique, who were standing beside each other on stage. I glanced behind them and noticed the dancers were still there. Catching Demi's eye, I blew her a kiss, and she winked at me, wearing a huge smile.

Kelsie smiled and waved us over. Once we reached them, she said,

"Girl, first of all, how did I not know *you* were the Jess Si was talkin' about? I love all of your work, boo. You're literally killin' the fashion game!" She turned toward the crowd before saying, "Make some noise if you've seen this beauty on your TV screens. Doesn't Jess look beautiful tonight, y'all?"

The crowd cheered, and I smiled, accepting the hug she offered me. I hugged Unique next, but it was short-lived because Julian quickly pulled me back and wrapped his arms around me from behind.

"How are you feelin' tonight, Jess?" she asked, holding the microphone toward me.

"I feel great. Oh my God, I love y'all so much!" I said, not caring about how badly I was fangirling at that moment. This was a legitimate once-in-a-lifetime experience.

"Well, anyone Si loves is a friend of mine, and he told me y'all are family, so we're locked in. Now Jess, I gotta admit, I already met your boo, and he told me you know all the words to this song I'm about to sing. I can't wait to see if he's right. You ready?"

I tilted my head back to look at Julian, and he silently kissed my forehead.

Focusing on Kelsie again, I nodded and smiled. "I hope I am."

She smiled briefly before it faded, and she closed her eyes. The music stopped completely, and she took a breath before singing the first line of the song a capella.

"Underneath the stars, just you and I."

My eyes widened, and I smiled as I turned toward Julian again.

This was my *song*, and he knew it. I bumped it in the shower so much that I was sure he knew all the words, too.

"Sang, girl," he said, laughing.

I turned around, and with my back pressed against him, I did just that.

"Through the highs and the lows, we'll weather the storm. In your arms, I've found my forever home."

I sang like my life depended on it, getting lost in the smooth sound of the live band and Kelsie's beautiful voice.

"Make me your forever. Say, baby, will you marry me."

I stopped singing because I could have sworn Kelsie and I just sang different lyrics. If I wasn't mistaken, she had just sung '*Jessica,* will you marry me,' and I was mad I missed it with my big mouth.

I turned to ask Julian if he had caught the shout-out, but I had to lower my gaze to find him.

"Ali, what the..."

I covered my mouth with my hands as the crowd's screams became deafening. This had to be a dream. There was no way Julian was kneeling before me with nothing but love in his eyes and the most beautiful ring I had ever seen in his hands. No way.

I wasn't sure when Kelsie moved, but she was now beside Julian, handing him the microphone. I patted my eyes when I realized there was a man with a camera recording my every move.

How long had he been there?

Julian, clearing his throat loudly in the microphone, brought my attention back to him.

"I'on know why you lookin' all surprised, pretty. You had to know this was comin'. I love you more than a lil bit, and I need you bad. This boyfriend-girlfriend shit is childish, and I'm done wit' it. I need you to be my wife, and I wanna make it happen ASAP, so gon' and say yes so I can make our appointment at da coat house."

Country ass.

Kelsie laughed, and I rolled my eyes and gazed at my man. I wouldn't have expected him to deliver his proposal any other way. As crazy as he was, I was right there with him, and it was perfect.

Still laughing, Kelsie got Unique's microphone from him and started chanting, "Say yes, say yes, say yes!"

She turned to the crowd, and before long, the entire stadium was saying the words. I knew my answer before he even asked the question, and so did he, but to appease the spectators, I nodded. Kelsie extended the microphone toward me, and I leaned into it and said, "Yes."

She started jumping up and down, clapping, while Julian slid the ring on my finger.

"Congrats, black people. Y'all make a beautiful couple, for real," Unique said into the microphone.

"'Preciate that," Julian said, his eyes still on me. Then, without warning, he gripped my chin and kissed me like we were the only two in the room. Eventually, he pulled away and hugged me.

"I love you, pretty," he said in my ear. A few tears fell from my eyes when I responded.

"I love you too."

***

Apparently, Julian wasn't playing about marrying me quickly.

After enjoying the rest of the concert, we went backstage with our VIP passes, and I was surprised to find our family and friends there, ready to congratulate us. We took pictures, then went to *Ace on Air* and turned up in a private room to celebrate our engagement.

Even though I wasn't able to drink, I still danced and partied as if I wasn't more than eight months pregnant. I was exhausted once we got home, and the adrenaline from the night's events wore off. Now, it was way too early in the morning, and this man was calling my name like the house was on fire. I placed a pillow over my head to muffle his voice, but it was quickly snatched away.

"Jessica Brielle. Get up, nie. We got stuff to do."

I finally opened my eyes and immediately rolled them. Of course, he was fully dressed, looking like a whole meal in a tailored suit. I rarely got to see him dressed up like that, but I always loved when he was.

"Julian," I said slowly. "Do you know what time it is?"

He chuckled and folded his arms as he stood over me. "It's seven fifteen, and our appointment is at nine fifteen. Davi is out there ready to do your makeup situation, so it's time for you to get up."

I groaned. Vi was here too?

How were they all able to function after the night we had? How was it that my sober behind was the only one suffering?

'Cause you're too pregnant to be twerking all night, that's why.

"It's Monday, Julian. When did you have time to make an appointment at the courthouse? You just proposed last night."

He grinned smugly, prompting me to cut my eyes at him.

"Girl, I made this appointment the day after our baby shower. What, you thought I was waitin' on your answer to make moves? You know betta than that."

I rolled my eyes. Of course he already knew I was saying yes.

Letting out a huff, I slowly sat up.

"You look good," I said to Julian, giving him a more thorough once-over. Had he had time to go to his barber that morning? Everything about him was crisp; I could sit in this spot and admire him for the rest of the day.

Julian smirked. "That's my line, pretty."

I laughed and shrugged. "You do. I'm not stoppin' you from sayin' it back, though."

He shook his head. "I can't say it right now."

I frowned. "Why not?"

"'Cause you lookin' a lil crazy right now, baby. Go let Sunshine do ya hair, then I can tell you how good you look."

Laughing, I kissed my teeth. "Kiss my butt, Julian."

I swung my feet over the side of the bed and placed one hand on my belly to steady myself as I stood.

He helped me up and replied, "You know I have no problem doin' that, Jet. I'on think you want Davi and J to hear you screamin' up in here, though, so don't tempt me."

His words and the seriousness in his expression made me shudder. Knowing he was low-key serious, I moved away from him and toward the bathroom before saying, "Whatever."

Once I entered the bathroom, I couldn't even start the shower because Julian was reaching over me and doing it himself. He then gripped the hem of the oversized T-shirt I wore to bed and pulled it up. I lifted my hands to assist him, and once it was off, he backed away.

"Hurry up, pretty. If you not outta here in ten minutes, I'm comin' to get you."

I rolled my eyes and turned toward the shower so he couldn't see my smile.

"Yeah, whatever."

He left the bathroom without another word, and I silently stepped into the shower. I couldn't help the smile on my face as I washed my body.

In just a few hours, I was gonna have his last name. *I couldn't wait.*

***

"You already know," Julian said once the judge recited the vows.

"Boy, you better act like you got some home trainin' and say it right," his mother said, making me laugh.

"My bad," he said and glanced at the judge. "I do."

I shook my head as the judge continued.

"And, do you, Jessica, take him, Julian, to be your lawfully wedded husband, to have and to hold, for better for worse, for richer or for poorer, to love and to cherish, from this day forward?"

Without hesitation, I delivered my response.

"I do."

Julian smirked. "You betta."

Ignoring him, the judge said, "By the power vested in me by the state of Georgia, I now pronounce you husband and wife! You may now kiss your bride."

My *husband* wasted no time claiming my lips. I expected it to be a short kiss since our parents were only a few feet away, but I should have known better. This man kissed me passionately, and although my mind was telling me to pull away, my body wasn't listening. When he slipped his tongue in my mouth, I knew I had to be strong and back away. When I did, he looked at me like I was crazy.

With warm cheeks, I avoided his eyes and glanced at my daddy. He was cutting his eyes at Julian.

"Save that for the house. I'on wanna see all that," my dad said, making us all laugh.

"My bad, Pops," Julian said, grabbing my hand.

The judge didn't stay in the room long after we wrapped up the ceremony, but we stuck around long enough to take photos. Davi had made me a beautiful white dress. It was short and flowy and fit my body perfectly.

The only witnesses in attendance were our parents, Davi, and Joseph. It was intimate and perfect, and I was officially Mrs. Jessica Tate. That sounded too good.

"What you wanna do for the rest of the day, baby?" Julian asked as we filed out of the courthouse.

I glanced at him as I thought about it.

I was sure the family wanted to go to brunch to celebrate our marriage, but I would much rather watch movies with Julian for the rest of the day.

Since Valerie went to jail, he and I had been outside. I missed the bubble we had created in his home for the last few months, and I wanted to get back to that a little.

"Lay up under you," I said honestly.

Winking at me, he replied, "Say no mo'."

Long Live Kaia Tate

♥

Tate

"Jessica, slow down," I said, kissing my teeth.

She looked back at me and laughed. Tightening her grip on the electric shopping cart handle, she continued to move forward, and I sighed. This girl was just about on my nerves.

She insisted on going grocery shopping today, but I wasn't with it. Jessica was two weeks past her due date and didn't need to be worrying about cooking a meal. The doctor encouraged us to go on walks at the park to try and induce labor, and that was what I suggested we do that afternoon, but nah...

My wife would rather try and be a racecar driver in the middle of a crowded grocery store. She had just asked me to bag up a couple of tomatoes, but as soon as I stepped away from her to grab a produce bag, she drove away, giggling the entire time.

"Childish," I said, approaching her.

Unbothered by my aggravation, she continued to laugh. "Am I childish, or are you just boring, baby?" she asked, glancing at me.

I couldn't help but smile as I gazed at her pretty face. I leaned down and kissed her lips before saying, "You're just childish. Leave me in this store again, and I'ma carry you outta here."

She kissed her teeth before readjusting her body on the seat.

"Boy, I'd like to see you try to carry me. I'm as big as a whale."

I cut my eyes at her. "Don't talk about my wife like that. And I can show you better than I can tell ya. Try me if you want to."

She smiled softly but said nothing else as we continued through the grocery store.

She stopped in the dairy section and said, "Can you get some heavy whipping cream for me?"

"I gotcha." I reached over her and grabbed the carton. When I dropped it in the cart, I noticed her rotate her hips the same way she had a few minutes prior. She exhaled deeply before pushing the cart forward, and I said nothing but continued observing her as we traveled through the store. She stopped at the cheeses and repositioned herself again.

"You good, pretty?" I finally asked.

It was clear that something was up with her, but I didn't want to overreact if it was only her being uncomfortable in the seat.

She let out another breath and placed a hand on her stomach. I watched as she lifted her body slightly and sat back down.

Nodding, she said, "Ooh. Yeah, I think so."

I was about to call her a liar because even her voice sounded weaker than it did minutes ago, but I couldn't get the words out because something else caught my attention. A small pool of clear liquid was forming just under her cart. I trailed my eyes from the puddle to her leg, and sure enough, her leg and the side of the cart were also wet.

A woman who was standing too closely behind us gasped. I turned to look at her. She was an older Caucasian woman. The look of disgust on her face as she stared at my wife had me about to cuss her the hell out.

"Who you lookin' at like that, lady? Gone somewhere before I thump your ass. I got too much goin' on right now." I was about to return my focus to Jess and make her aware of the fact that her water had clearly just broken, but I heard another rude muhfucka to the right of me. I snapped my head in that direction to see a group of people staring at my wife and me.

"Y'all's nosy asses ain't ever seen a pregnant woman's water break before? It ain't nothin' to see here, so y'all can all back up until we're up outta here."

Finally tuning them out, I focused on my woman. She was now gripping her stomach and breathing deeply with her eyes closed.

Rushing to her, I touched her arm, and she opened her eyes.

"Baby, I don't think I'm gon' be able to cook dinner tonight," she said, looking up at me with tears in her eyes.

I chuckled and scooped her out of the cart. Rushing toward the store's exit, I said, "It's all good, pretty."

As I got Jess out of the store and into the car, I took my own deep breaths. I could tell she was a little shaken up, and that meant I needed to be the calm to her storm.

I was trying not to focus on my thoughts—at least not until I got her to the hospital. If I took a minute to *really* process what was happening, I knew I would start going crazy. That wasn't an option. Not yet.

***

I'm 'bout to be a daddy."

That was my constant thought as I stared at Jessica. She was in the hospital bed and shaking her head from left to right. Every time she moved her head, her cheek made contact with the pillow, and she had a consistent hum going on that would randomly get louder whenever a contraction became unbearable.

I stood by her bed with my hands in my pockets to avoid touching her. We had been here for the last six hours, and she had gone from wanting me close to needing me to stop touching her. It was clear that she was in pain, and I didn't like the fact that I couldn't do anything about it. The only remedy to her pain was my daughter's entrance into the world, and that fact took me back to my original thought.

I'm 'bout to be a daddy.

I was blessed enough to be connected to some amazing ass fathers. J, his pops, and my own father were great role models in that department. I had admired each of them for so long, and the fact that I was about to join them in fatherhood was insane.

Was I capable of *raising* a child? I was a great godfather to my boys, but they went home to Davi and J at the end of the day. My baby girl would be under my roof twenty-four seven, and it would be on me—on *us*—to not mess her up. She'd be looking to me to make things right in her world when they were tumbling down, and I wouldn't have a choice but to come through.

"Hold my hand, please," Jess said, barely above a whisper. Her hand was extended toward me, and I quickly removed mine from my pocket and grabbed it. As I looked at her tense face, my heart felt bigger than my chest.

Sweat lined her forehead, and her eyes were filled with unshed tears. She had been emotional since she realized her water had broken, and because she wanted a natural birth, her pain was on ten. My baby was going through it, but she was taking it like a champ, and I was going to work overtime to pamper her when it was all said and done.

There was a knock on the door right before it opened. It was her mother.

She looked at me with tear-filled eyes before eyeing her daughter.

"We got here as soon as we could. This Atlanta traffic should be against the law. Oh, my baby is having a baby. This is going to be the best day," she said softly and approached us. I wrapped my free arm around her.

"Wassup, Ma?"

"Hey, baby. How dilated is she?"

I sighed. "Last time they checked, she was eight centimeters. Doc said she would be back in an hour, and it's been about that long now," I said.

Mama Nelly nodded, then turned to Jess. "How are you, feelin', baby girl?"

The tears that had been on standby fell from Jess's eyes as she looked at her mother.

"It hurts," she said in a voice that broke me.

I dropped my head as Mama Nelly covered Jessica's and my hand with hers.

"I know, sweetheart, but the worst is over. I promise."

Jess nodded as she cried silently, and my chest tightened. I hoped Mama Nelly was right, because I wasn't feeling the pain in my baby's voice or the helplessness I felt.

The door opened again, and the doctor was back. She came straight to the bed and examined Jess with a serious expression. I glanced at her and realized she was biting her bottom lip, and more tears were building behind her eyes. I could see she wanted to cry out, but she was attempting to hold out until the doctor gave us an update.

Just when I looked at the doctor to tell her to hurry and speak up, she stood with a smile.

"It's time, Mom. You're fully dilated, so we're going to begin pushing, okay?"

My eyes flew to my wife. I saw fear in her eyes, but she nodded anyway.

In a comforting tone, the doctor said, "It's going to be okay, Jessica. Now that we've made it to this point, it won't be much longer until you finally meet your baby girl. We're almost there, okay?"

Jess looked at me, and I squeezed her hand before blowing her a kiss. She inhaled deeply before letting out a shaky breath. Then I saw the fear diminish. It was still there, but determination was more prominent, and that made me smile.

My wife was a fighter, and I knew she wasn't going to let the pain of this experience get the best of her. She was going through this, and I was going to be right there to make it better once it was all said and done.

Nodding, Jess finally said, "Okay." She sounded more confident than she was moments ago, and that must have been enough for Doc because she immediately began giving directions.

"Okay, Mom. You're going to take a deep breath and push on your exhale.

Jess nodded again, and I watched silently as she drew air. She closed her eyes and exhaled while squeezing my hand.

"Great job. Let's do it again. Just like that."

My baby repeated her actions, and this time, she released a low groan as she pushed. She continued doing this, and on her fourth push, her groan turned into a scream. My eyes shot to the doctor.

"What's wrong?" I asked.

Without looking up at me, Doc shook her head.

"Nothing's wrong at all. The baby's head is crowning. This part feels intense for Mom, but it means we only have a few more pushes before she's out."

Finally looking up, Doc called Jess's name, prompting her to open her eyes. She looked tired, and sweat covered her forehead. I refrained from wiping it away because I didn't want to agitate her.

"Put everything into this next one. Take a few moments, then I need you to really push for me."

Instead of responding, Jess looked at her mother then at me. She said nothing, but tears rolled down her cheeks.

Reaching toward her with my free hand, I wiped her tears away, and she briefly closed her eyes.

"You doin' so good, baby. You almost there too. Let's make it happen, aight?"

"Okay."

She refocused, and it wasn't long before she let out a noise I had never heard her make before.

She began panting, and her chest rose and fell quickly.

Mama Nelly moved to the foot of the bed and stood behind Doc. Her eyes widened and teared up right before she covered her mouth with both her hands.

"Her head is out, baby girl. You're right there, sweetheart."

I glanced at Jess again. I really wanted to go see for myself, but the death grip she had on my hand let me know I would have to wait to get a look at my daughter.

"Your mom is right. This is it. One more push, Jessica. All I need is one more."

The doctor's words must have been music to Jessica's ears because she closed her eyes tightly and gave another hard push. The next few moments were a blur. I felt lightheaded and overcome with emotion as

I listened to my daughter's first cry and watched the doctor place her on Jess's chest. The nurses moved in immediately, low-key pushing me out of the way.

Instead of cussing their asses out, I rounded the bed and was right back at my woman's side. She was sobbing silently with her face pressed against our baby's. Finally, I was able to see our daughter with a clear view that was blurred with tears seconds later.

Perfection.

My daughter was perfection, and so was her mother.

Lowering myself to one knee so that I was eye level with them, I kissed my baby girl's forehead before doing the same to her mother.

"I love you so much, pretty. I swear I'ma spend the rest of my life tryna repay you for this blessin'. Thank you, baby."

She sniffled a few times, then whispered, saying, "I love you too."

"Dad," one of the nurses said. I looked her way, and she smiled. Holding up a pair of funny-looking scissors, she asked, "Would you like to do the honors and cut the umbilical cord?"

Her question prompted me to look at Doc, who was putting clamps on the cord.

I shook my head and frowned. "We can't leave that where it is for a minute? My baby girl already cryin'. I ain't tryna hurt her."

Laughing, Mama Nelly approached me and placed a hand on my shoulder. "It won't hurt her, baby. I promise. You got this. Go on, now."

I glanced at Jess, and she had her eyes open. With a smile, she nodded. "You got it, baby."

I stood with a sigh and made my way to the other side. The nurse handed me the scissors while Doc directed me.

"You're just going to place the scissors between the two clamps and cut. It's pretty chewy, so it'll take more than one snip, but I promise, the baby won't feel a thing."

I took the scissors from her and positioned them where she told me. Glancing at her, I asked, "Right here?"

She nodded with a grin but said nothing.

Leaning in closer, I began cutting. I was glad Doc prepped me first because I was almost ready to tell all of them that the cord was staying where it was when it didn't break, and my baby started crying louder.

Doc must have sensed my thoughts because she said, "Baby is okay, I promise."

I snipped the cord twice more, and finally, it broke. After that, I was right back to my girls.

"She's so perfect," Mama Nelly said, standing beside me. "Have y'all thought of a name yet?"

I chuckled because as much as we talked about and planned for our daughter's arrival, we had never discussed names.

"We never really talked about it."

Jess smiled softly and kissed our daughter's cheek, causing her to stir in her arms. Still gazing at her, Jess said, "Kaia."

I chuckled as I felt that annoying ass tingling behind my eyes. As I gazed at my baby girl, I realized everything about the name felt right. I couldn't think of a better way to honor my cousin's legacy.

"You sure, pretty?" I asked. Naming our daughter wasn't a small thing, so I felt the need to double-check.

"I'm positive. Your relationship with your cousin played a huge part in you becoming the man you are. The man I love. I think it's perfect."

I nodded and leaned in to kiss her soft lips.

"Aight, then. Kaia Brielle Tate."

Jess smiled softly. "I love it."

"I love you."

She puckered her lips, and I pressed mine against them again.

"We have a baby, Ali."

"We do," I said, glancing at Kaia. She was no longer fidgeting or crying. Her eyes were closed, and she breathed steadily while resting on her mother's chest. These two were my world. The love and happiness I felt gave me such an intense high I knew I'd spend the rest of my life chasing. These two were it for me, and I was beyond okay with that.

Lost Time

♥

Tate

Kaia's cry on the baby monitor woke me, and I stood immediately. I rushed out of our bedroom and was in her nursery, scooping her out of her crib within seconds.

"Wassup, daddy's baby? It's aight, I got ya."

I cradled her against my chest. Her tiny body squirmed for a minute before she settled down and closed her eyes. I let out a sigh of relief when the crying stopped. I couldn't take that, man. Every time I heard her little voice, and she sounded anything less than happy, I went on a mission to find out what was bothering her. Right now, it seemed that she just didn't want to be in that crib alone.

Kaia had been with us for over a month but had been sleeping in our bedroom for most of that time. Jess was against it, arguing that she needed to adjust to sleeping in her nursery, but I wasn't hearing that. Once I realized through my research that co-sleeping was actually a thing, I bought the bassinet that connected to our bed, and it was a done deal.

A week ago, Jess put her foot down and said we were going to put the crib we bought to use. Kaia hadn't been feeling it at all, and whenever she woke up, I made sure I was right there.

"I'm not gon' let you spoil our daughter, Ali."

I looked over my shoulder at my wife and smirked.

"You ain't got a problem wit' me spoilin' you, so I'on wanna hear nothin' when it comes to my baby girl," I said.

She shook her head and entered the dimly lit room. She wrapped her arms around me from behind and pressed her face against my back.

"I'm a grown woman who has no trouble sleeping through the night, so it's not the same."

I kissed my teeth and looked at my daughter again.

"She was cryin'. What you expect me to do, pretty?"

Jess sighed. "She was fussing, not crying. Either way, I expect you to give her at least a minute to self-soothe. She's never gon' get a full night's rest in here if we keep this up. And *you* won't either. Joseph told me you fell asleep in y'all's interview yesterday."

I laughed. "I ain't fall asleep. I just dozed off for a hot second."

Jess released me from her arms and moved in front of me. She gazed at our daughter with a small smile before she kissed her cheek.

"Same thing. If you would just go to bed and let me worry about Ky at night, it wouldn't be happening."

I frowned. "You worry about Ky all *day* while I'm at work. I ain't about to put the nights all on you, too."

She rolled her eyes. "Between your mother and mine, I barely lift a finger during the day."

That was probably true. Both of them were obsessed with their grandbaby and had low-key moved in. Today was actually one of the rare days one of them hadn't slept over.

"And," Jess continued, "since neither of them are here tonight, I'd like to spend some time with my husband. In *our* bed while our daughter sleeps in hers."

Her eyes fluttered, and she bit her bottom lip before tugging at it gently. I followed her movements as she placed one hand on my abs and began rubbing softly.

"Pretty," I said before clearing my throat—my voice was weaker than I intended. "Pretty. Don't play like that," I said, warning her.

Batting them eyelashes, she smirked. "I'm not playing, baby. It's been seven weeks. And I had a doctor's appointment yesterday."

I frowned, mentally calculating how long it had been since she gave birth.

Damn.

When I initially found out I had to wait six weeks before I could make love to my wife, I was heated. My obsession with Jess and her body existed long before we made things official. It only intensified since then, so the thought of not being able to touch her for over a month had me sick.

Instead of dwelling on that, though, I spent my time making sure she wanted for nothing so that she could focus on our daughter and her own recovery. My baby had been making sure my physical desires were met in other ways, even though I told her I had no problem waiting, but now...

"And what did Doc say?" I asked, holding her eyes with mine.

"She said I'm all good."

"You sure, pretty?"

She rolled her eyes before stretching up to kiss me.

"Yes. Ky is asleep again, so go ahead and put her back in her crib. Your other girl needs your attention now."

Chuckling, I allowed my eyes to trail to Kaia. She *was* sleeping soundly.

"Hurry up," Jess said before leaving the room.

Wasting no more time, I gently placed Ky back in her crib. She moved a little, and I held my breath, waiting to see if she would open her eyes.

She didn't, so I quietly left the room and headed to my wife. The doctor had given her the go-ahead, and I planned on spending the next couple of hours making up for lost time.

***

Jess

I had barely made it back down the hall when I was being swept off my feet. Julian immediately claimed my lips once I was in his arms.

We continued that connection as he carried me into our bedroom, and his lips didn't leave mine until he gently tossed me on the bed. He covered my body with his immediately and kissed me again.

As his tongue slipped into my mouth, his hands reached for the hem of my night dress. I shuddered at his touch and moaned as he grazed my skin and lifted the gown over my head.

I missed this.

Once I was completely naked, he pulled away from me, but I placed my hands on his shoulders, trying to bring him back into my space. He shook his head as he lifted completely on his hands.

"Hold on, baby. I haven't seen your body for real in a minute. Let me admire it," he said, his voice husky.

I felt my face heat at his words and unconsciously covered my midsection with my hands. He frowned immediately.

"The fuck you doin'?"

I sighed and shook my head, hating that I even cared. My snapback hadn't happened as quickly as I would have liked for it to, and although I wanted my man to make love to me, I didn't need him examining my flaws too closely.

"My body isn't what it was the last time we were together, Julian. I got marks I didn't have before, and there's still loose skin around my stomach. I've been workin' out, but I haven't—"

"Shut up, Jessica Brielle," Julian said, cutting me off. He took an arm and grabbed both my hands before placing them above my head. "You think I give a damn about some marks and skin? I'ma grown man, baby, and I'm insanely in love with every part of you. He lowered his head and kissed my stomach, making me shiver.

I resisted the urge to move his head to a different—more appealing—part of my body. He was already in the process of cussing me out, so I knew that would only make it worse.

He kissed another area of my belly, an area that held stretch marks I found myself observing anytime I was alone. I had used every oil in the book during my pregnancy to avoid them, but two small marks had still managed to find a home on my body.

He kissed my chest next, then rose to my lips. His eyes penetrated mine when he continued. "You're crazy if you think I would ever have a problem with the body that carried my daughter. You were sexy before and while you carried Ky. You're even sexier now 'cause I've only fallen deeper for you after watching you have her. The changes in your body are a result of our baby girl being brought into the world, and I fuckin' love 'em, pretty."

He slid his hands down my body and gripped my waist. Another moan escaped as he trailed his tongue across my skin. I gasped, but it got caught in my throat as Julian proceeded to kiss, lick, and suck every inch of my body.

Every. Single. Inch.

I had missed the feel of his lips on my skin so much, and he more than made up for the time lost.

"Don't ever hide from me, girl. The hell wrong wit' you?"

I nodded silently.

By the time he made it back up to my mouth, all thoughts of my body's flaws were nowhere near my brain. I just needed him inside me. Luckily, I didn't have to ask. After a brief kiss, I felt the head of his dick pressing my opening.

I rotated my hips to make his entrance easier, and he slid into me completely. It had been a minute, so it took a few moments for my body to adjust to the feel of him, but when it did…

He buried himself inside, then stilled himself and gazed at me. I figured he was waiting for me to tell him when to move, so I lifted my head and kissed his lips.

"Make love to me, baby."

With a smile, he pulled out slightly before diving in deep.

"*Damn*, girl." He changed the angle of his hips and thrust into me powerfully. He gripped my knees and pushed them forward, causing me to feel him even deeper. I couldn't even vocalize how amazing our reunion felt because I was too busy trying to keep up.

"I missed this, Jet. I missed you so much."

"I-I missed you t—"

My reply was cut short when he slammed into me hard. His mouth found my breast as he continued his assault, and I fully submitted to the pleasure he was delivering. His movements were intense, but I felt nothing but pleasure from them.

Not one to be shown up in the bedroom, I began moving with him, causing him to smirk as he thrust into me.

"You can't hang wit' me, Jet."

I laughed, allowing his words to fuel me. I felt my orgasm building, so I knew I didn't have much time to prove my point. I pushed at his shoulders, and he quickly got the message. Moving his hands to my hips, he laid on his back so that I was straddling him.

I hadn't taken him in a while, so I must have forgotten how much deeper he felt when I was on top of him.

His arrogant grin grew, and I rolled my eyes.

"Gone do ya thang."

Not willing to admit that the position was too much for me right now, I took a deep breath and began rotating my hips slowly.

I maintained eye contact with my husband, and although he was trying to hold his poker face, I saw the pleasure in his eyes. That was motivation for me, and I set out on a mission to make him scream my name.

Moving my knees off the bed, I planted my feet on it firmly and rose on my toes. I put both hands on his chest. I lifted up and swirled my hips before sliding back down powerfully. I rode him hard and at a steady pace until the tingling in my core intensified—then, my movements were wild and erratic.

I knew I was about to be done, but it was all good because my man was right there with me.

"Fuck, Jet!" he yelled loudly, and as my body collapsed and convulsed on top of his, I smiled.

Mission accomplished.

We lay in silence for several minutes, both of us breathing like we had just finished a marathon. After I was breathing steadily again, I lifted my head and looked at him.

"Who can't hang with you?" I asked with a raised brow, making him laugh loudly. He cupped the back of my head in his hand and brought me closer for a kiss.

"I'ma let you have it tonight, pretty." His voice was lazy, and his eyes closed as he spoke. Knowing he wasn't going to get up for a shower, I climbed off him and attempted to get out of bed.

"Where you goin'?"

"I was going to take a shower."

He shook his head. "Nah, we'll hit that in the mornin'. Ky prolly gon' wake one of us up in the next hour anyway, so lay down and try to sleep while she's out."

"Fine." I repositioned my body against his and closed my eyes as I listened to the thumping of his heart.

Just as I began to relax and doze off, my daughter's cries filled the room. I sat up, and so did Julian. I shook my head.

"Go to bed, baby. I got her."

He looked like he wanted to challenge me on that, but I glared at him, and eventually, he lay back down. "Fine, but next time, I'm gettin' up."

"Yeah, we'll see," I said as I put my nightgown back on.

Although I was tired, I walked out of the room and headed to the nursery, wearing a smile. My little family made me feel complete, and I felt blessed to call both of them mine. I wouldn't change nights like this for the world. I wanted this forever.

Epilogue

♥

Jess

"Calm down, Jet. Everything is gon' be smooth, so just relax," Julian said, taking Ky from me.

I rolled my eyes but took a deep breath. I wasn't relaxed at all. Ky had a doctor's appointment this morning, and we were running later than I intended, which had my anxiety on one hundred. I hated being late.

"I am calm. Leave me alone, goofy."

"Dadadada!"

I rolled my eyes again as Ky grinned and placed her hands on the sides of Julian's face. She was a little over seven months old and had started saying *dada* a few weeks ago. It was cute at first, but the fact that she had yet to call for *me* had me a little jealous of my own husband.

She was obsessed with her daddy, but I couldn't blame her—so was I.

Julian chuckled. "Don't be a hater all ya life, baby. That's prolly why she won't say your name. She feels that hater energy you got towards her pops."

"Julian... don't make me go off on you. Let's go." I slipped my hand into his, and we headed toward the venue.

Today was my brand launch day, and I was beyond nervous. Because the four pairs of sunglasses I designed gave summer vibes, I decided to wait until June to officially launch. I went all out with the summer theme and planned a private beachside brunch in California.

I invited ten top-tier social media influencers to attend the party and promote my eyewear. I had to fly four out while the others lived in Los Angeles. Each of them was getting free influencer boxes with all the shades and a good time. I also paid for their hotel rooms. This entire day had been planned to a T, but I was still feeling anxious about how it would play out.

I loved everything I designed, and my friends told me they did, too, but I needed *others* to love them, too. The guests attending the launch had huge social media followings, so if they posted good reviews, it could mean great things for my new business venture. That was what I was hoping for.

As we approached the private beach area, we were greeted by two security guards standing in front of a gate that enclosed the area I rented.

I smiled. "Hi, I'm—"

I was cut off when Shay approached the gate. She smiled at Kaia before turning to the security guards.

"This is Jessica Tate, CEO of *Tinesse Eyewear*, and the person throwing this party."

"Right this way, Mrs. Tate," one of the guards said, opening the gate.

"'Preciate ya," Julian said as we walked in. I gasped as I took the entire scene in. It was even better than I envisioned.

From the music to the tropical decor, every detail I mapped out had been executed perfectly.

"This is dope, pretty," Julian said.

Shay grinned. "It's perfect. All the influencers are already here, and most of your family is too. The party is pretty much in full swing. Everyone is just about done making their plates in the buffet line, so once you guys get settled, we can officially kick this launch off with a speech.

I wrapped my arms around Shay and squeezed tightly.

"Thanks, Shay. I feel like I've been overworking you for the last couple of months to get this launch together, but I appreciate you more than you know. This is amazing."

She hugged me back. "Girl, this is what I'm here for, and I'm glad to do everything I do. Come on."

My family and I followed her down the steps and toward the festivities. As we drew nearer, my daughter squealed. I looked over my shoulder and laughed when I saw Ky clapping and laughing with her eyes glued to the ocean.

She and I wore the cutest lime green beach outfits Vi designed for us. They matched my favorite pair of sunglasses from my launch, and I even had a tiny pair created for my baby girl.

Although this was a business event, it was also Kaia's first beach day, and once I addressed my guests, ate, and took a few photos, I was going to enjoy some family time by the water.

As we approached the party, Vi came running toward me, wearing a huge smile. My best friend looked beautiful in a pale pink ensemble that matched the shades she loved most from my collection. Vi had naturally long, curly blonde hair, and her wild coils gave summertime. I loved everything about her look.

"Jess! This is amazing, best friend! I'm so proud of you," she said, wrapping me in her arms. She then hugged Julian and promptly took Ky from him.

Ky giggled as Vi kissed her cheek and nuzzled her face.

I grinned. "Thanks, Vi. I low-key thought you were 'bout to cuss me out about you not planning the launch."

She and Paul wanted to do the planning, but realistically, they had both been caught up with their own work, so I told Shay not to bother them with it. I knew they would have made time to focus on the planning process, but it was a lot of work, and I didn't want to put that pressure on them.

She cut her eyes at me. "Girl, that's comin', but it can wait 'til after we're done celebrating you. It's going so well already."

I looked around and felt some of my anxiety subside. Some of our family and friends sat at the long rectangular dining table, while others were in the buffet line. Most of the content creators were walking around with their cameras, filming. I had a life-size version of the lime green glasses made for the event and was glad to see people using it as a photo backdrop.

A few of them brought a plus one to capture all their content, and I was cool with that too. I had also hired videographers to capture the event, and I noticed one of them moving closer to me with their camera on.

The brunch looked more like a party because of the large number of people in attendance. I invited everyone in my family, Julian's family, and Vi's family. Ace, Demi, Air, Crissy, and Paul were also here with their children, so it was packed. Everyone seemed to be enjoying the vibes, and that was all that mattered.

"Let's go eat. Me and my baby girl are hungry as hell," Julian said, grabbing my hand again. When we reached the buffet, I began making plates for us and was approached by one of the influencers. I smiled as she greeted me.

"Hey, I'm Hayley Pinn. It's so nice to finally meet you! I've literally been following your career since I was in high school."

I laughed and leaned in for a hug. "Ooo, girl, you just made me feel old, but I appreciate you so much for coming. I love all your content, so I knew I had to invite you when we started the guest list."

"I'm honored. You are one of my inspirations when it comes to content creation, so I wouldn't have missed this for the world."

My heart swelled at her kind words, and they stuck with me after she walked away. I had been doing this since I was in college, which was almost ten years ago. To know I could inspire people to take the same path I did and create a different life for themselves was humbling, to say the least.

After taking *way* too long in the buffet line—everything seemed to take extra time now that we had a little one—Julian and I took our seats at the head of the table. Once we did, the music faded out, and I heard Shay's voice over the loudspeaker, asking everyone to make their way to the table.

Most of the guests were already at the table, and the others didn't take long to make their way to their seats. Shay walked over to me and handed me the microphone. Taking a deep breath, I stood as everyone turned their attention to me.

"I apologize for my tardiness, y'all. I swear it's not my norm, but I'm still learning to balance work with this mommy life," I said, glancing at my husband and Kaia.

"Girl! Don't apologize for that. We understand," Aunt Tracee said from the middle of the table. I smiled at her and nodded.

"Yes, ma'am. Well, I just wanted to officially welcome you to the launch of *Tinesse Luxury Eyewear*. Anybody who knows me or has been following me for a while knows how I feel about shades. I—"

Two of the influencers cut my statement short and chanted, "The outfit don't hit the same without the shades!"

I couldn't help but laugh because that was a statement I lived by, and I said it all the time on my social media platforms.

"Exactly," I said, winking at them. "When I wasn't feeling the best about life or myself, this amazing man beside me reminded me of this dream. He encouraged me to put in the work and make it a reality." I glanced at Julian again. He gave a wink that made my insides flutter.

He had a way of making me forget everything but him with one look, but this wasn't the time to get distracted. Looking away from him, I cleared my throat and tried to refocus enough to make it through my speech.

"I'm so grateful for that because I'm beyond proud of what my team and I have produced. I hope you guys rock every pair and feel proud of them, too, because the process has been such a labor of love that I'm beyond excited to share with y'all. So, let's have a good time and celebrate today because it's been a long time coming. We're lit!"

Everyone stood and clapped as I laughed and handed Shay the microphone again. The music resumed shortly after that; some ate while others left the table to enjoy the beach, dance, and create content.

I tore off a small piece of the buttered roll and fed it to Kaia. She had been loving bread lately, and *Legendary* made the best. Julian and I watched as she chewed it, waiting for her reaction. Ky was so expressive, and she never took long to tell us how she felt about something.

Moments later, she frowned then looked at me. I frowned, too, because I just knew she would love the bread, but then her gaze went to my other hand, which held the rest of the roll. Before I could register what was happening, she reached toward me and snatched the bread from my hand before trying to stuff the entire thing in her mouth.

This little girl...

Julian's laughter triggered mine, and before long, all three of us were about to fall out of our seats from laughing. Kaia was giggling just as hard as we were, oblivious to the fact that she was the reason for our laughter.

A flash beside us caught my attention, and I looked up to see my mother snapping a picture of us.

"Hey, Ma," I said, wiping tears. I sat back up and tried to compose myself.

She leaned down and kissed my cheek, then Julian's. She saved her granddaughter for last, of course.

"Hey, baby girl. Y'all are so adorable over here I had to get it on the camera. Now give me my grandbaby and her plate. She said y'all don't know how to feed her right."

Julian handed Ky over, knowing better than to argue with her about her baby.

"Gone 'head and get her greedy butt, Ma," Julian said with a smirk. She grabbed the small plate in her other hand and went back to the end of the table.

My husband wasted no time tugging my chair closer to his and pressing his lips against mine briefly. Before pulling away from me, he said, "Your daughter is a trip."

I smirked. "I wonder who she gets that from."

He laughed and sat back. "Both our asses." He looked around before gazing at me again. "I'm proud of you, pretty. This is amazing, for real."

My cheeks obstructed my view of him as they rose. As a woman who prided herself on not caring about others' opinions, it was mind-blowing to me how great it felt to make my husband proud.

"Thanks, baby," I said softly.

"Girl, don't be over there talkin' like that. It ain't gon' do nothin' but have me take you into one of them bathrooms and shoot the club up. I'm ready to meet my son anyway."

I rolled my eyes. "Boy, we have a seven-month-old. We aren't ready for another baby yet."

He kissed his teeth. "Yes, the hell we are. I can see that lil nigga now—a real one like his daddy with features like his momma. He gon' be havin' all the girls at school goin' crazy."

I shook my head and licked my bottom lip as I considered his words. Honestly, if it happened, it happened. The thought of a new baby prompted me to reflect on the whirlwind of a year we had had. In the last few years, we had been friends with benefits, enemies, and everything in between. I never thought we'd be where we were now—happily married with our own little family—but I wouldn't trade it for the world. This man had my back like no one else, and he knew me inside and out. I felt extremely blessed to actually have a best friend for a husband, and our bond was one I'd never be willing to part with. I wanted to have as many of Julian's babies as the good Lord would allow.

Julian's chuckling brought me out of my thoughts. I refocused on him, and he stood and extended a hand toward me. I frowned but took his hand and let him help me to my feet.

"Where are we goin'? We haven't even eaten yet."

"We're goin' to work on my son, what you think? I told you to chill, but you over here bitin' your lip like I ain't a man of my word. Come on, now. You knew better than that."

"You are insane," I said, shaking my head in disbelief.

"And you married me. We're goin' in one of these bathrooms real quick, so just let it happen, baby."

He kissed my cheek and led me toward the small building where the restrooms were.

We walked past family and friends who weren't concerned about us in the least, and I shook my head. I didn't bother objecting because I knew it would do nothing to change his mind about what we were about to do. I'd be lying if I said I wanted to stop him anyway.

Julian was crazy and spontaneous, and more often than not, I was right there with him. Our relationship wasn't perfect by a long shot, but we were solid. We were *forever*, and I would bet my last on that.

The End!

Back Matter

♥

Thanks for reading!
Don't forget to leave a rating and review on Amazon.

Need more Jaimsss?
Jaimsss P. Catalog:
Davi + Joseph
Love That Saves
A Love That Restores

The Legend Brothers
A Legendary Love
Loving a Legend

Dream + Rhys
...And a Day (novella)

Cairo + Deanni
His Sweetest Escape

Connect with me on social media!

Facebook - Jaimsss P.
X - @jaimssswrites
Instagram - @jaimssswrites
TikTok - @jaimssswrites

Made in the USA
Columbia, SC
07 March 2025